FAITH'S SUGAR PLUM DADDY

Leanne Banks

This story is dedicated to Tony and Alisa.
Thank you for all the dinners, chocolate
and support during my deadline madness!

CONTENTS

Home
for the
Holidays

Leanne Banks
Dixie Browning
Kathie DeNosky

Published by Silhouette Books
America's Publisher of Contemporary Romance

Special thanks and acknowledgment are given to Leanne Banks,
Dixie Browning and Kathie DeNosky for their contributions
to the LONE STAR COUNTRY CLUB series.

 SILHOUETTE BOOKS

HOME FOR THE HOLIDAYS
Copyright © 2003 by Harlequin Books S.A.

ISBN 0-373-21826-5

The publisher acknowledges the copyright holders
of the individual works as follows:

FAITH'S SUGAR PLUM DADDY
Copyright © 2003 by Harlequin Books S.A.

CHRISTMAS EVE REUNION
Copyright © 2003 by Harlequin Books S.A

NEW YEAR'S BABY
Copyright © 2003 by Harlequin Books S.A

Visit Silhouette at www.eHarlequin.com

Printed in U.S.A.

LEANNE BANKS,

a *USA TODAY* bestselling author of romance and 2002 winner of the prestigious Booksellers' Best Award, lives in her native Virginia with her husband, son and daughter. Recognized for both her sensual and humorous writing, having received two Career Achievement Awards from *Romantic Times,* Leanne likes creating a story with a few grins, a generous kick of sensuality and characters that hang around after the book is finished. Leanne believes romance readers are the best readers in the world because they understand that love is the greatest miracle of all. Contact Leanne online at leannebbb@aol.com or write to her at P.O. Box 1442, Midlothian, VA 23113. A SASE for a reply would be greatly appreciated.

DIXIE BROWNING

Author of more than one hundred works under three pen names, both historical and contemporary, Browning draws from her experience as an award-winning painter, a country musician, president of a prestigious retail business and a variety of interests ranging from archaeology to politics. A wife, mother and grandmother, she's the daughter of a former big-league baseball player and the granddaughter of a sea captain. Both her grandfather and great-grandfather were keepers of the world-famous Hatteras Lighthouse. Contact Dixie at www.dixiebrowning.com, or at P.O. Box 1389, Buxton, NC 27920.

KATHIE DeNOSKY

lives in her native southern Illinois with her husband and one very spoiled Jack Russell terrier. Writing highly sensual stories with a generous amount of humor, Kathie has had books appear on the Waldenbooks bestseller list and received the Write Touch Readers' Award and National Readers' Choice Award. She enjoys going to rodeos, traveling to research settings for her books and listening to country music. Readers may contact Kathie at: P.O. Box 2064, Herrin, Illinois 62948-5264 or e-mail her at Kathie@kathiedenosky.com

Chapter 1

Dear Santa,
How is everything at the North Pole? We're being good down here in Texas. My brother Jason and I would trade all our toys if you could get our mommy a restaurant where she could cook. She's the bestest cook in the world. She can cook everything. She even makes broccoli taste good. She's the nicest mommy in the world and she takes very good care of me and my brother all by herself. She took care of my great-aunt Beth while she was sick too, but then my great-aunt had to

go to Heaven. I know you're busy, but my brother Jason wanted me to ask if you could get us a daddy for Christmas, too.

Sincerely,

Becky Donner

P.S. If you find a daddy, please tell him my mommy smells like cookies!

So earnest. So sweet. So out of place among the neat stacks of statistical and accounting reports, business development and strategy plans, and laptop computer on his gleaming mahogany desk. Gabriel Raines glanced up from the newspaper article that had been placed on his desk and waited expectantly for an explanation from his public affairs director, Rob Crandall.

Rob cleared his throat. ''One of the objectives we developed after the Enron mess was to take a more proactive approach to improving our company's image in the communities.''

''You think playing Santa Claus to some kid in Mission Creek is going to help our image,'' Gabe said doubtfully.

''It can't hurt. Plus this article made both the Dallas and Houston newspapers. If we move on it, they'll want to do a follow-up.''

''Okay. Write a check and accounting will take

care of it,'' Gabe said, lifting the article to return it to Rob.

Shaking his head, Rob cleared his throat again, betraying a tinge of nervousness. ''Actually, sir, charitable acts performed by the president of the company tend to have a greater impact.''

Gabe paused for a long moment and swallowed a sigh. He knew he made Rob nervous. He made a lot of people nervous. He didn't do it on purpose. A friend had once told him that his size and deliberate manner were intimidating enough without adding the power and wealth he'd gained from making his mark in the oil business.

''So what you're saying is that you want me to play Santa Claus to one of these kids?'' he said, feeling neither a spurt of interest nor scorn. The holidays meant nothing to him these days. Ever since he'd lost his wife and daughter... Like a cold draft of air in winter, a dull pain slid underneath the steel door of his defenses. He closed his mind to memories and focused on the moment. One moment at a time was the only way to survive.

''Yes, sir,'' Rob said hopefully. ''If you let me know when you'd like to go down, I'll make sure all arrangements are made for your lodging and with the press.''

Gabe checked his calendar. ''I'll head down on the tenth and return right after Christmas.''

Rob's eyes widened in surprise. "But that's two weeks."

Gabe nodded. "I've been planning to expand my restaurant business in that area. I'll just use the time to kill two birds with one stone." After all, Christmas was just another day to him, he thought, glancing at the letter to Santa. He couldn't, however, hold back a half grin at the postscript. So Becky Donner's mom smelled like cookies.

On December 10, Gabe walked into the Mission Creek Café. Shaking the rain off his Stetson, he took a quick look around and idly noticed the garland and lights in the windows and a Christmas tree in the corner. He spotted the Donners immediately. It didn't take a supersleuth to conclude that the two kids doing schoolwork and eating cookies in the booth against the far wall were Becky and Jason, and the slim woman wearing an apron and cleaning up Jason's spilled milk was Faith. A few other patrons sipped coffee or ate pie within the cozy confines of the café, but the establishment wasn't busy during the late afternoon between lunch and dinnertime.

Good, he thought. He'd planned it this way. As soon as Faith finished the milk cleanup, he felt three pairs of curious brown eyes trained on him.

"Who's he?" Becky asked in a stage whisper.

Faith laughed lightly and tapped her daughter's nose with her finger. "A customer, Curious George. You do your homework while I take care of him."

Gabe watched Faith Donner walk toward him and took in her purposeful, feminine stride. Her light brown hair was pulled back in a French braid and as she moved closer, he noticed she didn't wear a smidge of makeup on her fine-boned face. Even though the profile his PR manager had given him had reported her as a twenty-eight-year-old single mother, to Gabe, she looked all of eighteen, certainly not old enough to bear the responsibility of two active children on her own.

He noted the slight stubborn tilt of her chin and the glint of determined fire in her brown eyes and reconsidered. She might look like a fragile flower, but Gabe had read a full dossier on Faith Donner and her children and she'd survived more than a few rough knocks from life.

"Good afternoon," she said, pulling out a pad. "Have you had a chance to look at the menu on the table or would you like me to give you a couple minutes?"

He shrugged, opening the menu. "What do you recommend?"

"How hungry are you?"

There was a slight hint of huskiness to her voice. He liked it. "Very. I've been traveling."

"Okay," she said pointing to the inside page that listed daily specials. "We have one serving of the chicken potpie left."

"It must have my name on it," he said.

She smiled, revealing a dimple underneath her left cheek. "It must. You can choose a side and for dessert, I recommend the apple cobbler."

"Or cookies?" he mused, inhaling the scent of her. Damn if her daughter hadn't been right. The woman smelled like sugar cookies.

"Chocolate chip or sugar?" she asked.

"One of each. I'll take a side of the baked apples."

She nodded. "Done. Coffee to drink?"

"Black," he said, and glanced around the café in search of another employee. "You're the only one here?"

"Our regular waitress had an emergency, so I'll do everything for the next forty-five minutes. Then I'll get some help."

He raised his eyebrows. "Lot to juggle."

She met his gaze and he saw the determination rise again. "I'm stronger than I look."

She turned away and his gaze dipped to the sway of her tight little rear end. He felt an unfamiliar surge of curiosity that caught him off guard. He knew all the facts about Faith Donner, and while she wasn't a hardship to look at, she certainly didn't do anything to deliberately attract male attention. With her husky voice and dimple, she was a cute little package of feminine fire.

If it were left to him, he'd like to see a pair of earrings swinging from her delicate ears and a dress that would tell the tale on what he suspected was a nice pair of legs. Not that it really mattered to him, he told himself, surprised at the direction of his thoughts. He shook his head. He'd been working too many hours if a little waitress from Mission Creek could turn his head.

Faith swung around the corner armed with a coffeepot. She turned his cup over and filled it with the steaming brown liquid. "I'll have your chicken potpie in just a—" She whipped her head in the direction of her children. "Jason Donner, you sit yourself down before you fall sweetie," she said with a mix of stern rebuke and affection.

Gabe caught sight of Jason scrambling from his standing position on the bench in the booth.

"I told you to sit down," Becky said to him.

Jason made a face at her. "I wanted to see those guys on skateboards."

Faith groaned. "He needs a skateboard like he needs a hole in his head," she muttered. "Dear Santa, please don't bring my son a skateboard."

"Too late," Gabe said behind a chuckle as he lifted his cup to his mouth.

Faith looked at him in enquiry. "Pardon?"

He swallowed. "Thanks for the coffee."

She blinked. "You're welcome. Excuse me a moment," she said, and turned toward her children.

Hearing the stern tone in Faith's voice, Gabe surreptitiously watched Jason hang his head. She followed up the chastisement with a kiss on his forehead. Gabe saw the little boy throw his arms around Faith's neck and felt a strange tightening sensation in his throat. Odd, he thought, frowning at the response and turning away. Before he could ruminate for more than a couple of minutes, Faith reappeared with a piping hot stoneware crock of potpie and a side of baked apples. He eyed the flaky crust with approval. "Looks good."

"Tastes even better," she promised.

"You sound pretty sure of yourself."

She wiped her hands down the sides of her white apron and looked at him with just a glimmer of curiosity shining through the heavy fringe of her eyelashes. "You can see for yourself." She crossed her arms over her chest and waited expectantly.

He dipped his spoon into the potpie, lifted a bite of chunky chicken and vegetables to his mouth, and nearly singed his tongue. He drew in a quick hiss of cooling air.

"Oh, forgot to tell you. Don't burn your tongue."

He tossed her a dark look, but couldn't help

admiring the gentle kick of her dry humor. Spirit. She might be down, but she wasn't out. When the bite in his mouth cooled, he tasted a hearty, delicious combination of flavors. An idea slid through his mind.

"On second thought, I think I want to try the prime rib," he said. Beef was the true test.

She stared at him in consternation. "You want to send back my chicken potpie?"

He shook his head. "No. I'm just hungrier than I thought I was. I'll take the vegetable medley as a side and while you're at it, I'd like to try the apple cobbler and the chocolate pie."

She looked at him as if she were reassessing his height and weight.

"Six foot two and one hundred eighty-five pounds," he said, answering her unvoiced question.

Her cheeks flooded with color and she made a strangled little coughing sound. "Would you like your prime rib cooked rare?" she asked, and acknowledged his nod. "Okay, I'll bring it out in a little bit. You do understand that I'll have to charge you for another entrée and the two extra desserts?"

"I can cover it," he said.

Peeking through the serving window into the dining area, Faith Donner studied the male customer who seemed to have an appetite that would rival a whale's. She watched him take a bite and savor the food as if he were filling out a score card on each dish. If he weren't dressed so well, she might think he was a health inspector. If she worked in a different kind of restaurant, then he might be a food critic. She glanced around the cozy, but humble café and chuckled at the grandiose thought. No chance.

She hoped he didn't try to skip the bill. He might have a sense of humor, but he also had a take-charge air that reminded her of her late Uncle Lloyd, who had rubbed her the wrong way with his my-way-or-the-highway attitude. This man, however, held a totally different appeal than Uncle Lloyd. This man was hot. He oozed strength and masculinity.

Faith shook off the observation. He wouldn't look twice at her, and she shouldn't care, she told herself when she felt a little twinge.

She shot a quick glance over at Jason and Becky and breathed a sigh of relief. All was well for the moment. Becky was reading and Jason was coloring a Christmas tree. Jason, bless his soul, was going to be the death of her. He was more curious than careful. If he were a cat, then he would have already used up more than nine lives, and it was all Faith could do to keep him from using up any more.

Her heart twisted at the bowed heads of her two children. She'd been disillusioned and abandoned by her ex-husband, but the love and life in Becky and Jason's eyes gave her a reason to smile every day. A reason to swallow her pride and accept charity. Faith gnawed on her lip. She still had mixed feelings about accepting gifts from the oil corporation, because it made her feel inadequate as a provider, but she couldn't deny her children.

Picking up the pot of hot coffee, she made the rounds to the few customers in the café. Most had left. Taking in the sight of the broad shoulders of her last customer, she made her way to his table and refilled his cup.

"May I get something else for you, sir?" she asked, wondering what else she could dig out of the industrial-sized refrigerator in the kitchen.

He shook his head and pressed his large hand to his flat stomach. She wondered how he managed to maintain such an impressive physique with his appetite. She would bet he looked great shirtless. Not that she should be thinking such things.

"I couldn't eat another bite. It was all delicious," he said.

She felt a rush of pleasure at the honest appreciation she saw in his blue gaze. "Thank you. I'm glad you enjoyed it."

"It was so delicious I'd like to offer you a job

as head chef for the new restaurant I'm opening here in town. The Quartermaster. Have you heard of the chain?''

Surprise raced through her. "Of course. I've never eaten at one, but I've read about them in *Texas Monthly*. They're supposed to be fabulous. You're opening one here in Mission Creek?''

He nodded and named a jaw-dropping starting salary. "Would you be interested in the job?''

Her brain froze as she calculated the difference that kind of money would make for her children. "I—I—I don't know what to say.''

He cracked a half smile that transformed his rough-hewn features in a wholly distracting way. "Yes would be good.''

He looked like a man accustomed to hearing yes from women. Breathless, she shifted the coffeepot to her left hand and extended her right hand to the man. She would be crazy not to accept his offer. "Yes, Mr.—'' She lifted her shoulders helplessly. "I don't even know your name.''

He stood and enclosed her hand in his. "Gabriel Raines.''

Faith's heart stopped. "Omigoodness!'' she whispered. "You're our Santa Claus!''

Chapter 2

"No pot belly," Gabriel said firmly. "Although that might happen if I have too much of your food. No white beard. And no red suit."

Faith continued to gape at him in disbelief. The coffeepot tipped precariously in her hand, a stream of the brown liquid spilling onto the floor. He instinctively steadied her hand. "Whoa."

Faith glanced down at the puddle on the floor. "Omigoodness look at the mess I made. I just can't believe it's you." Her hand trembled within his and he moved the pot to the table. Pulling a towel from her pocket, she lifted her gaze to his. "Am I having an out-of-body experience or did you really just offer me a job at The Quartermaster?''

Her flustered reaction affected his chest in a strange way. "Yes, I did. And you accepted."

She shook her head. "This is amazing. First the gifts you're giving the kids and now this job. I don't know how to thank you."

"You just did," he said, uncomfortable with her gratitude.

"I don't think you realize how much this will mean to us."

Gabe grew more uncomfortable with each passing moment. "You know that the press is covering this."

She nodded. "There's supposed to be a presentation tomorrow. I've asked for time off from work and the house is mostly presentable."

"My public relations department deserves more of your gratitude than I do. They launched this particular project."

"But you okayed it," she pointed out, kneeling to wipe up her spill.

"Yes," he reluctantly admitted.

Rising, she met his gaze directly. "And whose idea was it to offer me a job at The Quartermaster?"

Gabe felt his collar growing tight again. "Mine, but—"

"But nothing, Mr. Raines," she said in that soft, husky voice that slid over him like a warm caress. "Thank *you.*"

He didn't know if he was more uneasy with her gratitude or the surprising way her voice affected him. Out of the corner of his eye, he saw two women walk into the café and don aprons. He nodded toward the employees. "Looks like your relief is here."

She seemed to tear her gaze from his. "Good. I'll, uh, get your check. Did you want anything else?"

Feeling the walls close in around him, he shook his head and pulled a hundred dollar bill from his pocket. "I don't need the check. Take this," he said, sliding the bill into her pocket. "Keep the change. I'll see you tomorrow for the press conference."

Gabe strode past curious gazes out into the pouring rain and got into his truck. A flood of memories rolled through him. A vision of his late wife, Charlotte, and young daughter, Michelle laughing bubbled to the surface of his mind. Michelle had been a blond mirror image of his beautiful, accomplished wife and Charlotte had kept little Michelle busy with every lesson imaginable: horseback riding, ballet and tap and piano.

Sometimes he'd wished Charlotte and Michelle

hadn't been such overachievers, but he'd figured they got it honestly. He'd been accused of being an overachiever since before he'd turned eighteen. With her education and cultured upbringing, his wife had been a perfect mate for him. She'd filled the social gaps while he'd built the business his grandfather had started. Charlotte had produced a beautiful baby and she and Gabe had discussed having another, but the time had never seemed right.

The time had never come for a lot of things, he thought, remembering the awful day Charlotte and Michelle had been killed in an automobile accident on the way to Michelle's dance recital. He should have been there. He should have been driving them. Maybe then...

The maybes tormented him. He stared out his window. It had been a rainy day, just like today. He watched Faith Donner and her two kids dodge raindrops as they left the café and climbed into an old Ford sedan.

He wrinkled his nose in disapproval. Several acronyms came to mind. *Found On the Road Dead. Fix Or Repair Daily.* He realized the company had come a long way, but he was still a General Motors man. He heard her make several attempts to get the engine running. Finally it started. She backed out of her parking space. He couldn't see the tires, but he bet they were worn.

Gabe frowned. A woman in her circumstance should have reliable transportation. It wasn't safe for her or her children for her to be rattling around in something undependable.

The following afternoon Gabe drove down the driveway leading to the ranch house where Faith and her children lived. He saw vehicles belonging to the press parked next to the house. He checked his rearview mirror to make sure that the other vehicle was still following.

Pulling to a stop, Gabe got out of his truck and held up his hand toward the driver of the vehicle behind him, who cut his lights and waved his hand in acknowledgement. With a sigh, Gabe walked toward the wraparound porch. A wreath hanging on the door exuded cheer despite the continuing dreary rain. Sometimes he felt as if he'd been walking in the rain since Charlotte and Michelle died. Today wasn't much different.

Gabe knocked on the hardwood door.

"Somebody's at the door," Jason yelled at the top of his lungs.

The sound of scrambling footsteps and a hard smack against the door made Gabe wince. That was definitely a kamikaze kid. The door swung open and Jason greeted him, nearly bursting with

excitement with his striped clip-on tie askew and
a tear in the knee of his pants. He furrowed his
little eyebrows in confusion. "You don't look like
Santa Claus."

"Thank goodness," Gabe muttered.

Becky and Faith rushed to Jason's side. "Mom
told you not to run," Becky said, pushing her
glasses back on her nose.

"Oh, Jason, your pants are torn," Faith said.

Jason gave a heavy sigh. "Sorry, but he don't
look like Santa."

"Doesn't," Faith corrected.

"That's what I said. He doesn't look like
Santa."

Faith met Gabe's gaze and gave an exasperated
smile. "I told you that he's not supposed to look
like Santa. He is just *acting* like Santa. Remember
he read Becky's letter in the paper and decided
he wanted to give you some gifts for Christmas.
Mr. Raines, please meet Becky and Jason."

"It's very nice to meet you, Mr. Raines,"
Becky said with perfect politeness as she fingered
the folds of her blue dress. "You're very kind to
give us gifts and a job for my mom."

Gabe extended his hand and gently shook her
smaller one. "It's my pleasure. You look very
nice."

"Thank you," Becky said, blushing prettily. "I

wanted my hair like Mom's. She says I got all the natural beauty with my curls, but I think she looks pretty, don't you?''

Faith's eyes widened in surprise and her cheeks colored with embarrassment. She cleared her throat. "Jason, say hello to Mr. Raines."

"Hi," Jason said solemnly shaking Gabe's hand. "Thank you very much."

"You're welcome," Gabe said, comfortable with the simplicity of Jason's response to him.

"We have cookies and cider in the kitchen," Faith said and lowered her voice. "Please forgive Becky for fishing for compliments. She means well."

"She was right. You do look pretty," Gabe said. With her hair pulled back from her face, she couldn't hide the nervous excitement in her brown eyes. She wore a modest burgundy print shirtwaist dress that concealed more than it revealed. For a moment, Gabe wondered how she would look in something that skimmed her lithe frame.

"Thank you," Faith said. "Now if I can just survive the press."

A young man entered the foyer and extended his hand to Gabe. "Mr. Raines, I'm Derrick Brown, an intern, and I'm here to help carry in the loot."

Gabe handed the man the keys to his truck. "It's wrapped and ready."

"Mr. Raines," a woman said as she rounded the corner. "I'm Carol O'Neil with the Houston ABC affiliate. Do you mind if we put a microphone on you?"

He stifled a sigh. "Go right ahead." He was led into the living room where the Christmas tree was decorated with lights, ornaments, popcorn and cranberry garland and stockings hung from the mantel on top of the large fireplace.

Gabe and Faith were positioned on chairs and given clip-on microphones while the wrapped gifts were hauled into the room. Gabe noticed that Faith's hands shook as she clipped her mike to the collar of her dress. He struggled with an odd urge to reassure her that the fuss with the press would be over soon.

"Ms. Donner, I'll start the interview with you and ask a few questions. I may ask your daughter a question or two about her letter to Santa then I'll interview Mr. Raines." She turned to the camera crew. "Everyone ready?"

For Faith, the interview seemed interminable. She hadn't slept a wink the night before. Although she was excited about taking a job with Gabriel Raines's new restaurant, she'd been troubled by thoughts about the upcoming interview and accepting gifts from Mr. Raines. Sure, she'd had it tough the past few years, but she'd always had a roof over her head and good food to eat. Her children wore clean clothing and had toys. She and her little family had a lot more than many people this Christmas. Knowing that, she felt guilty accepting Mr. Raines's charity.

Just as she sensed the end of the session, Mr. Raines pulled an envelope out of his suit pocket. "We at Raines, Incorporated are impressed with Ms. Donner's devotion to her children and her late aunt. That kind of commitment to family is the backbone of all our communities. We'd like to give a token of recognition with this check and one more gift for her."

Taken off guard, Faith stared numbly at Gabriel Raines. The agreement she'd made with his PR department had been that gifts for her children would be appreciated, but there would be no gifts for her. Feeling all eyes focused on her, she started to shake her head.

"I know Ms. Donner has been reluctant to accept gifts for herself, but I hope she'll make an exception."

Faith opened her mouth to protest, but the implacable steel in Gabriel Raines's gaze told her it would be useless. He placed the envelope in her hand and she was afraid to look inside, but the reporter insisted.

Faith hadn't thought she could be more surprised, but the zeroes on the check bowled her over. "I—I—I—" She gulped. "This is far too generous. You've done entirely too much."

"And there's more," Carol O'Neil said. "Are you going to give her the keys?"

The combination of the check and the word *keys* sent Faith over the edge. "Keys!" Faith echoed, jumping to her feet, heedless of the falling microphone.

Gabriel stood also, irritating her with his ability to loom over her. He pulled a set of keys out of his pocket. "You need a new car."

"I do not!" she said hotly. "Need is a word associated with food, clothing and shelter. Not a new vehicle. This is beginning to feel like *The Price Is Right.*"

His lips twitched, but his gaze remained serious. "Your car is old and I bet the tires are nearly bald."

"It gets us where we need to go."

"It's a safety issue. I would think you would want to make sure you don't break down on the road with your kids in the car."

She opened her mouth, but couldn't speak, couldn't breathe. "Are you implying I don't watch over the safety of my children?'' she asked, unable to keep the edge from her voice.

"I'm saying I'd like to make this part of the safety issue easier."

"And what's not to love about that?" the reporter asked with desperate enthusiasm.

Jason scampered into the room, bumping a camera man. "Mom! There's a big white car outside! Is that one ours?"

Becky poked her head in the room. "It's an SUV!"

Faith met Gabriel Raines's gaze and was torn between hugging him and ringing his neck. "I'd like a moment alone with you please."

He dipped his head and followed her onto the front porch.

"We had an agreement," she told him.

"I know, but these two gifts will still technically benefit the children. They will be riding in this vehicle. And it's not as if you're going to go buy a diamond necklace with the check. I'm sure you'll end up spending plenty of that on the kids."

"Yes, but—"

He swore under his breath. "Didn't anybody ever tell you how to say thank you?"

Faith stared at him then felt a strangled sound of exasperation bubble from her throat. "Okay, on one hand, you think I'm this wonderful devoted mother and member of the community worthy of a fat check and a new car. On the other hand, I'm a rotten mother because I'm driving an older vehicle. And don't forget I have terrible manners because you just want me to say thank you so you can get on your way. I'm curious, Mr. Raines. If someone wanted to give you a car and a big check, how would you feel?"

"That's different."

"Because you're loaded?" she asked and shook her head. "There are plenty of people worse off than me. I feel guilty accepting this."

He met her gaze and surprised her by taking her hand. "Trust me. This is a drop in the bucket when you compare it to what you'll be paying for college tuition. Think of this as winning a mini-lottery. Somebody else will win it next time." He turned at the sound of the door opening. "The camera crew is coming. Take a deep breath, stop snarling at me and try to smile."

The next moments passed in a blur. All Faith remembered saying was, "You did too much." When the news crew left, she slumped into a chair.

Jason tugged on her arm. "Can we open a present? Just one?"

"Oh, I don't know," Faith said, still overwhelmed from the events of the day.

"There's a big one to Becky and me."

"You might need some help putting that one together," Gabriel Raines said from the doorway. "My assistant briefed me on the larger items."

Faith sat up. She hadn't realized he was still there. "It needs to be put together?"

"I wouldn't mind doing it."

"Don't you think you've done enough?"

"Okay I'll trade labor for cookies."

"Can we Mom? Can we?" Jason asked, bouncing up and down.

Becky ran her hand over the package. "I wonder what could be in such a big box."

They found out in a matter of seconds. "A computer!" Becky said. "Mom, we got a computer!"

"We can play games on it," Jason said.

"And use the Internet," Becky said, whipping around to look at Faith. "Maybe we could find a husband for you on the Internet."

Faith felt her blood drain to her feet. Her precious, precocious daughter was going to drive her nuts. She shot a hard glance at Gabriel Raines. "Look at what you've started."

Gabriel roared with laughter.

The sound surprised her. She'd heard him

chuckle, but not this full-bodied, vibrant laughter.
It made him seem less like a CEO and more like
a man. An attractive, virile man, she thought as
he removed his jacket from his broad shoulders
and pushed up his shirtsleeves. Faith wondered
what his story was. Why wasn't he rushing home
to be with his wife or some other special someone? Or with that body, he could have several
special someones. No wedding ring on his finger,
she noticed. She wondered how many women he
had on a string.

"Hello, Faith," he said, waving his hand in
front of her face. "Are you okay?" he asked, as
if he'd been talking to her and she hadn't responded.

Faith felt her cheeks heat. She'd been lost in
speculation. Inappropriate speculation, she chas-
tised herself. "I'm sorry. I guess I'm a little
dazed. What did you want?"

He studied her for a few seconds too long and
she almost feared he could read her mind. Talk
about embarrassing.

"Cookies," he finally said. "The kids would
like some cookies while I hook up the computer."

Cookies turned into homemade vegetable beef
soup and sandwiches, and one opened gift turned
into three. The computer, the monitor and a computer game. Becky and Jason were thrilled.

Faith started to build a fire, but Gabriel stopped her. "I'll do it," he said.

"You'll mess up your suit."

"That's what dry cleaning is for."

Faith sank into a chair and fidgeted while she watched him build the fire. She wasn't accustomed to having anyone do anything for her. She tried to remember the last time anyone except her had built a fire in the house. Her aunt had been too ill, and her uncle had died several years ago.

She felt a pang of longing for a simpler time.

Gabriel looked at her and searched her gaze. "You sighed. What were you thinking?"

"I miss my aunt," she confessed in a low voice because she didn't want the children to hear. "Even though she was very ill this time last year, she was someone stable and sure in my life. Another grown-up. My uncle has been gone a long time, and my sisters and I lost our parents when we were very young." She closed her eyes and shook her head. "I shouldn't be complaining. This will definitely be a Christmas to remember. All the gifts you've given us, plus my sisters are coming home for a visit."

"How many sisters?"

"Two. Ann Elise is my type-A older sister, a veterinarian in Dallas. Marilou is the baby." She frowned. "I worry about her. She hasn't sounded right on the phone lately. But we'll take care of everything at Christmas. What about you? Any family?''

''My father is retired from the family business. He and my mother travel a lot. I have a younger brother in Chicago.'' He paused, staring into the flames. ''My wife and daughter died a few years ago.''

Faith's heart clenched in immediate sympathy. ''That's terrible.''

He nodded. ''Yeah, it was. Still is, sometimes.''

''I'm sorry,'' she said. ''That—'' She broke off at the sound of thundering footsteps on the porch.

''Give it to me!'' Jason called from outside.

''Oh, no.'' Faith felt the familiar sting of dread and stood, quickly moving toward the front door.

''What is it?'' Gabriel asked, following after her.

''They're chasing each other on the wraparound porch. Both of them have on dress shoes and the porch is wet from the rain. A disaster waiting to happen,'' she said, her words running together as she hurried onto the porch.

''Jason! Becky! Stop it this—'' Faith stumbled and her feet slid out from under her. She tried to break her fall with her hand, but her ankle turned, sending pain shooting up her leg. She fell back on her bottom with a thud just as the children rounded the corner.

"Mom!" Becky said, her face contrite as she gripped a computer game. Close on her heels, Jason slammed into her back.

Faith felt strong arms lift her to her feet. The solid wall of Gabriel Raines's chest at her back made her feel safe and protected. For at least thirty seconds. She tried to put her weight on her left ankle and pain shot through her. "Ouch!" The sound came out of her mouth before she could stop it.

"What's wrong?" Gabriel asked, his mouth close to her ear.

Her heart hammered in her chest. "I don't know. I think I hurt my ankle." Flustered by his proximity, she tried to gather her composure. "But I'm sure it will be fine. I probably just need to walk it out." She tried to hop a step away from him.

Gabriel looked at her doubtfully. "I don't know if walking is going to help."

"Well, I think I should try," she said, thinking this would be a terrible time for her to hurt her ankle. Actually anytime was a bad time. Taking a shallow breath, she gritted her teeth and tried again to put her weight on her foot. Pain shot through again. She bit her tongue to keep from

making a noise, but her face must have given
her away.

Gabriel shook his head. "Give it up. You're
going to have to give that foot a break. You can
see a doctor tomorrow, but I'm betting you are
out of commission."

Chapter 3

"I can't be out of commission," Faith wailed. "I don't have time to be out of commission."

"I don't think you have any choice," Gabe said, picking her up and carrying her inside. "You want me to carry you to your bedroom or—"

Faith felt a sliver of panic. The idea of Gabriel Raines in her bedroom even for something as innocent as setting her down on her bed and promptly leaving sent off an internal alarm inside her similar to a tornado warning.

"—the sofa's fine. Thank you," she said, trying not to notice the drugging scent of his aftershave, his broad shoulders, his bedroom eyes or full mouth. Upon such close inspection, the man evoked feelings she hadn't experienced in years. Feelings she hadn't thought she'd feel again. Feelings she had no time or energy for, her logical brain nudged her. When she realized she was resting her palms on his well-muscled chest, she pulled her hands back as if she'd touched a hot stove.

As if he sensed the commotion going on inside her, he studied her intently. "Something else hurt?"

"Uh, no," she said, feeling hot and uncomfortable. "I think I'm still just rattled from the fall. You can put me down now."

He gave a half grin. "I was planning on it, but I didn't think you'd want me to throw you on the sofa like a football."

Please do, she thought, appalled at her breathlessness. *Maybe it will knock some sense into me.*

Her eyes dark with worry, Becky hurried over as Gabe lowered Faith onto the sofa. She fidgeted with the computer game. "Mom, are you sure you're okay? Your face is red and your eyes look funny. I'm sorry. I shouldn't have fought with Jason. I wanted to get on the Internet and he wanted to play the game."

"I'll be fine, but you're right. You and Jason

shouldn't fight over the computer. You just got it.''

"When I was growing up, if my brother and I couldn't share, we had whatever we were fighting over taken away,'' Gabe said.

Both Jason's and Becky's eyes grew large with horror. Jason shook his head. ''We won't fight over it. You can get on the Internet, Becky.''

Becky pressed the game into his chest. "Oh, no, you play the game,'' she insisted.

Faith's lips twitched as she met Gabe's steady, but knowing gaze. Two points for backing her up, she thought, unaccustomed to any support.

"Do you think your ankle is broken?''

Faith shook her head and sent up a silent prayer. ''It will probably be better by morning.''

"Or a couple of mornings from now,'' Gabe corrected.

From the way her ankle was throbbing, she feared he might be right, but she sure didn't like him for it.

"I can fix you stuff to eat and drink,'' Becky offered.

"I can help,'' Jason said, pushing closer.

Faith tensed and hated herself for it. She adored Jason, but he was in a stage where he seemed like an accident waiting to happen. The idea of him carrying trays of food and drinks brought to mind a nonstop train wreck.

She put her arms around both Becky and Jason. "I'm sure I can hobble back and forth to the kitchen, and like I said, I hope I'll be all better tomorrow."

"But what if you're not?" Becky asked. "We go to school tomorrow."

"I'll get you some ice now," Gabriel offered. "And I can come over tomorrow."

Faith's heart slammed into overdrive. "Oh, no! Absolutely not," she said to his back as he headed for the kitchen.

"Why not? You're hurt. I'm not busy," he said over his shoulder.

"You've done too much already. Way too much," she emphasized. "Besides, I'm sure I'll be just fine." She glanced at the clock and looked at Becky and Jason. "I see two somebodys who need to get ready for bed."

"Oh, Mom," Jason complained.

"Not already," Becky protested.

"You're not going to make me regret letting you open a gift tonight, are you?" Faith asked quietly.

"I should get to go to bed later than Jason since I'm older," Becky said, jutting out her chin.

Faith nodded. "You can read for a while in

your bed after you brush your teeth and change into your pajamas.''

Becky's face fell, showing she was still hoping she'd get a few more minutes on the computer.

''Or if you don't like that choice, we can turn out the lights and you can count your blessings,'' Faith said.

Becky didn't pause a half beat. ''I'll read.'' She ran out of the room. ''I get the bathroom first!''

Jason tore after his sister and Faith cringed. ''I hope he doesn't—''

She heard the sound of a body colliding with a floor or wall or door. ''Jason!'' she called.

''Shoot! Becky beat me again. I'm okay. I tripped.''

Faith closed her eyes and shook her head. ''If I can just get him through this awkward stage.''

''How long has he been accident-prone?'' Gabriel asked as he gave her a bag of ice.

Faith placed the bag on her ankle. ''Since he started walking.''

Gabriel gave a wry smile. ''He hasn't even hit the early teen years when a guy feels like he's all arms and legs.''

Faith nodded, taking in Gabriel's broad shoulders and muscular build. ''I can't believe you ever felt that way.''

His eyes lit with curiosity. ''Why?''

"You carry yourself like you've always been an athlete."

He chuckled. "Trust me. When I was thirteen, I spent a lot of time tripping over my own feet." He nodded toward her hurt ankle. "What can I get for you?"

"Nothing. I'm fine. I meant it when I said you've done too much."

"I'll get you the remote for the television. What do you want to drink?"

"I said no—"

He shook his head. "You're going to get thirsty sometime. You might as well let me get it for you before I leave."

"Okay," she said, waving a mental flag of surrender. "Soda." She watched him leave the room and felt a wicked kick of feminine appreciation at the sight of his backside and body. The man had a great body. She covered her eyes, willing herself not to notice.

He returned with a can of soda and handed her the remote control for the television, but the kids popped back into the den ready for good-night kisses. When she rose to tuck them into their beds, Gabriel picked her up to carry her.

"I can hop," she protested, struck by a slew of uncomfortable feelings—embarrassment, frustration and a superawareness of him that bothered her.

"No need," he said and set her down on Jason's bed.

Trying to ignore Gabriel was ridiculous, but she did her best as she read a story to Jason. She kissed her son good-night and tucked his covers around him.

She stood and again, Gabriel picked her up to carry her into Becky's room where her daughter was furiously scribbling on a sheet of paper. Faith's stomach instinctively tightened. The last time she'd caught Becky scribbling on a sheet of paper with such concentration and passion she'd later learned Becky had been composing her letter to Santa.

"Last-minute homework?" Faith asked hopefully.

Becky looked up with a comically surprised expression on her face that screamed "caught" and pushed her glasses up her nose. She shook her head. "No, it's just a special project for all of us."

Gabriel set Faith down on the bed and Faith reached for the paper. "What is—"

Becky snatched it out of her reach. "You have to promise you won't get mad."

Faith opened her mouth in surprise. "Why would I get mad?"

Becky shrugged. "You can get touchy."

Faith prided herself on maintaining an even keel. "I'm not that touchy, am I?"

"No, but—"

"Then let me see what you're writing," Faith said, extending her hand.

Becky glanced at Gabriel then back at Faith. "I just want you to answer some questions."

Faith's heart twisted, surprised that Becky would doubt her. After all they'd been through, she and her children were extremely close. She wondered what could be bothering her daughter. "Honey, I've always been willing to answer your questions."

"You promise you will?" Becky asked solemnly.

"Of course."

Becky picked up her pencil and took a deep breath. "Okay, just remember you promised. Number one, what are the top five most important things you want in a man?"

Faith dropped her jaw, speechless for a full moment. She stared at her innocent-looking daughter in disbelief. "You tricked me."

"You promised!" Becky reminded her.

"What is this about?"

"You know Jason and I want you to get married again," Becky said.

Faith felt a twinge of guilt that she'd been unable to provide her children with a caring father figure. Their biological father had abandoned them years ago. "I've explained this to you before, sweetheart. I'm busy at the café and with you two. I don't need a man in my life."

Becky set her chin stubbornly, a bad sign. "But we want a dad, and I'm pretty sure Santa's not going to bring one down the chimney, so we've got to try to find one."

Faith shook her head. "This doesn't have anything to do with an online matchmaking service, does it?"

Becky shrugged. "I just want to know what kind of man you might like so I'll know him when I see him."

Faith bit back a groan. "Becky—"

"You promised you would answer my questions."

She heard Gabriel chuckle from behind her.

"Looks like she's got you."

Faith shot him what she hoped was a quelling look. It didn't do any good. His eyes glinted and his lips lifted in a grin that reminded her of the devil himself.

"Easy for you to say," she muttered, turning back to Becky.

"It's just a few questions. It shouldn't kill you," he said.

Becky cleared her throat, her pencil was poised over the paper. "Top five things you want in a man," she said.

Feeling Gabriel's gaze burn a hole through her back, she tried to ignore him. She sighed, feeling her cheeks heat with embarrassment. "Oh, Becky, I haven't had time to think about this in ages."

Becky rolled her eyes. "Okay, let's start with looks. How do you like a man to look?"

Faith frowned. "Well, appearance isn't the most important thing."

"Then what is?"

"Character," Faith said. "A sense of humor. Intelligence."

Becky scribbled her mother's response. "That's three. I need two more."

Faith had been stumped, but Becky's question unleashed a stream of wishes in her mind. "Strength," she said. "I want someone strong enough to take care of me and to let me take care of him." *Someone who thinks I'm pretty, someone who can't get enough of me.* Her cheeks burned as if she'd spent all day in the sun. "I think that's enough for now," she said.

"But Mom, you only gave me four and I asked for five," Becky complained. "And how am I gonna find you a husband if I don't know how you want him to look?"

Faith kissed Becky's soft cheek. "I'll have to think about number five and let you know later."

"Promise?"

"Promise," she said. "Twenty minutes of reading then lights out."

"Thirty minutes?" Becky asked.

"Or zero minutes," Faith said, countering her daughter's negotiation.

"Twenty," Becky quickly said.

Faith gave her a hug then stood. She wasn't on her feet more than a few seconds before Gabriel swooped her up in his arms again.

She gasped as he carried her out of Becky's bedroom. "This is really unnecessary. I can hop. I can crawl. You have to stop. What's going to happen when I go to bed or take a shower?"

"Good point," he said with an expression on his face that made her nervous. "Maybe I should stay."

Chapter 4

After extracting a solemn oath from Faith that she wouldn't overdo it with her foot, Gabe left her house. The second he stepped outside, he felt a loss of warmth, inside and out. It was the driving rain, he told himself, but it felt like more.

Faith's home had felt so warm. The smells of a homemade meal and baked cookies were comforting. Her laughter, even the children's squabbling, had felt as if someone had rubbed a soothing balm on a sore place inside him.

Ever since he'd lost his wife and daughter, he'd felt as if he'd been in deep-freeze. The advantage to being frozen, he thought as he got into his truck, was that he felt no pain. Gabe preferred to keep it that way.

Driving away from the small ranch, he concentrated on the road. The rain slapped at his windshield and he drove through knee-high mud puddles. As he approached the bridge, two police cars blocked the entrance and a man dressed in a poncho waved a lantern.

Gabe pulled his truck beside the man and lowered his window.

"The bridge is flooded," the man said. "No crossing tonight. You'll have to go back."

"Great," he muttered. "Is there another way into town?"

"There's another bridge twenty miles down the road, but it's rained out, too. Your best bet is to wait till morning or midafternoon."

"Great," he muttered again and turned his truck around. He thought about sleeping in his truck for the night and dismissed the thought. Faith wouldn't mind putting him up for the night even though she'd looked panicked when he'd suggested staying earlier.

After returning to her house, he walked up the steps to the wraparound porch and tapped lightly on the door so he wouldn't wake the children. No answer. He tapped again, slightly louder. Still no answer. He waited a few moments then tapped again.

He heard a hopping sound and the door swung open. Faith wore a towel around her head turban-style, and a wraparound terry robe dipped precariously low between her breasts, revealing a hint of cleavage. She smelled like something sweet, he thought and inhaled. Peaches. Her eyes were wide with surprise.

"Did I catch you in the shower?" he asked.

"Bathtub. Why—"

"The bridge has been rained out. Do you mind if I take your couch for the night?"

She opened her mouth, but no sound came out for a full three seconds. "Oh. Of course not. Come in," she finally said, hopping to the side to allow him inside. "Did they say how long they expected it to be a problem?"

She didn't want him around, he concluded and felt a twinge of humor. It was ornery as the devil, but he liked getting her flustered. She was so calm, implacable. It was fun to see her blush and stutter. When Becky had demanded to know Faith's top five most important things she wanted in a man, he'd wondered if she'd known her cheeks had turned the color of ripe strawberries.

"At least you won't have to hop as much. I can carry—"

"Oh, no." Her eyes widened in alarm and she raised her hand in a stopping motion. "Not necessary. I'm going to bed soon anyway. No need." She turned away and began to hop. "Let me get some linens for you."

A slice of protectiveness cut through him, pushing him to action. He swept her up in his arms and shook his head. "I thought you promised you were going to take it easy." He inhaled and caught another hint of peaches. She felt soft and warm.

Her eyes glinted with defiance as she squirmed in his arms. "I was just going for linens, not entering a bunny hop contest."

He tightened his grip slightly. "Could have fooled me," he said, taking her into the den and setting her on the sofa. "Stay there," he said firmly. "And point me in the direction of the linen closet."

"It's down the hall next to the bathroom, but…"

Gabriel headed toward the bathroom and caught a steamy draft of peaches. An image of Faith, naked and lounging in the tub, slid through his mind, catching him off guard. He scowled at himself. Where were these thoughts coming from? He'd successfully ignored his baser needs for a long time now, and it wasn't as if Faith was a beauty queen.

He opened the door of the linen closet and grabbed sheets and a blanket. There was just something about her. Something in the depths of her brown eyes that grabbed at him and twisted. Being in her house gave him the oddest feeling of finding home.

Gabriel rolled his eyes. It must be the Christmas season. All the holly-jolly, mistletoe and heart-plucking nostalgia. He was usually immune. He returned to the couch.

Faith immediately hobbled to her feet.

Gabriel glanced at the clock. "It's still early. You don't have to leave on my account."

"Oh, no, I—"

Cutting through her fluster, he waved his hand. "Are you sleepy?"

She opened her mouth then closed it. Her slim shoulders slumped and she sighed. "Not really. My head is spinning. I'm overwhelmed."

"Have a seat before I help you," he said with a half threat in his voice.

She sank onto the sofa.

"Is it the gifts?" he asked, moving to sit down on the sofa. He set the linens on the coffee table.

She nodded. "The gifts, the press, the SUV—" She closed her eyes then covered her face. "The check and you—"

"Me?" he echoed, interrupting her list. "What's overwhelming about me?"

Faith squirmed. "You just are. You come in here like some kind of superhero with all these gifts for my kids and a job offer for me—"

"I'm looking out for myself by offering you a job," he told her. "You know you're a damn good cook."

"I suppose," she admitted. "But the car and the check. And you keep picking me up and carrying me everywhere," she said, clearly exasperated.

"You're not used to having a man around the house," he said.

"I can't argue with that," she muttered, looking down at the sofa cushion.

"Do the kids ever see their dad?" he asked.

She shook her head and the disappointment he saw in her eyes grabbed at him. "He abandoned us. He couldn't handle the responsibility of a family." She sighed. "Even though my aunt was very ill during the last year and she couldn't do much,

I didn't realize how much I relied on her company. I love my kids, but I miss having another adult around.''

Gabriel thought about his too-quiet house and understood what she was saying. ''Makes sense,'' he said. ''Raising kids is hard enough to do with two people, let alone one.''

''Yeah, Becky says I need to get out more.''

''If she starts bringing home romantic prospects for you—''

Faith groaned. ''Oh, don't start. That's one of her Christmas wishes she's determined to make happen.'' She sighed and leaned her head against the back of the sofa. ''Christmas is a wonderful time of year, but it can be hard for some people.''

''For you?'' he asked, curious.

''Well, it's a time that I count my blessings and Jason and Becky bring so much magic to my life. But I also think about losses, like my parents when I was very young, my marriage and now my aunt.'' She glanced at him, her brown eyes reminding him of hot chocolate. ''I imagine it could be a tough time for you.''

He felt the familiar ache of loss and nodded. ''When I have time to think about it, it is. But I try not to think about it. The last several years I've been too busy to pay much attention to the holidays.'' He'd been busy because he'd made sure of it.

She met his gaze for a long moment then lifted her head. ''Do you ever think it might work better not to avoid thoughts about your wife and daughter?''

''What do you mean?''

She shrugged. ''I guess focus on the happy memories. Maybe give a donation in their honor. I've been told that if someone loves you, they will live inside you always.''

''You think it's true?'' he asked skeptically.

Her lips lifted and he noticed that her smile transformed her entire face. ''I like to think so. It's my way of keeping people alive who have been important to me. What about you?''

''I hadn't thought about it that way,'' he said. ''I try not to.''

''What was your wife like?'' she asked.

''Type A like me. She had our daughter in every activity imaginable. That kid barely had time to catch her breath. But they both loved it.''

''Did you have any special Christmas traditions?''

''In between the performances of *The Nutcracker*?'' He allowed his mind to drift back in time. He saw his wife brimming with happiness after a day of shopping, full of pride after trimming the tree. "My wife, Charlotte, always had to have the house perfectly decorated. She was in some women's club and our house was always on the Christmas House tour. She loved the hustle and bustle of that time of the year."

"It sounds like she made it fun," Faith said.

"She did." His heart lightened a fraction at the memory. "My daughter, Michelle, was always up before dawn wanting to see Santa Claus."

Faith nodded. "My sisters and I did the same thing. Used to drive my uncle crazy."

"I didn't mind. It was always a lot of fun watching her open her gifts. My wife would always leave very broad hints about what she wanted and it usually involved jewelry."

"But she always acted completely surprised when she opened it, right?"

"Yeah, how'd you know?" he asked, glancing at her.

"Female programming," she said. "It's in the chromosomes."

"You do the same thing with your gifts."

She nodded. "It's slightly different, though. I hint with small things like dish towels or hand lotion and I act very surprised when I get them. Jason likes to be more creative. Last year, he gave me the coolest rubber snake he'd ever seen. He traded a week's worth of lunches for it on the playground.''

He chuckled, picturing Faith's face when she opened the gift. ''What did you do?''

''Well, I screamed at first because I thought it was real. Then Jason reassured me it was fake.'' She shook her head. ''He was so proud that I screamed because that proved how cool the snake really was.''

''Where do you keep it?'' he couldn't resist asking.

''It's safely packed away right now. If we don't keep it packed away, then it somehow gets put in people's beds,'' she said with an expression that conveyed too much experience in the matter. ''In the spring, we'll pull it out and put it in the garden to scare things that want to eat my vegetables.'' Her lips twitched. ''I guess, in a way, you could say it's a useful gift,'' she said, but she didn't sound entirely convinced.

A memory of his daughter slid through his mind. ''My daughter gave me aftershave one Christmas. It was the rankest smelling stuff I've ever smelled.''

''But you did wear it?'' she asked as if there were no other choice.

"Yeah, for a while." He shook his head. "I swear I smelled like a dead fish when I wore that aftershave."

She chuckled. "The things we do for our kids."

He felt a bittersweet tug. His kid was gone. "Yeah."

She covered his hand with hers. "It's okay to miss them."

He stared at the sight of her small hand over his, but didn't reply. His throat was too tight.

"We put special ornaments on the Christmas tree for special people. My uncle was a very hard man, and a very hard worker. He loved carpentry work, so we put a couple of makeshift carpenter's tools on the tree in his honor. My aunt collected tea cups, so we have a few miniature ones on the tree. And I get to hang the teapot. Ever since I can remember, my mother, and then my aunt, allowed me to hang the teapot ornament."

She squeezed his hand. "So what was your daughter's favorite thing in the world to do?"

"Ballet," he said, remembering how Michelle had practiced twirls and leaps in the kitchen, in the foyer, just about everywhere. "She wanted to be a ballerina."

"And your wife?"

Gabriel chuckled despite the tight feeling in his chest. "I don't know what her favorite thing to do was, but her favorite thing to collect was diamonds."

She laughed with him, meeting his gaze. "And you, what do you like to do more than anything in the world?"

Work, so I don't have to think about what I've lost. He glanced away. "I don't know. I'll have to think about that."

"Something tells me it's not ballet."

He chuckled again. How did she do that? How did she make him laugh even when he was hurting? "What makes you say that?" he asked, turning his hand over and lacing his fingers through hers.

"I'm having a tough time imagining you in a tutu," she confessed in an almost-whisper that was surprisingly sexy.

He looked at her, taking in her towel-wrapped head, face bare of cosmetics, and terry robe and wondered how she managed to come across as playfully seductive. He wondered if she even knew she was sexy. He suspected not. "What do you most like to do?"

"Cook," she said immediately. "I love to bake."

"But that's work."

"Not always." She covered his hand with her other one so that his hand was cradled between hers. "Food iş more than work. It's more than just filling the belly. It nourishes, it brings comfort, pleasure. Certain smells can evoke childhood memories. In some cases, it can even be a very sensual experience."

"How?" he asked, too aware of how her fingers grazed his. The movement was both comforting and sensual. She seemed to be moving her hands without thinking about it. Each caress of her fingers cranked up his internal temperature.

"The smell of baking bread is definitely a comfort smell. For me, biscuits baking in the oven evoke childhood memories. Sugar cookies do the same thing. And fondue," she said, "eating fondue can be an incredibly sensual experience. Dipping tenderloin into a special seasoning sauce. Dipping fruit into a chocolate sauce. You just eat a bite at a time, so you're almost forced to savor it."

"Like slow sex," he murmured, and his gaze locked with hers. He felt heat and awareness flash between them like a shared crackle of electricity. The awareness sizzled in her gaze for a few seconds.

She looked down and her glance must have fallen on their entwined hands. He heard a soft gasp before she tried to pull away. Drawn to her touch, he instinctively tightened his grasp.

"You don't have to stop," he said.

She hesitated then slowly met his gaze. He read embarrassment on her face and wished he could take it away. He wished he could get back the easy growing intimacy.

She cleared her throat. "I should probably go to bed."

"I can take you," he said, brushing away a twinge of disappointment.

Her eyes widened and she shook her head. "That's not—"

"You know I'm not going to let you hop," he said flatly.

She swallowed and deliberately pulled her hands from his. "Okay. Will you be okay here on the sofa?"

A forbidden thought snuck through his mind. Maybe he would be a lot better than okay if he stayed in her bed.

Pushing aside the thought, he nodded. "I'll be fine. Are you ready for your ride?"

"I guess," she muttered.

He picked her up and carried her down the hall

to her bedroom. Her body was soft in his arms. Neat except for her discarded dress lying on her bed, the room beckoned with a soft bedside lamp and a cozy comforter drawn back partway. The curtains were ruffled and the top of her dresser was covered with photos of the children at various ages and a toy truck. Jason's, he suspected. A lady's vanity sat in the corner with a collection of nail polish and cosmetics. The location of the vanity suggested it had been shoved aside. Too busy caring for others to take much time to care for herself, he thought, setting Faith down on the bed.

"Ready to be tucked in?" he said, tongue in cheek.

"Not quite," she said. "All I need to do is brush my hair and get my nightgown, but you can leave," she added with unflattering speed.

"Here's the brush," he said, finding it on the top of the dresser. "Where's the nightgown?" he asked and saw the beginning of a mutinous glint in her eyes. "And you might as well go ahead and tell me, because I'm not leaving until you're in bed for the night."

She shot him a dark glance. "Third drawer down on the left," she said grudgingly.

He opened the drawer and pulled out a pink

cotton gown. Setting the brush beside her, he handed her the gown. It had been a long time since he'd held a woman's nightgown in his hands. A long time since he'd held a woman in his arms, all night long.

She clutched the nightgown to her chest. "Now, you really can go."

His lips twitched at the firm tone in her voice. "Stay in bed or else."

She lifted her chin. "Or else what?"

"Or else I'll have to kiss you."

Chapter 5

Every time Faith closed her eyes, she saw Gabriel's mouth.

She dreamed of kisses, all kind of kisses. Soft, gentle comforting caresses. Deep-drugging endless, sensual kisses. French kisses that echoed the physical act of lovemaking. Her lips burned. She rolled restlessly through the dreams, seeking his mouth, seeking release. Her body grew sensitive, her loose gown felt too tight. *Air* felt too tight.

She awoke wondering how he tasted, if he was a good kisser. Hot and bothered. It took several moments before she realized the embarrassing truth. She was aroused. Very aroused. All because Gabriel had *threatened* to kiss her.

Faith groaned and covered her head with her sheet. She had thought her sex drive was dead and buried. If her ex-husband's selfish approach to sex and subsequent abandonment hadn't killed it, then sheer exhaustion should have. Instead her hormones were churning like a tornado.

"This is not happening," she muttered to herself. "Gabriel is Santa Claus, and you absolutely cannot lust after Santa. Gabe will be your future boss," she told herself sternly. "You may *not* lust after your boss."

"Mommy, who are you talking to?"

Ack! Faith jerked the covers down, taking a breath of relief that only Jason stood in her open doorway. "Honey, I've told you that you should knock."

"I forgot," he said, picking up the truck on the top of her dresser. He yawned and rubbed at the cowlick sticking up straight from the crown of his head. "Who were you talking to?"

"Myself," she fibbed, rising to a sitting position. "I was making a list of things to do for the day."

"Okay." He walked over to her bed and crawled into her lap. "How's your foot?"

She wiggled it experimentally. Only a touch of stiffness remained. "I think it's mostly better."

"That's good," he said, snuggling against her. "Becky's fixing breakfast."

"She is?"

"Yep, and Gabe is helping her."

"Mr. Raines," she corrected. "What do you mean helping her?" she asked, oddly uncomfortable with the idea of Gabe in her kitchen.

"He told us to call him Gabe. They're making pancakes," Jason said, rubbing his stomach. "And I told them I wanted a million."

She tickled her son. "If you ate a million pancakes, you would explode."

Jason giggled. "Okay, half a million."

"Try four at the most," she said.

"How many do you want, Faith?"

Faith jerked her head up to find Gabe, all broad shoulders and tousled sexy hair, leaning against her doorjamb. Her heart jumped into her throat. The morning shadow on his unshaven jaw and the intent look in his blue eyes gave him a dangerous male look.

He lifted his head with an expectant expression. "Pancakes," he repeated. "How many do you want?"

He was offering pancakes, not his body, she told herself. "Two or three, thank you."

"How's the foot?"

"Great," she said swiftly. "I think I'm going to be fine."

"Let's see," he said in a skeptical tone.

"What do you mean?"

"I mean go ahead and get out of bed."

Prove it, he might as well have said. Resisting the urge to scowl at him, she urged Jason out of her lap and slid her legs out from under the covers. She carefully moved her feet to the floor, putting most of her weight on her uninjured ankle. She tested her other ankle and didn't feel the pain she'd experienced last night.

She smiled. "I'm all better. See?"

"A little stiff," Gabriel surmised, studying her.

"Not much," she insisted.

"You might want to wrap it and wear tennis shoes."

"That was what I'd planned to do," she said. "This means you don't need to carry me anymore."

"Well, darn," he said with a mocking glint in his eyes. "And I was just getting used to it."

Faith reached for her robe. "I'm sure you'll adjust. Jason, you need to get dressed, so you won't miss the school bus."

"I was hoping you would need me to stay home and take care of you today."

Faith smiled at her sweet, but wily son. "And

maybe watch a few cartoons in between right?"
She shook her head. "Scoot. You need to go to
school, so you can get smarter and smarter and
smarter. And if you don't get dressed, you won't
have time for pancakes."

Jason raced out of the room.

"I can be ready in just a couple of minutes.
Please just make sure Becky doesn't burn herself," Faith said.

"Will do. She's been giving me orders," Gabriel replied.

Faith winced. "She's assertive for her age."

"Wonder where she got that quality?" he
asked.

"I don't know," Faith said. "Sometimes I
think she's more assertive than I am."

"Well, I'll give you a little warning. She's got
a questionnaire she wants you to answer."

"Questionnaire about what?"

"About the kind of man you want."

Frustration rolled through her. "Oh, no."

"Looks pretty thorough. Height, weight, color
of hair, eyes. Age, occupation—"

She lifted her hand for him to stop. "I'll think
about that *later*." She was going to have to hold
a very firm discussion with her daughter on the
subject of finding a man. Or *not* finding one,
which was Faith's current outlook.

"Good luck," he said with a chuckle as she went into the master bath.

Just minutes later after both Faith and Jason had gotten dressed and Faith had tamed Jason's cowlick with gel and French-braided her own hair, Faith walked into the kitchen and found Becky setting plates heaping with hotcakes on the table.

"Becky, I'm so impressed," Faith said, filled with pride. "My goodness. I think you could manage a dozen people for breakfast instead of just four."

"Two dozen," Gabriel said, shooting a grin at her daughter.

Becky beamed. "Gabriel helped."

"I just followed orders from the chief."

Becky's smile broadened. "He was an excellent helper. I got out your favorite peach preserves too, Mom."

Faith's heart swelled and she pulled her daughter close for a hug. "Oh, honey, you're so thoughtful. What did I ever do to deserve you two?"

Becky shrugged. "Just lucky I guess."

Faith chuckled. "I guess so. Juice and syrup are already on the table."

Becky nodded. "Flatware, butter and napkins

too. Just in case Jason…'' She paused when Faith shook her head. Becky pursed her lips.

Faith didn't want Jason to feel anymore self-conscious over his clumsiness than he already did. One of her biggest fears was that he would develop an attitude of self-fulfilling prophecy. ''All of us need napkins,'' Faith said gently and took her seat.

Gabriel joined them at the table and Jason said the blessing. Everyone made appropriate sounds of approval and appreciation. Becky's face flushed under all the praise.

''When do you have to leave, Gabe?'' Becky asked.

Faith shook her head. ''Becky, it's not polite—''

''It's okay,'' Gabriel said. ''I'm actually staying until after Christmas because I'm opening a new restaurant in town. I'm going to use the time to finalize arrangements.''

''Don't you have kids?'' Jason asked over a bite of pancake.

Faith's stomach tightened at Jason's question. After talking with Gabriel last night, she knew this was a tender subject for him. ''Don't talk with food in your mouth, honey. Gabe had a little girl, but she isn't living anymore.''

Becky gasped. "She died? How horrible! How did she die?"

Faith cringed at the pointed questions. "Becky, Gabe might not want to talk about—"

"It's okay," Gabriel said quietly. "She died in an automobile accident with her mother."

"I'm sorry," Becky said, a slice of fear glimmering in her own eyes. "I hate it when things like that happen. It's terrible."

"It was terrible. I miss them very much."

Becky nodded solemnly. "We miss Aunt Beth."

Jason nodded. "We put some ornaments on the tree for Aunt Beth. Maybe we can put some ornaments on the tree for Gabriel."

"Would you like a pancake with chocolate syrup?" Becky asked. "Mom only lets us have pancakes with chocolate syrup when we're really upset."

Despite her fear that her children would open a raw wound for Gabe, she couldn't help feeling warmed by their sweet desire to comfort him.

Gabe smiled and rubbed his flat belly with one hand while he rubbed Becky's head with the other. "Can I have a rain check? You've already filled me up."

"Sure," Becky said. She adjusted her glasses. "But I do have a few questions for you."

"Okay," he said. "Why—"

"What's your favorite sport?" she asked.

"Football. Why—"

"Your favorite dessert?" she continued.

Gabe wrinkled his brow. "Hot apple pie with ice cream on top."

"Do you have a pet?"

"I used to have a golden retriever named Kelly when I was a kid, but my wife was allergic so…"

Becky nodded. "Favorite color?"

"Blue," he said, shooting a confused glance at Faith.

She decided it was time to intervene. "Becky, why are you asking all these questions?"

"Just because," Becky said firmly. "If I tell you why, it will spoil it, so don't make me tell you. Besides they're easy questions."

"My favorite color is green," Jason said, waving his hand.

Faith watched Jason's hand smack the side of his half-full orange juice glass and she instinctively stood and reached for it.

Gabriel grabbed it first.

"Great save," Faith said with a smile.

"I thought I'd gotten a little rusty, but Jason's gonna help me sharpen my skills, aren't you, bud?"

Jason nodded. "You're a good catcher. Maybe you can show Mom some tricks."

Gabriel met her gaze with a hint of sexy amusement in his blue eyes.

Faith felt her stomach dip.

"I might be able to show her some tricks if she's interested in learning," Gabriel said.

She felt the sizzle snap between them again. She couldn't tell if he'd meant the offer as a double entendre, but she could just imagine the kinds of things Gabriel Raines could teach her. If he didn't view her as a charity case. Which he did, she told herself.

"Are you coming back here for dinner?" Becky asked.

"Becky, Gabe may already have other plans," Faith said.

"Do you?" Becky asked.

"No."

"Well, can he come for dinner then? I need to ask him some more questions."

She felt pulled in two different directions. On one hand, she needed a breather from Gabriel. He was too overwhelming. He'd brought all these gifts to her and her children, he'd shared his loss with her and threatened to kiss her. On the other hand, she hated the idea of the pain she knew he was experiencing. She couldn't help wanting to make it easier for him. She swallowed a sigh. "Yes, but it's probably just going to be pot roast tonight," Faith warned him.

"If you're fixing it, something tells me it'll be good."

She felt a rush of pleasure. "That's kind of you to say."

"Nothing kind about it," he said. "I'm just speaking the truth."

So, don't be a ninny and read anything extra into anything Gabriel says or does.

That evening, as soon as Gabriel arrived at the house, the mouthwatering smell of pot roast greeted him at the door along with Faith. He looked at her and something inside him eased. It was damn crazy how he felt more at home here than he did in his own home.

He barely had a chance to say hello to her before the kids dragged him to the computer, wanting him to show them how to play more games. Becky asked him a bunch of strange questions, but he answered each one to the best of his ability. Jason asked to play just one more computer game…at least ten times.

Their lively chatter and enthusiasm made him feel lighter. He wondered if he'd spent too much time with adults during the past few years.

Faith called, "Dinner."

A stampede followed. He watched her as she helped the children take their places and greeted him again. Something was wrong, he thought, after a few minutes. He couldn't put his finger on it for a few minutes more.

She wasn't looking at him.

He wondered why.

She wasn't unfriendly. She always responded when he spoke to her, but she never met his gaze for more than half a second. After dinner, she allowed Jason to help her make sugar cookies for his class. After the children took their baths, she tucked them into bed and reappeared in the hallway.

"When do you stop?" he asked, amazed at her intense schedule. After work, he often found himself struggling to fill the hours. That obviously was not difficult for Faith.

She glanced at her watch. "In about two hours if I'm lucky."

"What do you have left to do?"

"More cookies and laundry." She smiled, revealing her dimple. "Always laundry."

"I thought you already made cookies for his class," he said.

"I made part of them. Jason likes to help, but he isn't interested in baking and decorating enough cookies for thirty kids and his teachers. Which is just fine. He likes to see lots of frosting and sugar on the cookies. Tomorrow night is Becky's turn and I'll need the assistance of Michelangelo.''

His lips twitched at her humor. ''A little ambitious, is she?''

She tossed him a weary look. ''You have no idea.'' She shrugged her shoulders and glanced away. ''I wish I could entertain you, but I've got cookies to bake.''

''I don't mind helping.''

Her head shot up and she met his gaze in surprise. ''Pardon?''

''I said I don't mind helping. You heard what Becky said. I'm a good helper.'' He lifted his hands and wiggled his fingers. ''Many hands make less work.''

She opened her mouth and moved her head in a circle. ''It's very kind of you to offer, but you really have done enough. I don't need your charity in this area.''

Her words dug at him, pinching. ''This isn't charity. I don't have anything to do except look at some remodeling plans for the restaurant and I can do that tomorrow.''

She bit her lip. ''Okay,'' she said, almost

grudgingly. "Thanks. I'll put a load in the washer and be right back."

Gabriel looked after her and frowned. Why was she acting so distant? It irritated him. He missed the genuineness he'd seen yesterday and last night.

When she returned, they made the rest of the cookies together, but she still seemed to avoid his gaze.

Gabriel grew irritated and curious. He couldn't take his eyes off of her. Spotting a bit of frosting that had somehow found its way to her cheek, he swiped it with his finger and lifted it to his mouth.

She looked up at him with an incredulous glance. "Are you eating frosting off my face?" she asked.

"Yep and it's good." He saw one more stray bit on her jaw and swiped it too. "Very good."

Her eyes darkened with a hint of awareness. She cleared her throat. "If you wanted frosting, there's still some in the bowl. Or here's a spoon."

He grabbed her hand and lifted it upward, locking his gaze with hers. "This way tastes better." He took her forefinger into his mouth and licked the frosting off of it.

Her jaw dropped and color rose to her cheeks. He liked the way she blushed. She worked her jaw, but nothing came out. "What are you doing?'' she finally managed in a high-pitched voice.

''Creative cleanup,'' he mused, running his tongue over her thumb.

Her eyes glinted with a dozen emotions he wanted to be able to read. He saw a hint of arousal, but he also caught a disturbing mix of anger and something else.

''You're playing with me,'' she said, her voice sounding husky and a little hurt. She jerked her hand away from him. ''We both know I'm a charity case to you, so why don't you just stop this—'' She huffed. ''This craziness.''

Appalled, Gabriel stared at her. ''I don't see you as a charity case.''

She rolled her eyes in disbelief. ''Oh, right. That's why you bought me a car and wrote that big check.''

''That was because of Becky's letter to the newspaper. My PR department thought this would be an opportunity to do some good and demonstrate good corporate citizenship.''

''Becky didn't ask for a car,'' Faith pointed out.

Frustration kicked through him. ''You need a new car.''

''There's a difference between need and—''

He waved his hand in dismissal. ''Yeah, yeah.

I know. That's my fault. Blame me. I thought you should be driving something safer.'' He sighed. ''But I don't see you as a charity case. How could I? You're successfully raising two terrific kids. You can cook like nobody's business. You can be damn sure I didn't hire you out of pity. I hired you because I always hire the best. You're an amazing woman.''

''Amazing,'' she echoed in disbelief and shook her head. ''I know I'm not anything like the women who cross your path on a daily basis.''

It hit him then, broadside. He was so surprised he couldn't speak for a few seconds. Faith didn't think she was attractive to him. She didn't think she was good enough. She didn't know that she had him wanting to be in her presence every spare minute. She didn't know that he wanted to get to know her...every way a man could know a woman.

''Did you ever think that it might be a good thing that you're not anything like the women who cross my path on a daily basis?'' he asked.

She gave a slow, hesitant shake of her head.

Gabriel felt a click of resolve. If she didn't know how she affected him, then maybe he should just show her.

Chapter 6

Faith watched Gabriel lower his head toward hers and nearly had a heart attack. She was trying to be sensible, trying not to do anything stupid. This man was way out of her league. Plus he would be leaving soon.

His mouth touched hers and all sensible thought left her brain. She tasted gentleness with an undercurrent of need that pulled at her. Her heart hammered in her chest.

He tugged at her bottom lip with his lips then slid his tongue over hers to taste her. A rush of heat ran through her like gasoline. It had been so long since a man had kissed her.

He gently pushed her against the wall and slid his hand behind her neck to tilt her mouth against his. His tongue slid inside her and her head began to spin. His hard chest felt so good against hers, and lower, he slid his knee between hers. The combination of passion and care in his touch made her feel like she'd been turned upside down and inside out.

"You taste so good," he said against her mouth. "Better than cookies."

She couldn't help smiling even though her heart was pounding.

"And your skin." He moved his hands up under her shirt to her bare torso and her breath stopped. His warm hands felt incredible on her bare flesh.

She couldn't withhold a soft moan and the sound seemed to crank up the temperature between them even more. She loved the feeling of being surrounded by him, his scent, his strength. He deepened the kiss and his hands wandered upward to the edge of her bra.

She felt her nipples tighten in anticipation, her skin burned like she'd been out in the sun too long. He slipped one finger beneath her bra and stroked the underside of her breast then pulled back.

She swallowed a choking sound of frustration.

He rotated his pelvis against her and she felt his hardness seeking her softness.

He slid his finger beneath her bra and stroked again. Instinctively arching against him, she wanted a fuller touch. She wanted more. He flicked his fingertip over her nipple and she moaned again.

"You like that?" he asked, stroking again.

His touch elicited a strange combination of satisfaction and restlessness. At the same time he stroked and kissed her, she felt like a flower blooming. She'd shut off her needs and wishes for so long.

Still fondling her breast, he slid his other hand to her bottom and guided her against his hardness, his tongue sliding in and out of her mouth. A steamy forbidden image of Gabriel and her, naked and locked in each other's arms singed her mind.

"I wish you were naked," he whispered.

A terrible thrill raced through her. This was getting way out of hand. She was already out of her mind. She pulled back slightly and dipped her head to try to clear it. Her heart was racing, her breath was unsteady and her mind was hazy with pure unadulterated want. She took a careful breath. "You've heard that expression. If you can't stand the heat…"

"Get out of the kitchen," he finished for her, his hand still on her bottom.

All too aware of his arousal, she took another breath. "I need to get out of the kitchen."

He met her gaze with blue eyes stormy with passion and lifted his hands to cradle her jaw. "You sure that's what you want to do?" he asked and kissed her so tenderly she could have wept.

"I can't think when you kiss me," she whispered.

"That can't be bad."

"Unless one of the kids walks in here," she said and sighed.

Faith could tell that it took a full moment for her words to register.

"Kids?" he echoed, looking at her in confusion. "Aren't they in bed?"

The arousal in his gaze tugged at secret places inside her. In her deepest secret places, she would love to be the one to take care of his arousal. Faith closed her eyes at the wicked thought. Now she *knew* she'd lost her mind. She gave herself a hard mental shake. "Just because Jason and Becky are in bed doesn't mean they'll stay there."

He reluctantly pulled away from her and walked to the other side of the room. "You wanna throw me some ice?"

She laughed despite the fact that she felt like

an overstretched rubber band. "You know this is crazy, don't you? Nothing good can come of it and—"

"Speak for yourself. For me, everything good has come of it so far."

Her heart dipped. "But there's no way it will work. We don't even live in the same town. It's insane and I—"

The intensity in his gaze made her throat close.

"Why don't we just see what happens?" he asked in a velvet tone that made her think of hot nights and lovemaking that never ended.

When she didn't respond, he moved toward her, took her hand and pulled her with him toward the den.

"I can think of a million reasons this isn't a good idea," she said.

"I can give you a few big ones to balance all that out," he said.

Faith gasped. If he touched her again, she was going to melt. "You've already demonstrated some of those. And I don't think you need to give me the big—" She sputtered, remembering exactly how large he'd felt against her.

He glanced at her in confusion, then realization crossed his face and he roared with laughter. "Get your mind out of the gutter, Faith. I'm not talking about sex."

Embarrassed, she pulled her hand from his. "My mind wasn't in the gutter," she protested. *Just all over his naked body.*

Guiding her to one end of the sofa, he gently pushed her down then sat across from her in a chair. "I'm not kissing you or touching you," he said, lifting his hands. "I'm just thinking about it."

His gaze raked over her, stripping her, kicking up the arousal inside her again. *And he wasn't even touching her.* Swallowing the urge to yell for help, she covered her eyes. "Faith, look at me."

She peeked between two of her fingers. "Do I have to?"

He nodded.

She lowered her hand to her lap. "I just have a hard time believing you'd be interested in a woman like me."

"Why?"

"Because I don't operate in your social or financial or even geographic circle. I'm not drop-dead beautiful. I'm not—"

"Enough of what you're not. You make me feel glad about being alive again. I haven't felt that way for a long time. You make it okay to miss my daughter and my wife at the same time that I enjoy life."

Faith was incredibly moved by his words, but she didn't want to be. Gabriel scared her. "You could get that from a decent therapist."

"I want to be with you as often as I can. I like the way I feel when I'm around you. I respect you. But I want you, too. A therapist can't give me that."

Her pulse beat erratically in her throat. She swallowed. "You scare me."

He looked at her in disbelief. "Why?"

"You're too good to be true. Any minute something's going to go wrong. And if something doesn't go wrong, you'll just *poof*, disappear one day."

His gaze held hers with a combination of compassion and exasperation. He stood and rubbed his hand over his face. "I'm gonna leave now. For the night," he added. "Because if I stay, I could end up giving your kids an eyeful, and I don't want to do that. But here's something I want you to think about. What if something doesn't go wrong? What if I won't disappear?"

Gabriel left and Faith stared after him. What was happening here? Had she just imagined what had occurred? Had she imagined that he'd kissed her? That he'd said those things that had blown her away?

She pinched herself hard.

Edgy, she stood and went into the kitchen where the dishes waited. Reality waited. This was her life. Baking cookies, caring for her children, working at the café.

Gabriel Raines was fantasy material and she'd do well to remember it.

The following afternoon after school, Faith helped Jason with his homework while Becky did her math at the kitchen table. Becky had seemed more distracted than usual, peering out the window.

"What are you looking at, sweetie? Do you see an animal?"

Becky shook her head. "No. I was just looking."

Fifteen minutes later, the doorbell rang.

Becky slammed her book closed and scrambled out of her chair. "I'll get it."

Faith exchanged a curious glance with Jason, but he just shook his head. Hearing the sound of a man's low voice, she rose. "I'll be back in a minute. You keep coloring."

She walked to the foyer to find Becky chatting with an attractive man in his mid-twenties. He glanced up at her arrival. "You must be Becky's mother, Faith. I'm Mike Wayland. It's nice to meet you."

Still uncertain why he was at her door, she accepted his handshake. "Hello."

"Mr. Wayland is the fireman I told you about," Becky said, giving an exaggerated nod.

Faith nodded slowly. Becky had never mentioned a fireman.

"Becky told me you wanted to make cookies for us guys who have to work on Christmas Day, and I just wanted to make a visit to personally thank you."

She smiled, tossing a questioning glance at Becky, who was innocently staring at the ceiling. "That's very kind of you, Mike," she said. "How many of you will be working on Christmas day?"

"It'll just be a skeleton crew of about ten, but we appreciate your thoughtfulness." He held her hand a bit longer than necessary and stepped closer.

If Faith didn't know better, she would say the man was sniffing her. She removed her hand from his.

"Well, darn if she wasn't right. Becky said you smell like sugar cookies and you do."

"Thank you," she said, for lack of anything else to say. "It was nice of you to stop by."

"I guess I should go," he said reluctantly. "You coming to the community party on Friday?"

"We were planning to attend."

He nodded and grinned. "Save a dance for me. Good meeting you, Faith."

He left and Faith immediately turned to Becky.

"Gotta go to the bathroom, Mom. Gotta go bad," Becky said and vamoosed out of the foyer.

Faith narrowed her eyes. It was definitely time to have a talk with her daughter. After checking on Jason and dinner, she parked outside of the bathroom waiting for Becky.

After several minutes, her daughter finally appeared. "I should get back to work on my math, mom," Becky said.

Faith snagged Becky before she escaped. "After you and I talk."

Becky's gaze held a tinge of desperation. "But I've got English, too."

"That can wait," Faith said, guiding Becky to her bedroom.

"But I need to get started on a science project," Becky said.

"You're a smart girl. I'm sure you'll get it all done," Faith said calmly, motioning for Becky to sit on her bed as she stood across from her. "What is this about me baking cookies for firemen for Christmas?"

"Well, you're always doing nice things for people, so I thought you'd like to do this, too."

"Becky?" Faith prodded in a warning tone.

Becky sighed. "He came to class today to tell us what firemen do and all my friends thought he was a hottie and that you should marry him."

Feeling the beginning of a tension headache, Faith squeezed the bridge of her nose. How to explain this to her eight-year-old daughter so she would understand? "Becky, do you like Brussels sprouts?"

Becky shook her head.

"Do you like liver?"

Becky made a face. "No!"

"Do I make you eat Brussels sprouts and liver?"

Becky shook her head slowly. "No."

"Do I put them on your plate at night for dinner for you to eat?"

"No."

"Do I let you choose when and if you will eat Brussels sprouts and liver?"

Becky nodded. "Yes."

"Honey, men are like food. What tastes good to one person doesn't necessarily appeal to another. Just because you think I should marry Mike whatsisname, doesn't mean I want to marry him. That should be my choice."

"But you never even date," Becky said.

"That's my choice."

"But Jason and I want a new daddy," Becky said, her lower lip trembling.

Faith's heart broke and she wrapped her arms around her daughter. "Oh, honey, I know you want a daddy. But daddies aren't like computers or toys or cars. You can't just call a number and order one. You have to find the right one. If you get the wrong one, it can be a big mess."

She squeezed Becky tightly. "I'm sorry you can't have a daddy right now, but I have to be very careful about who I date and especially who I marry. You and Jason are so precious. Whoever I marry will have to fall in love with the two of you. You two are too important for me to have it any other way."

Becky gave another heavy sigh. "I just wish it could be different, Mom."

Faith slid her hand through Becky's hair. "Is it so awful the way it is right now?"

Becky pulled back and shook her head. "No. It's actually pretty good. Everyone in my class knows my mom makes the best cookies."

Faith smiled. "You're the best daughter in the world, but no more matchmaking."

A shadow crossed Becky's face that made Faith a bit nervous. "But will you at least start dating?"

Faith thought of Gabriel and her heart raced. "If it's someone I choose."

That night, Gabriel didn't come to dinner or the house and Faith struggled with missing him. Ridiculous. How could she miss a man she'd just met? How could she miss a man about whom she shouldn't be thinking? Or wanting?

She couldn't, however, stop thinking about how close she'd felt to him, how natural it had felt to be in his arms. How right it had felt to comfort him when she sensed he felt sad. Her feelings for him had hit her too fast and too strong.

When she'd imagined herself in love again, and she hadn't allowed herself to imagine it very often, she'd pictured a slow, steady relationship. Nothing that would rock her boat, just something she could count on. Someone she could count on. She hadn't imagined fire, or a fast click. She hadn't imagined riding a roller coaster. She'd never imagined a man like Gabriel could be seriously interested in her.

"But it isn't serious," she reminded herself as she climbed into bed after baking cookies and folding laundry. She pulled up her covers, turned off her bedside lamp and closed her eyes.

The phone rang, startling her. She picked it up quickly. "Hello?"

"It's Gabriel."

"Hi," she said, her heart doing a silly Snoopy dance.

"I had dinner with the contractor for the restaurant," he said. "Got a lot of business done."

"That's good," she said.

He paused. "I would have liked to have seen you today."

She felt a melting sensation inside her and closed her eyes. She shouldn't encourage this. She absolutely shouldn't. "I would have liked to have seen you today, too," she said in a low voice.

"Then maybe we should see each other tomorrow," he said, his voice doing wonderful and horrible things to her nervous system.

"Maybe we should."

"Can I take you out to dinner?"

"That would be wonderful, but I need more notice to get a sitter. Would you like to join us for dinner?"

"Sure, but get a sitter for Saturday night."

Chapter 7

Faith saw Gabriel every night. He joined her and the kids for dinner, played board games with the kids, answered their incessant questions, chatted with her after she tucked Becky and Jason into bed, asked about her sisters, then kissed her senseless.

Every time she learned something new about him, she wanted to know more. Afraid of depending on him, she told herself not to get used to having him around. When she looked into his eyes, though, she forgot to be afraid. She forgot not to hope.

On Thursday night, just before the children

went to bed, Becky ordered Gabe to close his eyes.

"No peeking," she said. "We have a surprise for you."

"For me?" His mouth lifted in a pleased grin as he sat on the sofa.

"We can't bring it 'til you close your eyes cuz it's too big to wrap," Jason said.

Faith felt a dart of surprise. What had those kids been up to? She'd caught them whispering a few times lately and Becky had kept her door closed more often than usual.

"Okay, I'll close my eyes," Gabriel said with a grin.

The children ran down the hallway.

"I wanna carry it!" Jason insisted.

"You'll drop it," Becky said.

Faith cringed and rose. "Kids!"

Silence followed. "We'll both carry it," Becky said.

Both children entered the room carrying a small Christmas tree decorated with a variety of ornaments.

Stunned and moved, Faith shook her head. "Where did you find it?"

"In the cellar," Becky said. "We thought you wouldn't mind. Jason and I made the—"

"You can open your eyes!" Jason yelled.

Gabe opened his eyes and looked at the tree. "What's this?"

"It's your very own Christmas tree," Jason said, nearly jumping up and down with excitement. "Me and Becky made it."

"Becky and I," Faith automatically corrected, moving closer to look at the decorations.

"We decided since you weren't going to be home for Christmas that we would give you a Christmas tree. We put your favorite things and special people on it."

"I put on the football," Jason said, pointing to a miniature football.

"And that's a picture of apple pie with ice cream," Jason added, rubbing his tummy.

"We put on a ballerina slipper for your daughter," Becky said, pointing to the ornament. "And a diamond for your wife."

"Oh, and look, there's the logo for Raines, Incorporated," Faith said, amazed at her children's thoughtfulness. She looked at Gabe and saw him touch the ornaments on the tree.

"You two are something else, aren't you?" he said to Becky and Jason.

"Do you like it?" Becky asked earnestly.

"I love it," he said, his voice rough with emotion. "It's perfect." He stroked both their cheeks. "Thank you."

The kids set down the tree and he embraced them both. They scurried off to bed and Gabe met her gaze. He pulled her against him. "Your kids are incredible," he said.

"They are, aren't they?" Her eyes welled with tears of pride and emotion.

"Their mom is pretty incredible, too," he said and kissed her.

Friday arrived and she and the kids got ready for the community party. Jason had invited Gabriel the previous evening, so the four of them would be going. Faith walked into her room to find Becky going through her closet making clucking sounds of disapproval.

"What are you doing?" Faith asked.

Becky turned around with her hands on her hips. "Looking for something for you to wear to the party. Mom, all your clothes are so last year."

Her clothes were technically year before last, but Faith wasn't counting. "Buying new clothing for myself hasn't been my first priority," she said.

"But you got that big check from Gabe—"

"I intend to use that check for you and Jason and household repairs."

"But Mom, you could at least get one new outfit," Becky said. "The newest dress you bought

was that black one for Aunt Beth's memorial service.''

"I like the dress with frogs on it," Jason said
from the doorway.

Becky rolled her eyes. "That's a summer
dress.''

He shrugged. "I still like it.''

Becky looked at the closet again and shook her
head. "Mom, you have nothing to wear.''

"I'm sure I can find something," Faith said.
"The community party is casual, Becky. I won't
need an evening gown.''

"Yeah, but how are you ever gonna—''

The doorbell rang, cutting Becky off.

Faith's heart dipped in anticipation. "That
might be Gabe. Jason, would you—''

Jason was already running toward the door.

Faith turned to Becky. "I'll try not to embar-
rass you," she said with a smile.

"Well, maybe you could put on some eye
shadow and wear some earrings," Becky said. "I
need to call Amanda.''

Faith frowned as Becky left the room. She
hoped Becky wasn't cooking up another matchmaking scheme. She'd thought they'd settled that
issue the other day. Turning to her closet, she
glanced through her clothes and reluctantly had to
agree with her daughter. She needed to call Fash-

ion Emergency. There wasn't time tonight, though, so she pushed all the way to the far side of the closet and pulled out a black velvet dress. It was cut simply enough that it never went out of style.

Pulling it over her head, she fastened the buttons in the back then put on black stockings and stepped into a well-worn pair of black pumps. To relieve the stark color, she put on a glittery Christmas tree pin that had belonged to her aunt Beth. She looked in the mirror and the sight of her aunt's jewelry made her feel a sharp jab of loss mixed with warmth. Her aunt would be happy she was wearing the pin. She was so glad her sisters would be home for Christmas soon.

Taking a closer look in the mirror, she scowled at the shadows under her eyes. Maybe Becky was right. Maybe she should put on a little makeup. She dabbed on concealer, lipstick and coated her eyelashes with mascara. She brushed her hair and wore it straight.

Picking up a small purse to carry her keys and some change, she walked into the den. "I'm ready. Sorry you had to wait."

Three pairs of eyes stared at her in surprise.

Jason was the first one to speak. "Wow. You look pretty, Mom."

Faith smiled. "Thanks."

"You did really good, Mom," Becky said, sounding surprised.

"Amazing what you can do with a black dress, isn't it?" she said to her daughter, then met Gabriel's appreciative gaze.

"Very nice," he said. "A shame we're not going to dinner tonight."

Her stomach danced with butterflies at the thought of her upcoming dinner with Gabriel. She wouldn't have the protection of her children. Silly thought, but she felt nervous. "The community party will be fun," she said lightly. "I'll grab the cookies and we can go."

An hour into the party, after Faith had introduced Gabe to what seemed like a thousand people, she escaped to grab some punch. The local band had began playing and couples were starting to dance.

A man she hadn't met before approached her. "Excuse me, are you Faith Donner?"

She nodded. "Yes, I am. And you?"

"I'm Randy Allen. I'm the new assistant principal at Greenfield Elementary school. I believe your daughter and son attend school there."

Faith felt a surge of parental discomfort. "Yes, they do. It's nice to meet you. I hadn't heard there was a new assistant principal. I hope neither of my children have been sent to see you for some reason.''

He chuckled. ''No. I met Becky when I filled in for the P.E. teacher the other day. He had a family emergency and had to leave school early.''

''Oh, well I'm sure that made for an active afternoon for you.''

''Yes, it did. Becky mentioned that you were planning to send cookies in for the front office and administrators. That's really kind of you.''

Faith blinked. She wondered when Becky had made this kind offer on her behalf. She wondered how many other people Becky may have promised cookies. She smiled gamely. ''My pleasure. I've forgotten. How many are in the administration office?''

''Around twelve including the guidance counselor.'' Randy cocked his head toward the band. ''I like this song. Would you dance with me?''

Faith blinked again. ''I, uh—''

''Come on,'' he said, smiling. ''Don't be shy.''

Gabriel glanced toward the dance floor and did a double take. Faith was dancing. He felt a gut-tightening possessiveness that was totally inappropriate, yet he couldn't take his eyes off of her.

''Oh, sweet!'' Becky said as she took a bite of cookie. ''Mom's dancing with the assistant principal. I told him she liked to dance, but would need to be asked.''

Gabriel glanced down at Faith's little brown-eyed scheming matchmaker. ''You did what?''

Becky shifted from foot to foot. ''Well, I actually mentioned it a few days ago because Mom told me men are like Brussels sprouts. She doesn't make me eat Brussels sprouts, so I shouldn't make her date someone she might not want to date.''

He blinked, trying to digest the comparison. It was unique, but he could see it.

''Oh, and look there's the fireman who came by the house. He's one of the other ones I told about Mom.''

Gabriel felt a sinking sensation. ''Exactly how many men did you tell about your mom?''

''Only four,'' she said and munched a bit more on her cookie. ''Well, five if you include Jason's Sunday school teacher, but he might not be here.''

Gabriel swallowed a long-suffering sigh. By his calculations, Faith's dance card was going to be full for the next several numbers. Turning to the culprit responsible, he looked at Becky and shook his head. The little girl meant well, but he sure didn't like Becky recruiting all this competition. The more he got to know Faith, the more he felt as if he'd discovered the rarest of gems. The more time he spent with her, the more time he wanted to spend with her.

"So I wonder how many Brussels sprouts you'll have to eat for this," Gabriel said to Becky.

Her eyes widened in horror. "You don't really think she'll make me eat Brussels sprouts, do you?" She made a face. "Oh, no. She mentioned liver, too. If I have to eat liver…"

"You may want to be careful how many more men you recruit to date your mother," he said.

She nodded, wearing a slightly sick expression on her face.

She looked so miserable Gabriel almost regretted mentioning the Brussels sprouts. Almost. He took pity on her and decided to distract her. "You wanna dance?"

She looked at him uncertainly. "Dance?"

He nodded. "Would you like to dance? With me?"

Her smile started small, then grew so that it lit her entire face. She lifted her shoulders. "Yes, I would."

Faith's face began to hurt from smiling so much. She was going to wring her daughter's neck. Not literally, of course, but she was going to do something. Talking apparently hadn't worked. She glanced past the shoulder of her son's Sunday school teacher and caught sight of Gabriel dancing with Becky.

Her heart just stopped.

Becky was grinning from ear-to-ear, her eyes sparkling, and Gabriel was gently guiding her in a waltz. The sight of the two of them dancing made a knot form in her throat. She had longed for her children to have a father who loved them and enjoyed them. She had longed for a man who loved her and thought she was special, too.

She saw Becky and Gabriel laugh together, and at that moment, Faith fell hopelessly in love.

A slow song eased through the sound system and she stepped back. "Thank you," she said. "I think I'll—"

"May I have this dance?" Gabriel asked from behind her.

Her heart dipped and she turned around, unable to keep a smile from her face. "You certainly may."

He pulled her into his arms and Faith sighed. This was where she wanted to be.

"I'm warning you, if anyone asks to cut in, I'm going to be rude and say no," Gabriel murmured against her ear.

"Good," she said.

He chuckled.

"Easy for you to laugh. I've found out I'm

baking Christmas cookies for the school administration office, the firemen working on Christmas
and my son's Sunday school class. I'm afraid of
what might be coming around the corner.''

"I think it should slow down now. Becky and
I had a little discussion.''

Faith pulled back slightly so she could look at
Gabe's face. "I saw you dancing with her. That
was so...so...'' She swallowed over a lump of
emotion in her throat. "So wonderful.''

"I was trying to distract her. She'd just finished
telling me about the 'men are like Brussels
sprouts' discussion. I saw another guy ask you to
dance and said I wondered how many Brussels
sprouts she was going to have to eat.''

Faith laughed. "Very good, very good. I'm impressed.''

"I'm glad to hear that,'' he said in a serious
tone. "It goes both ways.''

Faith's stomach dipped again. Gabriel pulled
her closer and she closed her eyes, hoping against
hope that her time with this incredible man would
last a little longer.

The following day, in between making batches
of cookies, Faith took the children into town with
her while she shopped for a new dress. To keep
them from growing bored, she allowed Jason to

bring a truck and made a game of asking their opinions on the dresses she tried.

Luck was on her side and she found a beautiful winter-white sheath with simple lines that would last several seasons. Picking up shoes, stockings to match and a few stocking stuffers for her sisters, she headed back home to bake more cookies and tried not to think about how much money she had spent on the outfit.

As time for dinner grew near, Faith grew more and more jumpy. She told herself to chill, but she hadn't been on a date since she could remember. And she'd never been to dinner with a man like Gabriel.

Her fingers shook so badly when she applied her makeup that she allowed Becky to help her apply lipstick.

"Mom, you look like a movie star," Becky said in awe.

"You're sweet, honey," she said, laughing nervously.

"I'm sorry about the cookies," Becky said.

"That's okay. It could have been worse. It could have been Brussels sprouts."

Becky winced. "That would have been a lot worse."

The doorbell rang and Faith's stomach knotted. This was crazy. She was an adult, but she hoped she didn't drop a fork or do anything embarrassing.

"Hi Gabe!" Jason's loud welcome could be heard all the way from the foyer.

"It's time." Faith picked up her purse and just as she started to leave her bedroom, Becky threw her arms around her. Surprised, she hugged her daughter in return. "What's this?"

"I just wanted to give you a hug."

"Well, thank you for giving me one." She took a steadying breath and walked into the den.

"Wow, Mom!" Jason said.

Gabe gave a long, low whistle of appreciation. "You look great."

"Thanks. You do, too," she said, taking in his well-tailored black suit, crisp white shirt and red silk tie. Forget dinner. Gabriel looked good enough to eat.

"Ready to go?"

She nodded and he helped her with her coat. Faith relished the way he held the umbrella for her and helped her into his truck. He got in and started the engine and put on a Christmas jazz CD. "I thought we'd check out the competition at one of the restaurants at the Lone Star Country Club. Next time, we'll try Jocelyne's."

Just the mention of the name of the fine local French restaurant, Jocelyne's, was enough to catch Faith's attention. Two of the other words he'd said in the same sentence, however, made her heart jump. *Next time.* He'd said *next time* as if he was thinking about her past tonight.

They chatted on the way to the renowned country club, which was decorated with thousands of lights. With no hope of snow, the beautiful decorations took a close second in creating a winter wonderland. The valet took Gabe's truck and they entered the large club. Decorated in blues and ivory, the restaurant evoked an elegant, yet intimate atmosphere.

Gabe had arranged for a private corner table. His attentiveness soon made Faith forget her self-consciousness and they debated the finer points of the menu. He ordered steak and she ordered seafood with an agreement to share.

After they fed each other bites of their entrées, Faith ordered a gourmet lime sherbet.

"No apple pie à la mode," Faith said and shook her head because she knew that was Gabe's favorite. "They lose points for that."

"Exactly." The waiter served the light dessert and Gabe immediately picked up the spoon.

She laughed. "I didn't know you wanted any, but I'm glad to share."

"I'm going to serve you," he said, sliding the

spoon into the frozen treat. He held it in front of her mouth. ''Want a bite?''

She glanced around to see if anyone was watching, but they were safely hidden in a tiny alcove. She opened her mouth and he slid the cold lime dessert into her mouth. She closed her eyes. ''That's good.''

''Looks like it,'' he said, his eyes darkening with arousal. ''Another bite?''

She nodded and opened her mouth. He slid it inside her mouth and she licked the edge of the spoon.

He made a low sound of approval. She met his gaze and felt an undercurrent of electricity flow between them. A visual collage of all the times he'd kissed her flowed through her mind. Her temperature climbed.

His gaze holding hers, he offered another spoonful. Transfixed by him, she met his gaze and took the sherbet onto her tongue and swallowed it. She felt hot and the treat felt cool all the way down. She licked her lips and he set down the spoon.

Reaching toward her, he curled his hand around the back of her neck and French-kissed her. Faith had never felt more sensual.

''That's the way I wanted to taste the sherbet,'' he murmured. ''On you.''

He kissed her again and Faith felt the familiar buzz of arousal permeate her. Drawing back, he glanced up and motioned for the waiter. "You can put the check on my bill."

"Shall I take the sherbet?" the waiter asked.

Gabe shook his head. "We're not finished with it." As soon as the waiter left, he turned to Faith. "I can take you back your house. Or you can come upstairs to my suite. Lady's choice."

Chapter 8

"I can't stay the whole night," she told him after he led her into his hotel suite. *But heaven knows, I want to.*

"That's okay," he said, shrugging out of his jacket and gesturing toward the comfortable sofa in the lushly decorated living area. He'd already set the dish of gourmet sherbet on an end table. "I just liked the idea of having you all to myself for a few minutes. When do you need to be home?"

"Cinderella time," she said, joining him on the sofa. "After twelve o'clock I'll turn into a pumpkin and have a tough time getting this baby-sitter again.''

''Duly noted.'' He glanced at the sherbet. ''Would you like some more dessert?''

Still aroused from the way he had looked at her throughout the meal, Faith felt a surge of recklessness. ''I don't really want more of the sherbet,'' she said. ''But I do want more of—'' She bit her lip, losing her nerve.

''Of what?'' he prodded.

She swallowed over her nerves. ''Of you,'' she confessed in a low voice.

His eyes flashed with fire and he lowered his head. ''I wouldn't want to be accused of not giving the lady what she wanted.''

He took her mouth and the room began to spin. Faith felt the strain of her unexpressed feelings. Gabriel had changed her life in ways that had nothing to do with new cars, new computers and new toys, and everything to do with her heart and head. She wanted closer, oh so much closer. So close there was no room between his strength and her.

Her response to his seductive, mind-bending kiss must have conveyed her need. He groaned. ''I know I can't keep you here all night, but I want to.''

They had to be so careful at her house because the children could interrupt at any moment. Their passion had bubbled beneath the surface like a pot ready to boil over. Even though she knew she couldn't stay all night, the opportunity to kiss him and touch him freely was too tempting to resist.

She suckled his tongue deep into her mouth and swallowed his groan of pleasure. He slid his hands over the sweater dress that clung to her swollen breasts. He touched her nipples, and even through the barrier of her dress, they peaked against his fingertips.

"I want you naked," he muttered.

The heat of his touch raced through her like wildfire and she tugged at his tie and shirt, eager to feel his flesh against her hands. He helped her get rid of his shirt and undershirt so that she could slide her fingers over his muscular chest, enhanced with a soft spray of masculine hair.

She rubbed her open mouth against his throat and he swore under his breath. "You're making it hard for me to—" He groaned again. "To show any restraint."

"I didn't order restraint for dessert," she whispered.

He went very still then looked into her eyes. "Are you sure?"

She nodded. She'd never been more sure. "Except I can't get preg—"

He covered her lips with his finger. "I'll take care of you."

Following a combination of instinct and desire, she drew his finger into her mouth.

Gabriel took her hand and drew it to his chest. "Feel what you're doing to me," he said, his heart pounding hard against her palm. He drew her palm lower to where he was hard and swollen.

The intimacy of the gesture turned her inside out again. He took her mouth in an endless French kiss and pulled off her clothes and the rest of his. He fondled her breasts with his fingertips and mouth, making her breathless with need and pleasure. He took her intimately with his mouth, sending her over the edge.

Pulling a small package containing a condom from his wallet, he opened the packet and put it on, then slid between her legs. "I bought this after the night we made cookies together. I wanted you then and every night since." He thrust inside her. "You are so beautiful."

He made her feel that way by the love words he uttered and his sounds of pleasure. He made her feel like the only woman in the world. He made her feel like his dream woman.

By the time he took her over the edge with him for the last time, she could almost believe he loved her.

Like two teenagers who couldn't get enough of each other, they pushed Faith's "curfew." At five minutes before midnight, Gabe pulled in front of her house and escorted her to the door. His arm provided needed support. Her knees were still weak, and she knew she would be sore tomorrow.

He nuzzled her neck. "I only expected to take you to dinner. I didn't think you were going to blow me away in bed."

She felt her cheeks heat because she knew she had been totally wanton. "We weren't really in bed much of the time," she said. "Did you mind?"

"Hell no," he said. "I just hate you having to leave afterwards. I want to keep you by my side."

His words reassured her. "Me too, but duty calls."

He gave her a long, languorous kiss. "I'll call you tomorrow. Okay?"

She nodded, wondering how she could feel satisfied, yet still want him so much she burned with it. "Thank you for everything."

"Oh no, Faith. Thank you."

She watched him leave and sighed, wondering if she would be able to get her head screwed on straight by morning.

The following morning as she helped the children get ready for church, the phone rang.

Certain it was Gabriel, Faith picked it up on the first ring, her heart racing. She smiled into the receiver. "Hello?"

"Good morning, beautiful," Gabe said, his voice early-morning sexy.

Her smile grew. "Good morning, handsome."

"I have good news and bad news."

"Okay," she said, stepping into a pair of pumps.

"The good news is I'll be back by Christmas Eve, but the bad news is I have to take care of a minor crisis at headquarters. That means I have to go home today."

Her stomach sank with disappointment. She felt her smile fade. "Oh no."

"I know. I was bummed with the news and I would have liked to delegate, but I'm the best one to take care of this. Tell me you'll miss me."

"Of course I will," she said, wondering if he would miss her.

"I'll call you when I can, but it may be a little sketchy because I'll be in a hurry to get back."

Faith fought the childish urge to wail and took a careful breath. She needed to be supportive. Gabriel didn't need her to act like a clinging wuss. "Be extra careful driving back. The rain has made some of the roads a mess."

"I'll be careful," he said. "And Faith, I'll be thinking about you."

I hope so, she thought.

Faith spent every other minute thinking of Gabriel. He didn't call Sunday or Monday and she reminded herself he'd said he might have a hard time calling. But what if he'd already begun to put her from his mind? What if distance didn't make his heart fonder? What if it just made his heart more distant? She fought the ugly sense that she had just been a one-night stand for him. A hot night with a sexually deprived single mom. She cringed every time she thought of it and cooked up a storm in anticipation of her sisters' upcoming visit. She baked enough cookies to feed half the population of Mission Creek.

She cooked every dish imaginable in preparation for Christmas dinner. She wrapped gifts for her children and sisters. She even wrapped a gift for Gabriel. With Christmas music playing at top volume to drown out her doubts, she baked and wrapped…and baked some more.

The day before Christmas Eve arrived and Faith vowed not to think about Gabriel. Her sister Ann Elise was arriving today. It had been ages since she and her sisters had visited, and even though part of the reason they were gathering was to hold a special memorial for Aunt Beth, Faith couldn't wait to see her sisters. Ann Elise was her beautiful type-A older sister. She smiled as memories slid through her mind.

"Mama, tell me again about Aunt Ann Elise and Aunt Marilou," Jason said as he stuck out his shoe for her to tie it. Between her divorce and her sisters' busy lives, she and her sisters hadn't had an easy time connecting in person during the past few years. Jason didn't remember much about his aunts. Faith hoped that would change soon.

"Aunt Ann Elise is my older sister and she is a veterinarian in Dallas. An animal doctor," she interpreted for her son. "She's very smart and ambitious."

"What's ambitious?"

"A very hard worker," she said, tying his other shoe. "Aunt Marilou works with numbers."

"Math?" he asked.

She nodded. "And she's engaged to be married," she added. She'd often wondered why Marilou had never brought her fiancé to meet Aunt Beth. Something about Marilou's situation just didn't feel right.

Jason jiggled her shoulders. "Mama, sing 'The Twelve Days Of Christmas.'"

"Okay, but you sing it with me." She began the first verse and Jason sang every other word. She sang the second verse and the third. He always got the partridge part right. Faith loved watching Jason's face as he tried to learn the verses. He nodded his head and concentrated so intently.

He shifted from one foot to the other. "I gotta go to the bathroom, but keep singin' Mom," he said and dashed down the hall.

Faith laughed and sang at the top of her lungs.

She heard a male voice join in on the eighth day and jerked her head toward the door, stopping midverse. Gabriel stood at the door, wearing casual clothes and a smile that sent her pulse skyrocketing. The clock chimed 10:00 a.m. He must have been on the road early.

Striding toward her, he held her gaze and Faith was afraid to blink in case he disappeared. "You look like you've seen a ghost," he said.

She swallowed over a lump in her throat. "I guess I kinda feel that way. I wasn't sure if—" She bit her lip. "Or when—" Fear squeezed her throat closed.

He rushed to stand in front of her, putting his hands on her arms and looking down at her in surprise. "You didn't think I would come back?"

"I didn't know," she said.

"But I told you I would be back by tomorrow."

"I know you did. But when I didn't hear from you, I started thinking…" She shook her head. "Thinking about the differences between us. Thinking about how different your world is from mine. Thinking you might change your mind about how you feel about—"

"Aw, Faith." He pulled her against him. "You should have called me."

"I wanted you to call me," she confessed, unable to keep her voice steady. She felt her eyes burn with the threat of tears.

"Honey, I thought about you the whole time."

"I thought about you, too." She sank into his embrace and told herself to stop crying.

"I took care of the crisis," he said and she felt him brush his lips over her forehead.

"That's good."

"I came back to you early," he said.

"That's even better."

She felt his mouth lift in a smile against her forehead. "I brought you a gift."

Faith groaned and shook her head. "I don't want any more gifts. You've given me too much already. I'd just like you to stay around for a while."

He put his thumb under her chin and lifted it. "How long is a while?"

The expression in his eyes turned her knees to jelly. "A long, long time."

"How does forever sound?" he asked.

She swallowed, afraid to hope. "What are you saying?"

Backing away slightly, he pulled a small black velvet box from his pocket. "I know we technically haven't known each other very long, but I feel like I've known you forever. I know my heart has been looking for you. I want to marry you, Faith. I want you to be my wife." He flipped open the box to reveal a stunning diamond ring.

Faith couldn't stop the tears streaming down her face. "Oh, my! Oh—"

"Mom's crying!" Jason yelled from the hallway. "Mom, what's wrong? Why are you crying?'' He rushed to pull insistently at her jeans. ''Mom.''

Becky ran into the hallway too, her voice full of worry. She glanced at Gabriel, Jason and Faith. ''What's wrong? Did something bad happen?''

Faith swiped her cheeks with the backs of her hands. ''No, it's something wonderful.''

Gabe tenderly touched a tear she'd missed. ''You sure?''

She nodded. ''Yes, it's the most wonderful thing that could happen.''

''What is it?'' Becky demanded.

''I'm asking you and Jason and your mom if you'll marry me,'' Gabriel said.

Becky's eyes rounded. ''Sweet!''

Jason jumped up and down. ''You want all of us to marry you?''

Gabe nodded. ''If you'll have me.'' He met Faith's gaze. ''Will you marry me?''

''Yes.'' All three answered at once, and Gabe slid the ring on Faith's finger.

Late that afternoon, Gabe stayed with the children while Faith drove to the small airport to pick up her sister Ann Elise. It was raining cats and dogs, but she couldn't be happier. The weight of the stunning new engagement ring on her finger felt both strange and wonderful. She kept looking at it to make sure she wasn't in a dream.

"It's real," she told herself. "He's not going anywhere."

Her heart expanded in her chest and she struggled with another urge to cry. She wondered how long it would take for her to really believe everything was going to work out.

Pulling into a parking place, she walked inside the small terminal and waited for her sister's commuter jet to arrive. Minutes passed and she felt her eagerness build.

A small jet landed and Faith watched the passengers unload. Spotting Ann Elise's blond head, she waved madly. Ann Elise smiled and ran toward her.

Faith pulled her sister into her arms for a big hug. "I'm so glad you're here."

"I know. It feels like it's been forever," Ann Elise said.

"How was your flight?"

Ann Elise's smile faded and her eyebrows furrowed. "Strange." She shook her head and waved her hand. "I'd rather hear all about you and the kids. Tell all."

The two sisters collected Ann Elise's luggage and Faith drove them back to the house. Along the way, Ann Elise pointed out familiar sights and the few changes that had been made in the past few years.

"How's your practice?" Faith asked, sensing an underlying restlessness in her sister.

"Very successful. Sometimes too successful. It seems so quiet here. What about you and the kids? Are they excited about Christmas?"

"Extremely," Faith said and told Ann Elise about how Becky's letter to Santa Claus had caught the attention of the CEO of Raines, Incorporated. "He's been embarrassingly generous." She chewed her lip, trying to figure out how to tell Ann Elise the rest of the incredible story.

"I'll say," Ann Elise said, pointing at the diamond ring on Faith's finger. "Looks like he has excellent taste. You better be careful about wearing that ring on your left hand, though, or people will think you're engaged."

Faith took a quick breath. She should have known her sharp-as-a-tack sister wouldn't miss anything. "They would be right," she said in a low voice.

With the exception of road noise, complete silence followed.

"Are you kidding?" Ann Elise asked in a

shocked, high-pitched voice. "Didn't you just meet him?"

"Yes. I'm not sure I can explain it, but it's right," she said, pulling into the drive to the ranch. "He loves me, loves the kids. I never dreamed I would meet anyone like him."

"When are you getting married?" Ann Elise asked as Faith pulled the car to a stop.

Faith smiled, her heart still bursting with joy. She turned to look at her sister. "Valentine's Day. Please say you'll come."

Ann Elise nodded her head incredulously. "Of course, I will." She hugged her tight. "You deserve some happiness. You've been a saint to take care of Aunt Beth."

"I just feel lucky right now," Faith said, blinking back tears. "First Gabe and now you and Marilou home for Christmas. It couldn't be better."

Hours later after Ann Elise met and approved of Gabe, and had reacquainted herself with Becky and Jason, everyone except Gabe and Faith went to bed.

"You think I passed?" he asked Faith, pulling her onto his lap.

"With Ann Elise?" she asked, wrapping her

arms around his neck. She nodded. "With flying colors. Nice of you to save the Christmas tree after Jason ran into it."

"He's a fast one. I think he's going to end up running track," Gabe said.

"Think so?" she asked, allowing him to draw her mouth close to his.

He nodded, nuzzling his face against hers. "He can chase the track. I'll chase his mother."

She tilted her lips to his for a kiss. He took the offering, and his mouth warmed her all over. "I haven't said this in years, but it's truer than ever."

"What's that?"

"I love Santa."

He gave a low, sexy chuckle. "I love you, too, Faith."

*   *   *   *   *

CHRISTMAS EVE REUNION
Dixie Browning

Chapter 1

The moment the seat-belt warning went off, Ann Elise Baker scrambled through her purse to find her pillbox. Requesting a glass of water from the single attendant on the crowded commuter, she swallowed two acetaminophen capsules, tilted her seat back and closed her eyes. Last year on her way to a veterinarian conference in late November, she had vowed never again to travel during the holiday season. It was a headache. Literally.

This time she'd had no choice. Through no fault of her own she had missed her aunt Beth's funeral earlier in the year—she simply couldn't afford to miss the memorial service.

But another reason was even more compelling.

Her sisters needed her. She knew Faith had been struggling to make ends meet after ending a disastrous marriage, but her middle sister had more pride than the law allowed. Ann Elise had even offered to sell her practice and move back to Mission Creek to help take care of Aunt Beth, but Faith had been adamantly opposed.

Twenty years ago, after their parents had been killed in a plane crash, Ann Elise, who'd been twelve at the time, had bottled up her own grief and tried to comfort and reassure six-year-old Marilou and eight-year-old Faith. Over the years, that pattern had continued until they had gradually pulled away, confident that they no longer needed comforting and encouraging, not to mention a big sister's advice. Even though they were scattered from Dallas to Corpus Christi to Mission Creek, they were all still in Texas.

Ann Elise applauded their independence, she really did. After all, she'd done her best to encourage it. But what she wanted more than anything now was to draw her small family close again. They might not realize it, but they still needed her. She certainly needed them.

Busy establishing her practice as a companion animal vet, she hadn't realized how quickly time sped by. She hadn't seen Faith's two children since little Becky was in kindergarten and Jason was only a toddler. Sad state of affairs, she mused, when it took a dear relative's memorial service to bring them together again.

Aunt Beth's house, once the center of a prosperous ranch, was certainly a better place to spend the holidays than her own apartment. Especially now that she'd found homes for all the strays and survivors she'd temporarily adopted. The corgidachshund mix she'd called Longshot was the last to go. Her chair rungs would forever bear the marks of his teeth, but he'd certainly livened up the place. Uncle Lloyd would've banished him to a pen, but Aunt Beth would have adored him.

Aunt Beth and Uncle Lloyd had given the three little girls a home after their parents died. Ann Elise had initially worried that Uncle Lloyd's wife, who was no blood kin and therefore not obligated to take them in, would ask them to leave. Tall for her age, she'd conceived some wild idea of dropping out of school, claiming to be sixteen and getting a job at the Hamburger Hangout, kidnapping her sisters and looking after them herself.

Not very practical. In fact, not practical at all. Fortunately she'd never been forced to act on her plans. Uncle Lloyd had been...well, stern was a kind word to describe his temperament. But not unkind. He'd built them a playroom in the attic, after all. Probably to get them out from underfoot, but still…

Uncle Lloyd and Faith had clashed right from the start. As for Aunt Beth, although they were related only by marriage, she'd been unvaryingly kind and patient, never once alluding to the fact that while she was a Wainwright, one of Mission Creek's founding families, they were only Bakers.

Of course, Aunt Beth had married a Baker. In fact, Ann Elise had once heard it whispered that her aunt had married beneath her, but then, Mission Creek was inclined to be cliquish.

True or not, it had served to put her even more on the defensive in the beginning. As a result, she'd spent those early years preparing for the future and waiting for the rejection that never came.

Lord, she thought now, opening her eyes to massage her throbbing temples, where had all that ancient history sprung from?

Well, that was obvious. For the first time in too long she was returning to the big, rambling ranch house they'd all shared until she'd left for college. In the meantime, Faith had married and moved away—more to escape Uncle Lloyd than for any other reason, Ann Elise had always suspected.

Marilou had gone off to school and surprised them all by not only doing well, but by becoming a financial consultant.

Soon after Uncle Lloyd had died, Aunt Beth had moved to New York, so there'd been no reason for Ann Elise to come back to Mission Creek. Besides, she'd been busy establishing herself as a veterinarian.

Excuses, excuses...

Eyes closed as she tried to will away her headache, she started putting together a mental to-do list. She'd turned into a compulsive list-maker, which probably said something about her that wasn't too flattering. Here it was the twenty-third of December and she hadn't even started her Christmas shopping, but she did have several half-finished lists.

For Faith, something pretty. A silk negligee and matching slippers, perhaps—or maybe something more practical, but still nice.

What about Marilou? What did CPAs like? CPAs who didn't look like CPAs and didn't act like CPAs? A chocolate calculator?

An irreverent thought crept in and she bit back a drowsy smile, her eyes still closed against the glare coming through the small Plexiglas window.

Why not simply raid the local shelter and give everyone a pet?

Okay, back to reality.

Had she left anything on that shouldn't be on in her apartment? She'd gone through her check-list before locking the door behind her. She was compulsive about security, too, at least when she wasn't distracted by other duties. All a part of her stress-related symptoms, according to Dr. Hodges, friend and physician.

Ann Elise wasn't sure she bought into the di-agnosis. On the other hand, a brand-new year was bearing down on her and she wasn't even done with the old one yet. As soon as she could clear her calendar she vowed to spend a solid month on a beach—any beach at all, but the more de-serted the better. That way, no one could make demands on her, real or implied. No telephones, no e-mail, no persistent sales reps. For one whole month she would do absolutely nothing but sleep in the sun, float on the water, and read purely for pleasure—nothing even faintly resembling litera-ture, certainly nothing educational.

And of course she would end up with a million more freckles and a blistered nose. She'd always hated her freckles, but even without them, she'd never have been called pretty. Big eyes, long legs and good teeth didn't make up for freckles, glasses and straight hair—not when every other girl in Mission Creek High had 20/20 vision, bouncy curls and knew how to use makeup to enhance any shortcomings.

Uncle Lloyd had frowned on the use of makeup. She'd tried lipstick a few times, but with her colorless lashes and brows it always made her look like a clown.

At least now she knew what to use and how to use it with discretion. Contacts didn't hide her eyes, and the right shade of lipstick made a difference. She'd finally grown into her cheekbones so that the hollows didn't look so cadaverish. She had even learned how to minimize her freckles and put on a few pounds so that her five-foot-eight frame didn't look quite so gawky.

Of course, she'd recently lost the same pounds. Stress again. Too much to do and too little time. She couldn't remember a time in her life when she hadn't been in a hurry. Hurry up and graduate from high school in case she had to make a home for her sisters. Hurry up and get away from Mission Creek before she made an even bigger fool of herself over Joe Halloran.

Oh, God, Joe Halloran...

Along with every other girl in Mission Creek

High, she'd had a monumental crush on the gorgeous hunk, and he'd been only a rising junior the year she'd graduated. Hello, Mrs. Robinson.

After that, it was hurry up and get through undergraduate school, which she'd done in three years. Get through vet school, and then establish a practice as quickly as possible in order to pay back her student loans. She'd been determined to become financially independent.

Practicing veterinarian medicine had hardly been the quickest route to riches. Looking back, she had to blame her career choice on an adolescent crush. Joe, the son of a small rancher, had told her on their one and only date that he'd made up his mind to be a vet when he'd been in fifth grade, after watching his father's careful breeding plan fall apart after an outbreak of brucellosis. He'd probably be amused if he ever learned what she'd done with her life.

She yawned, heard her ears pop and touched her throbbing temples. Flying had never agreed with her, especially on top of what her doctor called stress-related symptoms, which included insomnia and tension headaches.

"So much to do, so little time," she remembered joking after hearing the diagnosis. "Story of my life."

''Yes, well, it's your choice, Ann Elise. You're a doctor—you know the risks. Kick the habit before it kicks you even harder. Your blood pressure's nothing to brag about, either.''

After that she'd tried to ease up, she really had...when she wasn't too busy. She probably could have squeezed in time to do her Christmas shopping before she'd left Dallas, but the thought of trying to get through security with a stack of gift-wrapped boxes seemed totally impractical when she would have a full day to shop in Mission Creek. She'd decided to make a list while en route, then set out first thing tomorrow morning and whip through the stores, getting everything done in short order. If there was one thing she was good at, it was organizing her time and using it to the best advantage.

She yawned again and tried to remember where she'd left off. Definitely something pretty and feminine for Faith. Lord knows, she deserved it. And for the children... Baby gifts were easy—she always gave new babies savings bonds, but older children wanted something they could unwrap.

Her head fell forward in a doze and she jerked upright again, then adjusted the seat back so that she could recline. As the plane droned steadily southward, Ann Elise drifted in and out of sleep, picking up threads of nearby conversations and weaving them into her strangely intense dreams.

"—*told him if he ever come near me again I'd*—"

"*Lawsy, if it was me, I'd'a sicced the law on him.*"

She stood helplessly on a strange sidewalk watching Faith running down the middle of the street, two bulging suitcases beating against her legs. Looking up at the Christmas decorations on the streetlights while someone beat on a drum, Ann Elise kept calling her sister's name, but no matter how hard she tried to make herself heard, she couldn't seem to speak above a whisper.

The drone of the engines melded with voices as she drifted deeper into a familiar dream, where a much younger Ann Elise appeared wearing her first formal...

The whole thing had been an accident, her one and only date with Joe Halloran. Not that she hadn't dreamed about him ever since the first time she'd watched him sauntering off the football field, his thick, chestnut hair damp with sweat. He couldn't have been more than fourteen, but he was as tall for his age as she was for hers, only in his case, it all went together. The broad shoulders, the narrow hips, the long, muscular legs. Not to mention a smile that could light up a small city.

Unlike so many of the Mission Creek kids whose families belonged to the Lone Star Country Club, Joe wasn't snobbish. Later she'd learned that his dad wasn't even a member of the club, not that that mattered at all to Ann Elise. Once when she'd stood behind him in line for a movie, she'd wanted to touch him so much her whole body tingled. When he'd smiled at her and said, ''Hi,'' she could only stare at him and stammer while her face turned fiery red.

Of course, he'd been with another girl. He'd turned back to his little cheerleader and they'd gone on laughing and talking about football strategy, something she'd always found totally mystifying. She had envied the petite brunette with all her heart.

Her fertile imagination fast-forwarded to the night of the senior prom. Too shy to ask anyone, she'd been resigned to staying home, but on a Wednesday before the big night, Billy Kiner from her math class had invited her to be his date. And although she hadn't known him well she had recklessly said yes. Recklessly, because she didn't date. An honor student, she'd rated a big fat F when it came to a social life.

Still did, in fact, but back then she'd been pain-fully shy and insecure. Even after five years of living with the Bakers, she'd taken nothing for granted. No wonder she'd had so few dates. Lord, she must have been a mess. Afraid to make over-tures in case they were rebuffed, she'd been called snooty, stuck-up and several less flattering things.

When Billy had asked her to the prom, she'd surprised herself by saying yes and then tried to get Faith to call him and tell him she'd come down with the flu and couldn't go.

Faith refused, and Aunt Beth wouldn't hear of letting her pay for her own prom dress with the baby-sitting money she'd been hoarding for emer-gencies. Instead, they'd gone shopping together, and Aunt Beth had insisted on buying her the most beautiful gown in all of Mission Creek. It had been blue-violet. "Exactly the color of your eyes," her aunt had told her. "That gown was made for you, honey."

She'd felt like Cinderella. After the shopping spree, her aunt had steered her to the Texas Belle and instructed the hairdresser to trim her hair so that instead of hanging straight and heavy down her back it brushed her shoulders and feathered around her face.

Staring at her image in the mirror afterward,

she'd confronted a stranger whose blond hair shimmered, whose eyes, even with the hated glasses, looked impossibly large, incredibly blue, and whose mouth appeared full and vulnerable instead of merely too big.

And then the night of the prom arrived. Faith and Marilou were so excited for her they could barely sit still. "Is he handsome? Is he taller than you?" That from Faith.

Marilou had chimed in with her own string of questions, mostly regarding the car he drove, whether or not he had a horse and whether he smoked. Patiently, Ann Elise had said, "I don't know what kind of car he drives, I don't know if he has a horse, but I'm pretty sure he doesn't smoke."

Just because she'd never been close enough to smell it on him, that didn't mean he didn't. He probably did. Probably drank, too. Billy Kiner wouldn't have been her choice for a first date, but she'd had to start somewhere, and he'd been the only one to ask her. It was as good a way to break in her social life as any. If the date turned out to be a dud, her heart wouldn't be broken because it wasn't involved.

Billy was supposed to pick her up at seven-thirty. Dressed and ready a full half hour early, she'd had to race to the bathroom twice from sheer nerves, each time checking her image in the medicine cabinet mirror to be sure she hadn't devolved into her old self. Was her lipstick too bright? So much for a dress to match her eyes. You couldn't even see their color behind her round, gold-framed glasses. Aunt Beth had advised her to leave them at home, but she was blind as a bat without them.

Oh, Lord, what if she had to go to the bathroom in the middle of a dance? What if he asked her to slow dance? She'd only done it with other girls, and she'd always had to lead because she was always the tallest. She should have practiced more.

The hands on the grandfather clock brushed past seven-thirty and moved relentlessly toward eight. Gripping the edges of the seat with sweaty hands, she opened her mouth and took in a great gulp of air.

He wasn't coming. He'd only asked her on a dare, she just knew it. He was probably laughing his head off with all those wild boys he hung out with.

"Stop gulping, Ann Elise," Aunt Beth said. "You swallow air that way and you'll be belching all over the dance floor. Boys don't have any sense of time.''

But she knew. She just knew in her bones that Billy was standing her up. And as it turned out, she was right.

Headlights swept across the front of the house. Tires crunched on gravel of the circular drive. She gulped again. By that time she'd twisted her lace-edged handkerchief into a damp rope.

The big brass knocker on the front door could be heard all the way to the back of the house. ''I'll get it,'' squealed Marilou as she and Faith raced to see who would reach the door first.

Instead of her date, there stood Joe Halloran in an obviously rented tux, his longish hair gleaming under the porch light. He beamed that slow, friendly grin at her and said, ''Ann Elise, can I take Billy's place? He's been, uh—delayed.'' Joe and Billy had been friends back then, even though Joe was a few years younger. She later learned that Billy's father worked on the Halloran's ranch.

What Billy had been, was picked up for shop-lifting, although she hadn't known it at the time. Assuming she'd be meeting her real date at the school gymnasium where the prom was being held, Ann Elise had allowed Joe to assist her into his father's pickup truck that he was too young to drive, but drove anyway. She scarcely dared breathe in case all that air she'd gulped came rushing back out.

Just before they pulled into the school parking lot, Joe told her that Billy was tied up and wouldn't be there at all, and would he do? He could dance pretty well, but if she would rather just dance with older guys, he would understand.

She must have said something, but for the life of her, she couldn't remember what. They'd gone inside, and she would never forget the way the gym had looked, decorated with banners, balloons and streamers. They had drunk punch—rumors were that at least one of the huge bowls had been spiked, but Joe had dipped hers from the bowl in the middle. He'd told her that all the guys were drinking from the one on the end, so he was pretty sure the middle one was okay. He'd brought her samples of all the goodies, most of which were too sweet or too salty, but she'd thanked him and nibbled persistently, hoping she wasn't eating off her lipstick or getting crumbs stuck between her teeth.

They had line-danced and slow danced, and she hadn't once stumbled, tripped or belched. Joe was even taller than she was, which made it heavenly. He'd smelled faintly of Old Spice and he hadn't once sneaked outside for a drink like most of the other boys had done.

By the end of the evening she was head over heels in love. Serious, grown-up love, never mind that he was only fifteen and she was going on eighteen.

Between dances Joe told her his dream of becoming a veterinarian. "See, there's no money in ranching these days unless you're one of the big guys, and my dad's not, but he loves it. It's all he's ever done. So I thought if I could be a vet, I could stay there on the ranch and help him and have a practice on the side. I'm planning on getting a football scholarship—leastwise, I'm hoping I can. I guess that doesn't sound like much to you, you being a Wainwright and all."

"I'm not a Wainwright, and Uncle Lloyd's ranch is even smaller than your daddy's. In fact, it's not even a ranch anymore, mostly just the house, the outbuildings and some trees."

It had to have been the sparkling lights and the noisy, mind-numbing music. They had talked nonstop, even while they were dancing. Breathless bursts of chatter whenever they were close enough. She'd forgotten all about her shyness, her plainness—about being stood up and having a junior high school substitute date. They'd been as different as two people could be, yet for one magic night they had been best friends...and more.

Now, as the DeHavilland's twin engines changed pitch, Ann Elise's dream segued into a collage of pompom-waving cheerleaders and yapping miniature poodles wearing rhinestone collars. The pilot came on to report "a spot of turbulence" up ahead and she opened her eyes, shards of her dream still clinging as she looked out the window to see lightning streak down from the dark clouds ahead.

It wasn't the fact that both her parents had been killed in a crash that made her uneasy. Rationally, she knew that far more people died in automobile accidents every year. All the same...

She fastened her seat belt, shut her eyes again and tried to pick up her dream where she'd left off.

Chapter 2

In her dream, the prom was a kaleidoscope of laughter and loud music—mostly just a pounding beat surrounded by hoards of young voices all vying to be heard in a swirling rainbow of colorful gowns and tuxedoes that ran the gamut from traditional to wildly nontraditional.

Spilled punch. "Oh, wow, sorry! Here, lemme mop you off."

Someone screaming, "Bobbie, stop that! Oh, gawd, you broke my strap," was followed by screams and giggles.

No one took offense. No one appeared to notice when the boys—not Joe, but most of the others—

would slip outside and come in several minutes later smelling of whisky or beer and cigarettes. On that one memorable night, people who had never even bothered to speak to her before had stopped by their table to talk—mostly to Joe, granted, but she hadn't been excluded.

And wonder of wonders, she'd talked right back. Probably nothing brilliant, but she'd felt like a butterfly freshly emerged from her chrysalis. Showing up with a younger date hadn't hurt her image at all, especially when that date was Joe Halloran.

Oh, how she'd hated to see the evening end. Back to the pumpkin, she remembered thinking as Joe helped her into the old red pickup truck. He'd talked on the way home. About football and his science teacher's attempts to get his father's breeding program underway again. She'd mostly listened, afraid if she opened her mouth she might say something gauche and break the spell. Either that or burst into tears.

And then he'd kissed her good-night. Out beside the truck, because Aunt Beth had left the porch light on. Joe had opened the passenger-side door and held out his hand, and when she'd stepped down from the high running board in her barely-there sandals, he'd slipped his arms around her.

She hadn't even tried to resist. Even then, as her magic night came to an end, she'd still been drifting in a dream world. Joe had spoken her name, ''Ann Elise,'' sort of quiet and raspy, and then he'd kissed her.

Seventeen and a half years old, and it had been her first real kiss.

And oh, my mercy, had it ever been *real!* To this day she didn't know how she'd managed to make her way up the front walk to the house. She was fairly certain her feet hadn't touched the ground.

On Monday morning she'd spent a full hour getting dressed for the next-to-the-last day of school. Over breakfast, which she hadn't been able to force down, Aunt Beth had offered to buy her a secondhand car for graduation. She was practically the only senior in the entire school who rode the school bus.

Deeply touched, she had nevertheless declined, asking for the money instead to go toward her college fund. No matter how hard she'd worked, she'd only been able to get a partial scholarship. Ann Elise had insisted the insurance money from her parents be set aside for her younger sisters' education.

She still remembered climbing down from the school bus that bright spring morning and casually lingering outside, searching without appearing to, for a glimpse of a certain shaggy chestnut-brown head. She'd been half afraid he wouldn't be there waiting for her, half afraid he would.

Joe had been there, but he hadn't been waiting for her. Clinging to his arm was the petite brunette sophomore he'd been dating all year. Feeling as if she'd just slammed into a wall of ice, Ann Elise had hurried over to where a group of seniors were rehashing the prom. One or two of them had smiled. She didn't know if she'd smiled back or not but she'd managed to look vitally interested in what they were saying, nodding at the appropriate times so that no one would think she'd been looking for Joe.

The next time she'd seen him was when they happened to meet outside the school library. "Hey, Ann Elise," he said, sounding almost shy, that melt-your-bones smile in full evidence.

Pretending she hadn't seen him, she'd lifted her nose in the air and marched off to the girls' bathroom, where she'd locked herself inside a stall and cried herself sick.

Fool, fool, fool! What did you expect—a genie to burst from a bottle and change you into a beautiful princess? "Get real," she remembered muttering. The phrase had been new then, and she'd told herself that if she couldn't be beautiful, at least she could be cool.

The plane rocked in the turbulent air as they descended through the low cloud layer. The attendant touched her shoulder, reminding her to put her seat in the upright position, then hurried forward to take her own seat. "Won't be long now," she assured her passengers.

Ann Elise pressed the seat release, then closed her eyes again. Behind her someone said, "Mumble, mumble—got another raise. That makes... mumble, mumble. But man, this IPO, I mean, I made a killing on it, I kid you not."

Money.

The last thing she remembered thinking before she drifted off to sleep again was that no amount of money was worth what one had to give up in exchange. Even after her sisters had no longer needed her, she'd been driven to succeed. Force of habit. She'd paid a small fortune for her practice when the vet she'd worked for decided to retire. By then she'd finished paying off her student loan. Now that she was no longer in debt, she was still putting in more hours than most other companion-animal veterinarians, and on top of that she did pro bono work for a local shelter in her free time.

And what did she have to show for her driving

ambition? A thriving practice, certainly. A professionally decorated suite of offices in an upscale section of Dallas. The satisfaction of having helped scores of animals that would otherwise have been euthanized.

A few friends, but no lovers. Without quite realizing how it had happened, she'd turned into a lonely, isolated workaholic in pursuit of riches she wouldn't know how to spend even if she'd had the time.

"On a clear night you'd be able to see the lights of Mission Creek by now, folks. Town's all gussied up for Christmas." The pilot's voice, sounding chipper, but somewhat tired, resonated through the cabin. "Air temperature on the ground is a balmy forty-seven degrees Fahrenheit, with more rain in the forecast. Sorry I can't promise you snow, but on behalf of first officer Sara Shoemaker and myself, I'd like to wish you all a merry Christmas and thank you for flying TTAir. And now, if you'll fasten your seat belts we'll have you on the ground shortly."

Shortly couldn't come soon enough for Ann Elise. Dallas-Fort Worth airport had been a madhouse, with rain delays and security jams combining to create thousands of angry, frustrated travelers. Even the small feeder line that served the Mission Creek area had been overbooked with home-for-the-holiday travelers, plus those returning after a Dallas shopping trip.

The child in the seat behind her was whining again. "But Mama, I hafta pee!"

"Honey, you heard the man, we're getting ready to set down. You can go when we get to the airport."

Ann Elise had to go, too, but it wasn't worth the effort of crawling over old Scrooge in the aisle seat. He muttered something about kids in a tone that hinted at a lack of patience. Something about him—not his looks, but his tone of voice—reminded her of Uncle Lloyd.

From day one her uncle had insisted on strict discipline. Until they'd come to realize that his bark was far worse than his bite, she and her sisters had tiptoed around the big, rambling house, speaking in whispers; afraid of being turned over to social services.

Now Faith had two children of her own and they were back in Mission Creek, living in the same house again. Becky and Jason were what— five and eight? Six and nine?

Ann Elise hadn't a clue what kind of toys children that age liked, much less what her niece and nephew already had. So much for finishing her shopping list. She'd scribbled four names and stopped.

Ann Elise was still working on the list when the engines changed pitch, signaling the final descent. Tucking her notebook back into her purse, she let her thoughts off the leash. Not surprisingly, they homed in on Joe Halloran again. Had he married his cute little cheerleader? If so, did they have children? Visions of a good-looking kid, tall for his age, with Joe's world-class smile, appeared unbidden. A daughter would probably inherit what'sername's turned-up nose and long, curly black hair. For a girl, it was probably the better alternative, she admitted, trying for fair and balanced when jealousy was what she truly felt.

Lord, you're a mess, woman, she thought scornfully. Imagine, wasting all this time thinking about a man she hadn't seen in more than a dozen years instead of completing her Christmas shopping list with less than a day to go. Just went to show what a vast wasteland her social life was. The hackneyed phrase ''Get a life'' came to mind, and she promised herself she would, she really would, just as soon as she got back to Dallas.

All the same, she couldn't help but wonder what might have happened if Joe hadn't already been spoken for, and if she hadn't been too stiff-necked with pride to risk a snub. Or if he'd been three years older or she'd been three years younger.

He'd probably moved away by now. She almost hoped he had—not that their paths were apt to cross. Still, there was no point in wasting time thinking about what might have been, now that it was too late.

A madly waving Faith met her inside the airport. After a big hug, they collected her luggage and hurried across the gleaming parking area, chattering and catching up. Faith murmured, "There's someone I want you to meet when we get home."

Ann Elise thought about the children, wondering if they would remember her at all. A few years was an eternity in a child's life. When Faith asked about her flight, she shrugged off the question. "Strange," she said. How did you describe old memories?

They talked about her practice and they talked about the children, and Ann Elise sensed an undercurrent running through her sister's chatter. Staring at the showy diamond ring on her third finger, left hand, she said, "Are you going to tell me about him?"

For several minutes Faith remained silent. Negotiating holiday traffic on a rainy night claimed her attention, and Ann Elise didn't press her. Sooner or later, though, she intended to hear every

single detail. If anyone had ever earned a happy-
ever-after ending, it was her middle sister.

''Darned fool,'' Faith grumbled as a car cut in
front of her.

''If you think this is bad, you ought to see Dallas.''

''No, thanks, I'll stay where I am.'' Faith cut
her a quick glance. ''There's someone I want you
to meet when we get home.''

Not until they were nearing the turnoff to the
Baker ranch, or what was left of it, did Faith
speak again. Ann Elise had been busy absorbing
all the changes that had taken place since she'd
last been home. ''Marilou's due sometime tomorrow. She said she's bringing a surprise.''

Ann Elise twisted in her seat to stare. ''My
gosh, is that a new shopping center?''

They zipped on by the strip mall with its gaudy
decorations reflecting on wet pavement, talking
about all the changes that had taken place in the
small, prosperous town of Mission Creek.

''Next time don't wait so long between visits.
A lot of things change, but the welcome mat's
always out.''

And then they were pulling into the driveway
of the large, southwestern-style ranch house.
''Tah-dah! Do I hear applause for my decorating
efforts? Just goes to show what you can do with

nine miles of tinsel and ten thousand tiny lights. Here, come on inside and have something hot to drink.''

Ann Elise had scarcely got through the front door before the children appeared. ''You remember Becky, don't you? She's nine now, going on thirty-nine. Hon, say hello to your aunt Ann Elise.''

Taking a good look at the tall, thin little girl wearing glasses and a solemn expression, Ann Elise thought, Oh, my mercy, she reminds me of me at that age.

''Hello, Aunt Ann Elise. Do I hafta call you both names, or can I just pick one?''

''Hush, you can settle that later,'' Faith said. ''And this is Jason. I guess the last time you saw him he was, what—two? Three? He's a big boy now, aren't you, honey? Say hey to your aunt Ann Elise.''

Six-year-old Jason Donner had the smile of an angel, only instead of a halo, he was wearing a cowboy hat—pint-sized instead of ten-gallon. He beamed up at her and said, ''Hey, Annalise. You know what Santa's bringing me? A fire truck with a ladder that raises up and down like a real one. I wanted a snake, but Mama said no.''

''Hmm…a boy after my own heart,'' Ann Elise said. ''Remind me to tell you about Splotch.''

Just then a dark-haired, blue-eyed man wearing jeans and a Western-style shirt Ann Elise easily recognized as custom-made, sauntered into the hall. He touched Jason on the shoulder, shook his head at Becky and looked at Ann Elise. "And this must be your sister?"

"Ann Elise, meet my fiancé, Gabriel Raines," Faith said breathlessly, giving him a quick kiss. "He's going to be spending Christmas with us. Gabe, this is my older sister, the one I told you about."

"You told me about two sisters," he reminded her, and Ann Elise was struck by the warmth in his voice.

"Yes, well, this one's the vet from Dallas."

Gabe smiled and extended his hand. Ann Elise hesitated only a moment before accepting his handshake. His smile was certainly friendly enough, but his cool blue eyes were difficult to read. She would reserve judgment for the time being. Old habits died hard.

The noise of the children galloping through the house woke her early the next morning. Ann Elise opened her eyes, glanced at the tall window to confirm what her ears had told her. It was still raining. Gray, wind-driven sheets of water pounding down from a leaden sky, probably drowning thousands of Christmas decorations.

Briefly, she considered turning over and going back to sleep. But only briefly, because rain or not, it was still Christmas Eve and she had too much to do to procrastinate.

Reluctantly, she sat up, raked her fingers through her hair and wished she hadn't skipped her last appointment. It was just long enough to be a bother, not quite long enough to tie back. Maybe once she finished her Christmas shopping she could stop in at the Texas Belle—if it was still in business.

Fat chance. The place would be packed with last-minute customers getting ready for a round of parties. Aside from all the private festivities, there was always a ball at the Lone Star Country Club. She had never even seen the club's fabulous ballroom, although Aunt Beth had been a life member.

Yawning, she eased one leg out from under the duvet. Somewhere in the house, a radio blared Christmas music. Faith yelled, ''Turn that down, Aunt Annie's still in bed!''

''No'm not,'' Ann Elise mumbled. Aunt *Annie?* Well, why not? The alternative was a mouthful for a kid who didn't even have all his permanent teeth yet.

Last night she'd managed to stay awake long enough to eat a sandwich and toast her sister's engagement with a single glass of champagne. "Good luck, little sister," she whispered now as she yawned, scratched and stretched. After her first disastrous marriage, Faith deserved the best. Whether or not Gabriel Raines was the best remained to be seen. She would watch closely, just in case. Faith had said he was "in oil," which could mean almost anything from oil-field roughneck to service station attendant to tycoon.

On the other hand, being "in" anything was a lot better than Earl Donner, who'd been "into" nothing more productive than mooching off his wife and drinking up every penny she earned.

"Ham and eggs?" Faith greeted from the kitchen some twenty minutes later. "Hash browns? Grits? Pancakes? Cinnamon rolls?"

"How about one bite of all the above?" Ann Elise said, laughing. Her middle sister was a genius in the kitchen, always had been. "I'm really not hungry."

"How's your head?"

"Better. Fine, in fact, as long as you don't expect the gray cells to function anytime soon. I've got to do my Christmas shopping, which means—"

"You haven't done it *yet?*" Faith handed her a heaped plate.

"You ever try getting through airport security with a stack of gift-wrapped packages?" Ann Elise shook her head. "Don't even consider it. I need to call a cab. How long do you think it'll take to get one out here?"

"Hush, you sit down here and eat your breakfast first. When you're ready, you can take Aunt Beth's car. The thing needs driving anyway, and I always use mine."

Chapter 3

It was late that morning before Ann Elise managed to get away. First she had to see every toy either child possessed and hear their wish lists. All of which helped her decide what to buy, but failed to lessen her apprehension about driving in weather that appeared to be worsening by the minute.

Gabriel had offered to drive her, but she refused to hear of it. Besides, she'd heard him promise Becky to help redecorate the Christmas tree that Jason had accidentally knocked over the day before. Gabriel was good with the children, a big mark in his favor. And they obviously adored him, which was an even bigger one.

Lucky Faith.

Still thinking about those odd dreams that had haunted her on the trip south, she backed out of the garage and was soon speeding along the wet highway toward town. Half-mesmerized by the monotonous sweep of the windshield wipers, she found herself thinking about Joe Halloran again. Priding herself on her pragmatism, she decided that by now he would have developed a paunch and lost all that wonderful chestnut hair. She might even look him up while she was here, just to see. At least maybe then she could finally quit dreaming about him.

Or maybe not. Aside from his essential sweetness, so at odds with his rugged features and tall, rangy build, there was a strength about young Joe Halloran that had held enormous appeal. She didn't know if he had younger siblings or not, but if so, they were lucky.

A gust of wind rocked the car. Was that sky growing darker, or was it only her imagination? Her fingers gripped the steering wheel as she peered through the preternatural gloom. Hers was the only car on the road so far as she could see. Even so, with the shoulders on either side of the road filling with rain, she'd better stop mooning over Joe and pay closer attention to her driving. Tornadoes weren't entirely unknown in this part of Texas, either, although she'd never heard of one on Christmas Eve.

The middle-aged sedan shuddered and pulled to one side as she drove through a long stretch of standing water. If memory served, the only place for miles was the old Camden place, long since abandoned. Didn't there used to be a creek along here? Not much of one, just a big double culvert under the highway. All the same...

Suddenly uneasy, Ann Elise fumbled for the defroster and sent a streak of air over the inside of the windshield to clear away the fog. Of all times to be without her cell phone, but the thing had run down and she'd left it on charge back at the house.

Rounding a curve, she caught sight of a line of cars several hundred feet ahead. A festive display of red lights came wriggling toward her as several drivers hit their brakes at once. Reacting instinctively, she used her left foot and felt the little car fishtail before coming to a stop.

"What the devil?" The defroster was barely keeping up with the job. Leaning forward, she cleared a patch of glass, peering ahead to see what the holdup was. Probably a fender bender, considering the conditions. She just hoped no one had been hurt.

Then one set of taillights pulled away from the

others and crept forward. A few moments later, another set followed. She closed the space between her and the other two cars just as a momentary letup in the rain allowed her to see that what was holding up traffic was no accident, but a river of muddy water.

"Well, shoot," she muttered. Leaning her head on the headrest, she closed her eyes and wondered about her chances of getting same-day delivery if she went back and called in her orders. Probably on a par with her chances of being airlifted over the mess up ahead.

"Santa, where's your blooming sleigh? I need some help here."

One of the vehicles turned around on the highway and headed back toward where she sat, the engine idling quietly. When the white Miata slowed beside her, Ann Elise lowered her window a few inches, flinching as cold rain struck her face.

"Honey, if I was you, I wouldn't risk it," the driver yelled. "Them trucks made it through awright, but ask me, it's getting deeper by the minute."

"Oh, well. Thanks for the warning."

What now, she wondered, gnawing her bottom lip. Try to get through before the water rose any higher? Give up and go back? In her trusty van she might have tried it, but not in a borrowed car.

After a moment's deliberation, she took her foot off the brake and inched forward. She would just have to judge for herself. Flash floods were notoriously dangerous, but in this mess it would be easy to mistake a few inches of surface water for something more serious.

Two sets of taillights disappeared in the rain-shrouded distance, which meant that the other drivers had managed to get through. The insides of the windows were still steaming up faster than the defroster could handle the moisture, which didn't help visibility. She smeared another patch of glass and tried to see what the roadside looked like. If the creek was seriously over the banks...

Nothing to do but get out and look.

The wind caught her hair, whipping it across her face as she struggled with the door. Her black silk raincoat was more fashionable than practical. An umbrella wouldn't have lasted five seconds— not that she'd thought to bring one.

Shielding her eyes with one hand, she edged closer to the rushing, mud-colored water in an effort to gauge her chances of crossing. Trouble was, there was no way to tell how deep the stuff was. At least three vehicles had made it through in the past five minutes, but they were probably trucks, higher off the road and more powerful.

Why on earth had she put off shopping until the last minute?

Well, she knew why, of course, but that didn't help matters now.

A high, keening note reached her, raising goose bumps down her spine. The wind, she assured herself. Not an animal, just the ferocious wind howling through the hedgerow. It came again, and she whispered, "Oh, please, God, not a child."

Cupping her ears, she tried to block the wind and tune into whatever it was she'd heard. Moments later, it came again. A whine—ending in a sharp yip.

Edging closer to the side of the shoulder, she peered at the river of muddy water racing toward its eventual goal—the Gulf of Mexico. Either the creek was much higher than she'd first thought, or there was a tree down some fifty feet down the bank. Something—a dog, maybe a coyote—or maybe only a pile of trash—was caught in the branches.

Scarcely aware of the headlights coming toward her at a slow, steady pace, Ann Elise gauged the distance, trying to see a way to reach the poor creature. If it was a creature. It definitely sounded like a dog, but the whining and yipping could be coming from anywhere. She'd be a fool to risk drowning for a sack of trash someone had tossed out of a car. On the other hand, if it was an animal hanging on to that tree branch, it didn't have a chance of swimming against all that current.

She edged closer until water lapped at the toes of her boots, peering through the unnatural gloom. That was no sack of trash, it was a dog, and it was in serious trouble.

Moving carefully to keep from slipping, she hurried back to the car, searching frantically for something—anything. A rope!

There was nothing at all in the back seat, but maybe— She grabbed the keys from the ignition and blundered her way to the rear of the car, praying to find something in the trunk that would help.

Nothing. A spare tire and a jack. If she'd had some rope, she might have tried using the tire as a life ring, but that was stupid. The thing probably wouldn't even float, and even if it did, a terrified, half-drowned animal would hardly climb aboard and wait to be hauled ashore.

"Well, shoot," she whispered to herself. Closing the trunk, she tossed the keys in the car. They landed on her purse, and on impulse, she stripped off her wet raincoat and tossed it inside, too. If she was going to go plowing through a muddy field and try to scramble down a ditch bank, she didn't need all that excess material flapping around her legs.

"I know, I know, honey, I'm thinking," she called, hearing the pitiful whimper again. She had to do something, she simply had to, even if it meant her family would have to do without gifts.

Her new boot-legged jeans were already muddy and her yellow cashmere turtleneck was beginning to sag. As for her favorite pair of boots— gray snakeskin with a classic tulip design—they were probably history. They'd been an indulgence she'd allowed herself after spending her last birthday operating on an overfed Shih Tzu bitch with an abdominal obstruction. She was pretty sure the designer had never intended them for wading around muddy creeks.

It couldn't be much past noon, yet it was almost too dark to see clearly. Her foot slipped and she flapped her arms to regain her balance, then glanced over her shoulder, noticing for the first time the oversized pickup that was slowly creeping through the flood, headed her way. Whoever he was, if he happened to have a rope she could beg, borrow or steal, she'd figure out what to do with it later.

Stationing herself in the middle of the road, she waved both arms, trying not to think about the possibility that the driver might be a predator instead of a Good Samaritan. Several years ago she'd taken a course in women's self-defense, but her rusty, untried skills might not be a match for an armed thug.

Blinded by the headlights, she turned and pointed toward where the poor creature still clung to the branches, then gestured for the driver to roll down his window.

On his way home from making a call, Joe had stopped off in town to pick up a prescription for his mom. While he was there he'd bought a few last-minute stocking stuffers. If he'd known the weather was going to worsen he might have left off shopping for extras.

No, he wouldn't. His mama needed her chocolate fix and his dad would enjoy putting a few hundred old snapshots into a new album. Their lives were restricted enough these days. He wasn't about to deny them the few pleasures they could still appreciate.

Seeing the flooded creek, he'd eased off the gas and touched the brakes, trailing a wake behind him as he inched forward. Some fool woman on the other side was standing in the middle of the highway waving her arms. Either she was out of gas, or she'd had a breakdown. The question was, was it mental or mechanical?

Hell of a time for it, either way.

And then his own mind started playing tricks on him. For a minute there she almost looked like...

"Ann Elise?" He whispered the name, not really believing the tall, bedraggled creature looking up at his window could be the same woman he had held in his arms exactly once—kissed exactly once—and dreamed of for the past fourteen years.

There couldn't be two women with that face. Haunting eyes, elegant bones, girl-next-door freckles. Not even her two kid sisters had looked like Ann Elise. "Trouble?" he asked.

She's not out here sunbathing, jerk.

Obviously she didn't recognize him. Of course, he was wearing his hat, and it was dark inside the truck. Outside, too, for that matter. But if she hadn't recognized him the day after their only date, there was no reason to think she would recognize him now.

"There's a dog—I think," she said breathlessly. "It might be a coyote—whatever—it's caught up in those bushes downstream. Do you have a rope?"

God alive, it *was* her!

Brushing aside any personal feelings, he nodded and said, "Let me pull off the road."

She stepped back as he negotiated space for

another vehicle to pass, if anyone else was fool enough to be out in conditions like this. When he'd checked with the highway patrol before leaving town, they had already begun to set up roadblocks. Unless the rain stopped in the next half hour, flooding was going to be a problem throughout the county for the rest of the day, maybe even into Christmas.

Opening his big aluminum toolbox behind the cab, he took out a coil of rope and a heavy-duty flashlight and thought, she hasn't changed at all. Same cheekbones, same freckles, same big blue eyes, as guarded as ever. For one magic night he'd seen those eyes lose their wariness, and it had marked him for life.

Her hair was clinging to her scalp now instead of dancing around her shoulders, and that rig she was wearing wouldn't pass as prom dress by anyone's standards.

"Here we go," he said, trying to sound more like twenty-nine than fifteen. At least his voice didn't break. So far. "Now where's this animal you spotted?"

"Oh, my God—*Joe?*" For a moment she looked stunned, but then, recovering quickly, she turned and hurried to the edge of the pavement, pointing to a spot about a dozen yards downstream in what was normally a well-behaved, two-culvert creek.

"Oh boy, we got trouble," he muttered. Drenching a mean-tempered bull with the scours was nothing compared to rescuing a big, terrified dog from drowning in a rushing river of muddy water.

Quickly, he peeled off his leather coat and shoved it back into the truck, then removed everything from the pockets of his jeans.

"What are you doing?" she asked. Her boot slipped, she flailed her arms to regain her balance and sat down hard.

"Your bidding, ma'am," he said grimly, and gave her a hand up.

"But what—you can't—!"

"Got a better idea?"

"Can you— Can't we—?"

"Here's the way it works. I'll tie one end of this line onto the front bumper, patch on a loop for me, and then another one for your friend. Once I get hold of your critter, I'll secure him and then overhand back to shore, pulling the dog along with me. If the current's too strong, you might have to start the truck and back up, real slow, but watch for my hand signals. If I get tangled up in something down there, you need to stop instantly, you got it?"

"Then what?" Her face was the color of wet marble. Even her freckles were pale.

"Then we'll figure out how to get me untangled. Chances are, we'll be back on dry land in less time than it takes to worry about it."

"There's no such thing as dry land," she replied, watching the flood victim as Joe hurriedly rigged the rescue line. "Hang on, honey, help's on the way," she called.

Standing up, he tested the knots, attached one end to the bumper, then tightened one of the loops around his chest. "Honey?" he repeated quizzically.

She looked startled for a moment, then shook her head. "I'm pretty sure she's female."

He shucked off his boots and socks and tossed them into the back of the truck. They couldn't get any wetter. And then he edged out into the rushing stream. Grinning over his shoulder, he said, "Not even sure what species we've got here, but you're positive of the gender, right? Wish me luck. Remember the drill. If I get into trouble I'll signal. Whatever you do, don't try to pull me out with the truck unless I tell you to, okay?"

Joe could think of several things he'd rather be doing than wading out into muddy floodwaters after an animal that might or might not be wild, or even rabid, but that would sure as hell be scared, and therefore dangerous.

Funny thing, but he trusted Ann Elise not to panic. She might look like an ice princess, but she had what it took to get through vet school and set up a fancy practice in Dallas.

Oh, yeah, he knew all about that. She hadn't been hard to track once they'd both gone into practice, her a couple of years earlier, as she'd had a head start. He'd occasionally seen her listed in various professional publications. She'd attended a conference down in Orlando last fall that he'd missed.

Something—a piece of brush—struck him on the hip, but rushed by without snagging his jeans.

It was a dog, all right. "Easy, sport, I'm coming," he called softly to the terrified animal from some ten feet away. Golden retriever, from what he could see, which wasn't much. Head, shoulders, one forepaw. God, if she was caught in a steel trap down under there...

The animal whimpered, and Joe risked a glance over his shoulder to see how much slack he still had. The line wasn't taut yet. With any luck, he'd have enough, as long as the bitch didn't fight him.

And even if she did. "Smart girl, we're almost there, hang on another minute for me, will you?"

Like Ann Elise, he was assuming the gender. Something about her eyes…

His mama still teased him about what she called his romantic streak, claiming it was going to land him in trouble. Course, Mama was still hoping for grandkids.

A dog's eyes, for cripe's sake.

"Take it easy now, sweetheart, we're going to get you out of here in short order." As he neared his target, he widened the end loop and held it high over the bitch's head. Somehow he had to work it over her shoulders and under her forelegs, else she'd strangle. Any way he did it she was probably going to leave her mark on him.

"Smart lady," he muttered, working the loop over one foreleg and at the same time trying to keep her from climbing all over him. The good thing was, he could touch bottom here. Bad thing was, it was too muddy to gain any real traction, which meant that he and the princess here were doing a clumsy water ballet.

"There you go," he said, holding the big, half-drowned animal an arm's length away. She tried to clamber up onto his shoulders again but the current separated them as he began hauling them both upstream. It occurred to him that he might have worked his way to the shore and slogged through the flooded field back to the highway, but once ashore, she'd have taken off. He had a feeling she needed attention before she was turned loose again.

They made it at approximately the same time, the dog lunging ahead to drag herself up onto the bank. From the looks of her he figured she was mostly golden retriever. She shook herself off just as Ann Elise knelt in front of her, making soft noises that were probably meant to be reassuring.

"Better give her some space," he said. "You two haven't been formally introduced yet."

"Oh...my...goodness," she said softly, "Do you see what I see?"

Oh, yeah. He saw, all right. Talk about complications.

Chapter 4

Ann Elise was experienced in dealing with distressed animals, but never before had she been confronted with one that was both half-drowned and in the first stage of labor. "We have to get her in out of the rain."

Joe shot a speculative glance at his truck. "Crew cab," he said. "It'll be a close fit, but I can shift enough gear to make room." Then he looked back. "Mind telling me what the hell you're doing out on a day like this?"

"Not that it's any of your business, but I'm going shopping. This is Christmas Eve, remember? Children expect to find presents under the tree, right?"

"Yeah, well—kids don't always get what they want."

The bitch shook herself again, sat and then sprawled over onto her side, gazing up at them through patient, pain-filled eyes. "The back seat's not going to work," Ann Elise murmured, picturing the two of them on their knees in the front seats, ministering to the patient.

"Alternative?" Joe collected his boots, emptied them and then shoved them on to his bare feet, bracing his lean butt against the grill of the 4x4 pickup.

"Aunt Beth's car's awfully small. The trunk's roomy, but…"

"Right," he said. *"But."*

She couldn't believe she was standing here on the side of a flooded highway in the pouring rain, talking to Joe Halloran for the first time in fourteen years about, of all things, a dog. How many times had she pictured such a reunion? In her daydreams she'd always been wearing something elegant, understated and wildly flattering, her hair freshly styled to make the most of her ordinary features.

Instead, she was soaked to the skin, her makeup a victim of the rain, wearing a soggy sweater that was stretched almost to her knees, and a pair of

mud-caked boots. As for her hair, the less said,
the better.

"If you'll help me get her inside the car I'll
take her back to Aunt Beth's," she said, thinking
that at least there she could work in a dry garage.
It was still Aunt Beth's place, even though Beth
Baker was gone now. "I hate to close her up in
the trunk in case she panics, but if you have a
tarp, I could spread it over the back seat."

"I have a tarp and you're welcome to it, but
the Baker place is out of the question."

She had never dealt well with ultimatums, but
this was no time to take offense. The dog whimpered, and she knelt and rested one hand on its
head, meanwhile easing her bedraggled tail aside.
"Oh, Lordy," she murmured. "This can't wait
much longer."

"My bag's in the truck. We could slow things
down, but I don't recommend it."

Under the circumstances, neither did Ann Elise.
The poor creature had been through enough without interfering with her labor. She stood, glanced
at the car parked on the shoulder some fifty feet
away, then at the nearby pickup. "It'll have to be
the car, then. At least it's dry."

Joe shook his head. "Out of the question.
Look, don't even think about getting her back to
your place. Before I left town I checked with

Highway Patrol. So far, this is the worst spot, but half the road between here and your place is under water now. North of here there're already two washouts. I'm surprised you made it this far in that little thing.''

Ann Elise could have taken offense on behalf of her aunt's compact car, but she only nodded. Flash floods weren't called that for nothing. There was a good reason why so many people in this part of the country drove SUVs or pickups. Already the water had risen several inches closer to where they'd parked and the rain showed no sign of letting up. Within the next hour—maybe sooner—every creek south of San Antonio could be out of bank.

Ann Elise laid a hand on the retriever's head, sliding her other hand along her distended side. The bitch struggled to her feet and tried vainly to reach around her swollen belly and sniff out the state of affairs. Then, with an apologetic look over her shoulder, she limped away and tried to crawl under the pickup.

''All right, little mama, let's get you out of this rain,'' Joe said softly. Moving quickly to bar her way, he lowered the tailgate, shoved a block and tackle aside and carefully scooped up the desperate creature. Arms full of roughly eighty pounds of wet retriever, he grunted, "Once you start launching cargo, girl, we're stuck here for the duration, so try to hold back, y'hear?"

Ann Elise hoisted herself up onto the side of the truck bed and shifted a crowbar and a length of chain farther out of the way just as Joe arched his back in an effort to clear the tailgate with the animal's paws. "No good place to hold on to her," he grunted, easing her onto the truck bed.

Balanced on her midsection on the side panel with one toe hooked onto the rear tire, Ann Elise leaned over to help ease the dog down onto her side. "Next time we'll try for a beagle, they're easier to handle," she said. "Shh, you're all right now, sugar, you got lucky."

"Damned right," Joe affirmed as he stepped back and wiped his hands on the legs of his jeans. "Two vets, what're the odds? Go lock your car, Al. You want to drive, or you want to ride with the patient? I don't think she needs to be left alone in case she panics and tries to jump out."

Al? As in "Hey, Al, good buddy, do me a favor, will ya?"

"I'll ride back here," she said. "I just hope this truck bed of yours has scuppers, else we both might end up afloat." The rain was still coming down in a solid deluge.

Al? In her wildest dreams, he had never called her Al.

"We're not going far. She'll do better with as little handling as possible."

Ann Elise had to agree, still it seemed heartless. "You're going to run the roadblocks?"

"Nope. No creeks between here and the old Camden place. Remember it?"

She remembered it. The local haunted house. "Whatever," she said, "Just get us out of this rain."

She hurried over to lock the car, her mind racing over a dozen possibilities. She didn't have a single instrument to deal with a situation like this. Who would have expected—

"Let's move!" Joe yelled.

"I'm moving!" To someplace warm, hopefully. The temperature was plummeting, and frozen slush would be disastrous. They needed shelter, needed it soon. Call Faith, she reminded herself as she reached inside the door and automatically punched the button that locked both doors.

Joe was waiting to help her up into the high truck bed. He swung her up in his arms and for one brief moment before he set her down beside the dog, she felt his warmth, inhaled the unique scent of warm, healthy male and cold, muddy water.

Oh, lawsy, I'm plum crazy. Just plain certi fiable.

Half a mile down the road Joe stopped to clear away a branch that had blown down across the highway. Before climbing back into the cab, he checked his two passengers. Ann Elise—was this a wild dream, or what?

He'd called her Al in an effort to defuse the old familiar spell she'd cast on him so long ago. It hadn't worked. She was leaning against the tool compartment, legs spread wide, the retriever lying between them with its muzzle on her thigh. She was crooning to the animal.

Joe had been known to try a few unorthodox treatments in his career, but singing to a patient— that was a new one. Back inside the cab, it occurred to him that she might be cold. Soaking wet, sitting in rain fit to strangle a catfish with the temperature dropping steadily? Hell, of course she was cold.

Climbing out again, he dug his coat out from behind the passenger seat and draped it around her shoulders. She thanked him without looking away from the patient.

"How much farther?" she asked.

"Not far now. Don't take that coat off,

y'hear?'' he warned, guessing that as soon as he turned his back she'd take it off and spread it over the dog.

Funny thing, he mused, downshifting to creep through a patch of bumper-deep water—he didn't really know her. And yet, on a deeper level, he did. Knew her well enough for her to have busted his heart wide open before he was even old enough to get his driver's license.

Calling her Al in an effort to break the spell of all that cool, enticing femininity wasn't going to work any more than dating half the women in Lone Star County had helped. Fourteen years. Nearly half a lifetime, and there was still something about her that got to him. Back then, most of the kids had considered her a real snob. He was pretty sure that wasn't the case. Hell, she'd gone out with him, hadn't she?

Still, they used to make jokes about her. Serious attitude. Princess Four-eyes. Stuff like that. It had made him fighting mad before he'd ever spoken a word to her. Made him want to bust a few noses.

He'd done it once, too. The guy who'd dared Billy Kiner to ask her to the prom and stand her up still sported a hump on the bridge of his nose. They'd planned to let her get all spiffed up and then leave her waiting all night for a date that never showed up.

Oh, yeah. Big joke.

As it turned out, Billy had done him a big favor by getting himself hauled in by the cops the afternoon of the prom. Joe had thought about going to the Baker's place and explaining why her date wasn't going to show up.

Instead, he'd got the idea of taking Billy's place. It had required some hasty scrambling, but with the help of his dad and a waiter over at the Country Club, he'd made the grade, tux, flowers and all.

Now here she was again, little Ann Elise Baker, all grown-up. He'd called her Al to try and break the spell.

It wasn't working.

She'd mentioned doing last-minute Christmas shopping for kids. He wondered how many she had. He could have asked around and probably found out who she'd married, but he'd chosen not to. She wasn't wearing a ring, but that didn't necessarily mean anything. Maybe she had an allergic reaction to gold. Maybe she was a single mother who'd sold her jewelry to support her kids. Last he'd heard, her name was still Baker.

Yeah, right. And maybe some other Ann Elise Baker owned a fancy practice in Dallas's high-rent district.

One thing he did know—he wasn't about to let

her screw him around again. No way. He'd already paid too high a price for a single date that had ended up in a lot of laughs, a few shared confidences, some hands-on stuff on the dance floor and one long, mind-blowing kiss.

In the back of the truck, Ann Elise stroked the bitch, murmuring to her as she watched rain puddle in the corrugated truck bed. Murphy's Law strikes again. Here she was with Joe Halloran, and this time he was definitely old enough to drive.

And she was definitely old enough to know better.

This time, instead of wearing a prom dress and smelling of Aunt Beth's lily-of-the-valley, with her newly styled hair wisping around her face, she was soaked to the skin, wearing muddy jeans and a ruined sweater, her hair plastered to her head. The only detectable smell was mud, exhaust fumes and wet dog.

"You two okay back there?" Joe yelled through the back window he'd insisted on leaving open, even though everything in the back seat was probably getting soaked. She knew he was driving slowly to keep from hydroplaning, but she wished he'd hurry and get them somewhere...anywhere!

"Fine! Just get us out of this rain, will you?"

"Two minutes. Hang on, I'm fixing to turn off, but it looks like the dirt road's a mess."

"So's this one," she muttered, hanging on to the side of the truck with one hand, using the other to soothe the dog.

Oh, she was fine, all right. All her lofty resolutions to forget the past and get on with the future might as well have been tossed in the washer and set on spin cycle.

Darn it, she'd had everything planned. Shop today, help Faith with any last-minute preparations and find out if she was really, truly okay with this Raines fellow. Sometime today Marilou was due in, and once the children were in bed they could catch up on all the news. Next week she might even visit a few old friends—acquaintances, actually, as she didn't really have any close friends in the area.

Then on New Year's Day, the memorial service for Aunt Beth, and after that, head back to Dallas and the practice she'd worked so hard for, that she had almost come to despise.

Not the animals—never those. But too many of her clients saw pets as status symbols instead of as the unique individuals they were. From Afghans—elegant to look at, but surely the stupidest breed alive—to classic poodles, to every exotic that came along, to the sporting breeds that were enjoying new popularity thanks to a recent president.

A few of her clients actually bonded with their pets, but too many led such active social lives that they had neither time nor room in their busy schedules for a close relationship. Those were the animals she felt sorriest for—those that were looked on as accessories, not companions.

"And what about you, sugar babe—what's your story? Do you have a dear friend who's frantically trying to find you?"

Nearing the end of the rutted, overgrown road, the truck slowed. "Looks like the house is out of the question," Joe called through the window. "I'm going to head for the barn. If it checks out, I can back part way inside."

As she couldn't see ahead, she murmured an agreement that was lost in a rumble of thunder. When he began backing toward the barn she knelt and leaned over the tailgate, watching for anything that could cut a tire. An old rake, for instance. All they needed now was a flat tire.

"I'm going to get as close as I can," Joe yelled. "Watch for hazards."

"Already watching," she called back. And then, before she could stop herself, she added, "I'm just glad it was you."

Oh, God, I didn't really say that, did I? "You

who happened along, I mean. What I meant was—'' Just shut up, woman, while you're ahead.

Only she wasn't. Far from it.

"Better the devil you know, right?" Joe's voice reached her over the sound of the rain as he switched off the truck's engine.

"No comment."

The main section of the barn underneath the hayloft was comparatively dry. Joe took out a battery lantern and searched the area, selecting a pile of ancient straw. The dog whimpered, but Ann Elise laid a hand on her side, caressing, soothing, examining, gauging from the movement and rigidity that labor was well underway.

Joe quickly spread a tarp over the straw and set the lantern off to one side, illuminating the immediate area. "Delivery room's prepped and waiting," he said, sizing up the best way to transfer the patient.

It took both of them, but they soon had her settled.

"Notice the scars?" she murmured.

Joe nodded. "Looks like our friend hasn't led the easiest of lives. Wouldn't be surprised if she needs a whole battery of shots, but those can wait."

And wait, they did. Waited while the gray daylight gradually faded. Waited while the wind eased around so that rain blew through the door. They were far enough from the opening so that it didn't reach their corner, but the air was uncomfortably cold. Even wearing Joe's leather jacket, Ann Elise was shivering. When she'd tried to give it back to him he'd refused to take it. Told her to toss it aside if she didn't want it.

Code of chivalry, she thought, and sneezed.

"Bless you. I've got a blanket somewhere."

"It's just the straw. Dust does that to me sometimes." She needed to remove her contacts, but she'd left her glasses back at the house. Without them she was...well, hardly blind as a bat, but things would be pretty darn fuzzy. Something told her she would need all her senses at their sharpest for the next hour or so.

Time was measured not in ticks of the clock but in raindrops splashing on something metal in another part of the barn. After a while Joe said, "You mentioned shopping for your children. I guess your whole family's here with you?"

She recognized it as a leading question. "Most of my family is already here. Faith and her two kids live here. And her fiancé. Marilou's supposed to be coming in sometime today—certainly by tomorrow." She sighed. "I'd better call and let Faith know what's happened, if I may use your phone?"

Uncoiling his lanky six-foot-three frame, he crossed to the truck and retrieved the cell phone just as a flash of lightning lit up the entire universe. It was coming more frequently now, but no closer, fortunately.

Ann Elise punched in the numbers and waited. Faith's voice, backed by Christmas music, came on. Quickly Ann Elise explained what had happened, fielding questions and assuring her sister that no, she didn't need a helicopter, and no, she wasn't hungry—which was a lie. "Look, we'll be fine, okay? We're safe and dry, and as soon as the roads are clear, Joe'll get us home."

"Joe? Not Joe Halloran! You mean he's the one who came along and—" Ann Elise winced, wondering how acute his hearing was. "No kidding, you mean the same guy you went to the prom with back in the dark ages?"

Closing her eyes, Ann Elise fielded her sister's questions and ignored Joe's knowing grin. Finally she broke in to say, "Look, tell the kids I want to see that tree fully decorated and vertical when I get there. Tell them I'll take them shopping day after tomorrow at their favorite toy shop."

She ended the call and handed Joe his cell phone. "I just hate that, you know?" She was blushing. "I mean not being able to shop for Christmas. I should have done it before I left Dallas, but I kept having these visions of thousands of people lined up at security, having their carefully gift-wrapped packages ripped open.'' She sighed. "I thought I was being so smart. Story of my life.''

He chuckled softly, and mentally she translated the sound as callused fingers stroking velvet.

God, woman, you are hopeless!

"What about your family?'' she asked brightly. She didn't want to know, she really didn't, but perhaps a shot of reality could dampen a few impractical dreams before they blazed out of control.

In the brief silence that followed, the rain seemed to have let up, but the sky was still leaden and occasional rumbles of thunder sounded in the distance. Joe said, "They're both doing pretty well,'' and her heart plunged. "Considering Pop's in the early stages of Alzheimer's. Mom and I manage between us, but her arthritis gives her trouble, especially when the weather's like this.''

What about your wife? Ann Elise wanted to ask. Do you have one? And if not, why not? You must know you could have any single woman in Lone Star County, not to mention a few of the married ones.

She wondered if he had, then decided she didn't want to know. Lordamercy, thirty-two years old, and still clinging to an adolescent crush.

It spoke volumes about the quality of her social life.

"You didn't mention a husband," he ventured just as lightning illuminated the ruined farmhouse and a section of broken fence.

It was surprisingly comfortable inside the barn, thanks to the army blanket Joe had supplied that smelled ever so faintly of horse. Fortunately, she wasn't squeamish. Never had been, come to think of it, otherwise she might not have chosen to study veterinarian medicine.

"No husband," she said. "Past, present or future. What about you?"

"Me neither. No husband in any of those categories," he said, shooting her a grin. "No wife, either, for that matter."

"Oh, that's nice. I mean…"

"I know what you mean," he said gently, and she was pretty sure he did. With anyone else, she would have come right out and asked if he was married, but Joe was different. With Joe, the question was intensely personal.

They decided to call the dog Goldilocks until they found out her real name. She wasn't wearing a collar and there was no sign she'd worn one in the recent past. Now Goldie struggled to stand, circled twice and lowered herself onto the tarp again. Joe felt her ear while Ann Elise checked another area. "So far she seems to have survived her dunking with no ill effects," he said quietly.

Ann Elise nodded, "Another few minutes and we're going to start seeing some action. Once she starts, it should be—"

"Like popping popcorn," he finished.

So they waited quietly in the dim, musty-smelling barn. Ann Elise sneezed occasionally, and Joe blessed her and teased her. There were birds on the rafters. Something small—probably mice—scrambled in the dark corners. Oddly enough, it only added to the coziness. The intimacy. She was every bit as aware of the man beside her as of the patient before her, which wasn't her nature at all. The animal always came first. *Always,* as more than one owner had learned to their discomfort.

Simply put, Joe was a major distraction, the older version even more intriguing than the young Joe of her dreams. The crow's feet bracketing his eyes and a shadow of beard on that rock-bound jaw only added to the attraction. One of the things that had fascinated her most about the younger version was the contrast between his rugged features and a slow, sweet smile that could melt glaciers.

Goldy wasn't the only lady present who was panting.

Joe rose and retrieved a box of latex gloves and a stack of clean, ragged towels from the truck. "Mom saves these for me," he said, placing the towels on the edge of the tarp.

"This obviously isn't her first litter," Ann Elise observed, and Joe nodded agreement. "That helps." They both knew that first timers could be tricky, especially when they were seriously distressed.

Now both watched for the first sign of trouble. The contractions were clearly visible. "I'd really like for her to do the job with as little outside interference as possible," Ann Elise murmured, and again Joe nodded. He was a solid, reassuring presence at her side. His specialty was large animals, hers small, but in case help was needed, there were four experienced hands ready to take over.

Now and then he voiced an observation. Now and then she did. Mostly they talked shop, although she was dying to ask about his personal life, past, present and future.

But she didn't, and so he related a few of his more memorable moments as a large animal vet, and she described some of the pitfalls of working with animal rescue. "For one thing," she said, fluffing her drying hair with her fingers, ''I live in an apartment. No yard, not even a patio. Animals are allowed, which was the only reason I took it, but animals in wholesale lots are discouraged. Most residents have a single pet—a few don't have any. There are two African gray parrots in the apartment across the hall from mine, and let me tell you, they can make up in volume what they lack in size.''

He laughed, and she went on to tell him about the schizophrenic Hillside Setter she'd had to find a home for, the three-legged Australian sheepdog, a Silky rooster that insisted on living inside and eating at the table with the two women who shared the apartment.

''Who's keeping the menagerie while you're here?'' Joe asked, amused because he'd done more or less the same thing in his early days. Adopted all the unwanteds, telling himself he'd find a home for them. Which he usually did—his own.

''Believe it or not, I placed every single one. Dolly was one of the last to go—she's a deaf kitten. I still miss her, but she wasn't happy in my place. It faces north.''

''Right,'' he murmured. It faces north?

Her hand had found its way inside his and absently—or not so absently—Joe caressed her knuckles with his thumb. He heard her catch her breath as if she'd just noticed what he was doing.

"I happen to know this woman with a severe hearing loss," she continued in a breathless rush. "Her husband's somebody big in one of the energy companies, so he can afford it."

"Whoa, back up. He can afford his wife's hearing loss?"

"No, silly, the house. See, he built her this house that's almost entirely of glass, because she's so visually oriented. It's like being outdoors, it's so bright and sunny."

"Hmm, I can see a few drawbacks, but go ahead."

"Well, Dolly just loved it. Poor baby had been so withdrawn while I had her, but as soon as I took her to see Mattie she became a different animal. They both compensate the loss of one sense by sharpening others, so with all that light, all the visual stimuli—Dolly was curious, the way cats are. My place is not really dark, but it's not real bright, either, especially in the winter. Like I said, Dolly just sort of moped when she was with me, but bless her heart, she explored every corner of that big old glass house in the first few minutes we were there. Then she curled up in the middle of the living room floor and watched everything that went on, inside and out." Ann Elise leaned over and hugged her knees, warm with remembered satisfaction. "The two of them bonded right away, so that's probably my very best real success story."

"Until now," he said softly.

They continued to watch Goldie. Somehow, Ann Elise's head had found its way to Joe's shoulder. "Here we go," Joe whispered after a quarter of an hour passed in comfortable silence.

She sat up and leaned forward as Joe moved around to the other side of the tarp.

Chapter 5

Outside, the rain tapered off. In one corner of the barn, marooned in a small circle of lantern light, Goldie attended her new family, nursing, nudging and bathing. Ann Elise wanted nothing so much as to cuddle each one, but the cuddling could come later, as could a closer examination. So far, Mama Goldilocks had done everything just right. For now, the bonding process was strictly a family affair, no strangers needed.

"They're beautiful, aren't they?" she murmured. Exhausted and hungry, she felt contentment steal over her like a warm blanket. It was enough to have played a part in the rescue of a half-drowned animal and to assist in the delivery when it became necessary. The rest could wait.

And if there was another reason for her feeling of contentment, she didn't want to think about it, not just yet.

Seated beside her in the dusty old barn, Joe flexed his shoulders, then stretched both arms over his head. It occurred to her that he must have been under a terrific strain in that flooded creek, pulling his own weight along with Goldie's eighty-odd pounds against the current. When he lowered his arms, one of them fell casually across her shoulders. Was he even aware of her as anything more than a convenient armrest?

"Oh, yeah?" he jeered softly. "Wait a few months, you might change your tune. These guys aren't going to win any beauty contests. I'm thinking boxer and maybe some German shepherd."

She shrugged. "They'll be beautiful, regardless of their genes."

"Granted."

"Besides, mongrels are a recognized breed. I know I can spot one every time."

"Yeah, but can you name the ingredients?"

"We're not talking recipes here. At least Goldie's babies probably won't have the usual genetic flaws from overbreeding."

"Granted," he said once more. "Doesn't necessarily mean they're going to be flaw-free."

"I know," she said and sighed. "I'll think about that tomorrow...or the next day."

"Merry Christmas, Scarlet," he said softly, laughter lacing his baritone drawl.

His hip was pressing against hers and the weight of his arm was burning a brand across her shoulder. "You know what?" she exclaimed, feeling compelled to break the spell of intimacy. "I'm starving! How much longer do you think we need to stay here?"

"I'll check with Highway Patrol, but don't get your hopes up." When he eased his arm away, she wanted to snatch it back. "Little Mama needs some time to recuperate, anyway."

Feeling the cold again, she wrapped her arms around her body. "It's Christmas Eve. Back at the house they're all pigging out on ham and barbecue and mince pie, and I don't even have a stick of bubble gum."

"Whine, whine, whine," he teased. "I got you in out of the rain, didn't I?"

He unfolded his length and stood as she flopped onto her back on the army blanket. From her perspective he looked enormously tall. His damp jeans clung to his body, delineating his masculinity in a way that took her breath away. Tired and hungry she might be; she'd have to have been dead not to notice.

"Did you have lunch?" she called after him.

"Chili dog."

"I hate you."

"No, you don't." His smile didn't help either.

But the empty feeling inside her wasn't entirely due to hunger. She'd tasted everything on her plate at breakfast, and had planned to grab something in the food court for lunch. "No, I don't," she whispered.

"Hang in there, I've got just the thing." She watched him walk stiffly toward the truck. Now that the rain had almost stopped there was a faint glimmer of daylight outside, but it was fading fast. She didn't know how long the batteries in his lantern would last, but she didn't relish spending the night in a pitch-dark barn that was probably home to more than one variety of rodent.

On the other hand, with Joe to keep her company…

"Here you go," he said, handing her a flat gift-wrapped box. "Mom won't begrudge you a few pieces once I explain how her Christmas chocolates saved a woman from starvation."

"Candy?" Ann Elise sat up and reached for the gaudy box. "Oh, I shouldn't," she murmured, ripping off red foil, gold ribbons and the inner cellophane cover. Lifting the top, she stared down at the contents. "Fondants, nougats, almonds, cherries... Oh, my mercy, I don't know where to start."

"Start at the southwest corner and work your way northeast," he suggested dryly. Crossing his long legs, he lowered himself beside her again and reached for a foil-wrapped morsel. "No more than three at a time, though—then wait for your blood sugar to adjust, okay?"

"I'm in heaven," she crooned, biting into a chocolate covered cherry.

Joe reached over and switched off the lantern. "We might need the batteries more later," he said. A watery shaft of daylight slanted through the wide, west-facing doorway. Even after the rain ended it would take a while for the water to go down. By contrast, the barn felt warm and cozy. "How long, do you think?" she asked, licking chocolate from her fingertips.

"How long for what, your blood sugar?"

"For the water to go down. Oops."

"Sloppy," Joe teased and used his thumb to catch the cherry liqueur that dribbled onto her chin. Earlier, he'd shared his antibacterial liquid soap with her, but the towels had all been used up, so he did the next best thing. He licked it off.

And then, because her lips were so close to his,

and because she was feeling mellow and disassociated from reality, she kissed him. He let her have control for all of ten seconds before he took over.

It was better than any chocolate. Slow and languorous because they were both exhausted. Sweet and rife with old memories—on her part, at least. His lips eased away, and he murmured something that sounded like, "Not again," and she rolled into his arms, trapping him on the old army blanket on the pile of ancient hay, in the dark, deserted barn.

Other than a few near misses and a single relationship that had ended by mutual consent, Ann Elise was inexperienced. She refused to let it stand in her way now. If she let this chance go by she knew she'd spend the rest of her life regretting it.

This time Joe was in command. He kissed her lips, her temples, her eyes, exploring slowly, as if determined not to leave any part of her face unkissed. By the time he found her mouth again she was all but catatonic, a puddle of throbbing desire.

"Could you possibly...please...make love to me?" she whispered. Cheeks flaming, she hid her face in his throat, waiting for a response that didn't come immediately. Tomorrow I'll move to the Australian Outback and never, ever have to face him again, she thought desperately.

"Are you sure that's what you want?"

"You want me to beg? All right, I'm begging."

Instead of replying, he kissed her again, and this time there was nothing exploratory about it. This time it was purely carnal. He tasted of chocolate, and so did she. He smelled earthy and damp and sexy, with only the faintest medicinal hint of the antibacterial soap. If he'd smelled like old shoes she would have wanted him anyway, because he was Joe. And rational or not, she had always wanted him. Joe and Ann Elise, the two went together like—like grits and gravy.

Brushing her hair from her face, he kissed her eyelids and then her nose. He kissed each corner of her mouth, and then eased her lips apart once more with his tongue. This time, the chocolate was all used up. This time, it was pure Joe she tasted.

And that was only the beginning.

"Might be scratchy," he said, tugging her damp cashmere sweater over her head. He had spread the wool blanket over the straw pile a few feet away from where Goldie and her litter dozed fitfully.

For Joe, she'd have lain on a bed of nails. She waited until he'd stripped off his flannel shirt, then reached for him. In the near dark, she could barely see his silhouette, yet every cell in her body recognized the man who had evolved from the boy she'd fallen in love with so long ago.

He stroked her cheek, then his hand moved down her throat and found her breast. She wasn't overly endowed—in fact, she barely had enough to cleave, yet she could almost feel her breast swelling to fit his palm. Magic…sheer magic.

And this time, she wasn't dreaming.

"I, um—I have protection, but it's in the truck."

She said, "Hurry," and held him back. Ann Elise the pragmatist reminded her that they needed to be sensible, but Ann Elise the dreamer of impossible dreams whispered that if he left her now, he might never return. She didn't have fourteen more years to waste.

He slipped from her restraining hands and she caught a single glimpse of his naked body silhouetted against a gray-gold sky. I can't believe what I'm about to do, she thought wildly. Then she wondered why he carried protection in his truck, picturing hurried couplings on a blanket spread hastily over the truck bed before remembering that he'd left his wallet there before wading out into the creek.

Of course he carried protection. All men did, unless they were celibate or married. Or stupid.

He was none of the above—which set her to wondering about the women he must have known. Was he was currently involved? Did he have a sweetheart? Lovers in the plural?

Was this going to be a one-night stand?

What else could it possibly be?

She was drowning in second thoughts by the time he came back, but then he knelt beside her again, and it was too late. It had been too late fourteen years ago, when she'd been a high school graduate and he'd been an overgrown, sexy boy.

No promises, she thought fleetingly. If this is all I can have, it will still be the best Christmas ever.

While the dark clouds moved eastward and the sun settled into the west, he made love to her. By the time he braced his hands on either side of her body, leaned over and brushed his lips across hers, back and forth, dragging like damp velvet, she was drowning in need, desperate with a hunger that blocked out all hope of rational thought.

Her hands stroked his back, moved down to his narrow hips and pressed him closer to where she needed him most. "Please," she begged.

"Easy, easy, we'll get there." Sweet, patient Joe.

She didn't want sweetness and patience, she wanted him! She wanted release from this driving, mindless hunger!

Curling downward, her fingertips scraped across his nipples. He sucked in a shuddering breath and she felt tension rip through his lean body. Positioned over her, yet still not quite touching her, he radiated heat like a furnace.

Supporting his weight on one arm, he reached down and found her. "Ah, sweet—I can't wait much longer," he groaned.

"Yes! No—just...please," she begged. She, who had never begged in her life, was begging a man to make love to her.

I love you, love you, love you...

The words echoed silently down the canyons of her mind as he entered her, found the core of her heat, and enflamed her with an escalating, mind-destroying desire that had her crying his name.

He was incredibly gentle. Sensitive to needs she was hardly aware of having. How could she have imagined such an all-consuming urgency? Without Joe's deliberate pacing, she would have gone up in flames the instant he touched her. While her inner storm had her clinging and pleading, with the small portion of her mind still capable of rational thought, she realized that he was exerting almost superhuman control.

He moved slowly, thrusting, lingering, with-drawing, while fire gnawed at her center, blazing up, burning down only to flare up again. The pow-erful arms that supported his weight trembled. Her hands slipped on his sweat-slick flesh. He tasted her mouth, lowered his face to suckle her breasts, and she knew the instant he went over the edge.

Straining over her, he rode her wildly, fiercely, the sound of his breath like tearing canvas in the silence around them. She might have screamed—

She *never* screamed.

But then, it had never been like this before.

He collapsed on her, the full weight of his trem-bling body echoing the beat of his thudding heart. Still reeling from a pleasure so profound it was almost pain, she held him to her. She could scarcely breathe, but she would have held him forever if Goldie hadn't chosen that moment to intrude.

"Something just nudged my foot," she whis-pered. "Was it you?"

"Just a rat, go to sleep."

"I can't sleep with a locomotive lying on top of me." Keep it light, she warned herself silently. Don't tell him how you feel, he never bargained for that.

"You implying I'm heavy?"

"Well, all that candy…"

"Mmm, I never realized chocolate was such an aphrodisiac." He adjusted his weight so that he was mostly lying beside her instead of on top of her. The moment he did, she wanted to drag him back and start all over again.

"Joe, something just licked my foot," she whispered.

His teeth gleamed in the darkness as he grinned at her. "Well now, if you want to play that kind of game, I'm your man. But I think we're being called on to baby-sit." He sat up, and reluctantly, so did she.

Goldie stood, stepped carefully over her nest of squirming babies and left, glancing over her shoulder just once before disappearing into the gloomy dusk. "She trusts us," Ann Elise said, feeling around for her clothes.

"Smart dog. You all right?"

"Of course I'm all right," she said airily. "Why wouldn't I be?"

"No reason. Just checking."

Ann Elise felt around for her sweater. Joe handed her his shirt, and she put on that instead. For the time being, it would do. He found her bra and held it out and she snatched it from him.

Joe shrugged and reached for his jeans. Back to business as usual, he thought, wondering if he'd just proved himself to be the world's biggest fool. A single kiss more years ago that he cared to remember had pretty much ruined him for other girls. He'd dated a few, sure, because that's what boys his age did, hormones being what they were. But even when he'd gone from "dating girls" to "seeing women," he'd never quite been able to forget the vulnerable girl he'd discovered hiding behind freckles, glasses and a thick layer of shyness disguised as pride.

His first year out of college he'd drifted into a relationship with a schoolteacher that had nearly led to marriage. Fortunately, Mary had felt something lacking and had broken things off before they could go too far. Later he heard she'd moved east, married a Coast Guardsman and started on a family.

As for him, he'd been too busy establishing and keeping up with a thriving veterinary practice, not to mention running the ranch and looking after his increasingly dependent parents, to worry about what he might be missing. Only lately had he stopped to wonder if life was passing him by. At twenty-nine, he was still young, but by nature he was probably too set in his ways to settle down with a wife and raise a family, even if he could have found a woman he liked enough who would have him.

This is a fluke, he warned himself, hanging

back to watch Ann Elise lift each pup, check the gender and do a quick examination in the dim light provided by the lantern. She'd be leaving in a few days, going back to her fancy big-city practice and her fancy big-city friends. They might happen to share a profession and a few memories, but that's all they shared.

For all he knew, she might not even remember the night of the prom, when a wet-behind-the-ears kid had risked being arrested for driving without a license just to spare a shy upperclassman from being humiliated. He had threatened to beat the tar out of any jerk who even whispered that the whole thing had been a setup, a big joke. That Billy had never intended to show up, even if he hadn't gotten hauled in for shoplifting.

Hell of a lot of water had passed over the dam since then.

And over the highway.

Chapter 6

"Five little boys, including the runt—and four big, pretty girls," Ann Elise announced, examining a limp lump of grayish fur that promised to be wiry. "Oh, look at this darling, already she's got personality."

"With those genes, she'll need it," Joe said, amused.

Reluctantly she restored the whelp to its mother. "All sorely in need of the usual, of course. I suspect Mama's been on her own for some time now."

"Yeah, I noticed. Battle scars, worms—no sign of a recent collar, so it's anyone's guess about her

shots.'' Joe was doing his best to sound noncha-
lant when that was the last thing he felt, seeing
her kneeling beside the tarp-full of whelps, bare
from the thighs down. Even her feet were sexy—
long and narrow, with high arches and small pink
toes.

You've lost it, man. ''I called Highway Patrol—some of the roads are clear now. Anytime
you're ready to give it a go, we'll start loading
up cargo.''

For a long time she didn't answer. She just
looked at him in a way that put him immediately
on the defensive. ''Unless you want to spend the
night and try in the morning,'' he added lamely.

''Sure, why not?'' Standing, she looked around
for her sweater and jeans.

''What, go or stay?'' Great. As if it hadn't been
bad enough before, now he'd had to go and com-
plicate things, squared and in triplicate.

''Let's just get out of here,'' she muttered.

Turning away, she managed to wriggle into her
bra without taking off his shirt, then she peeled
off the shirt, flung it at him and tugged her stained
and baggy sweater over her head. It hadn't im-
proved over the past few hours. He didn't know
if you could bleach something like that or not, but
those mud stains were going to be tough to
get out.

She should have looked like hell. Instead, she looked like one of those leggy fashion models with her skinny, shapeless tunic and her tousled hair.

Well, hell.

"Where're my jeans?" she muttered.

He pulled on his shirt, still warm from her body—still smelling faintly of whatever fragrance she'd started out the day with, overlaid with nuances of sex and dog.

She found her jeans and wriggled into them, then jammed her feet into her muddy boots. "Those pups don't need to be in the back of any truck," she said, daring him to argue.

"I'll make room in the cab."

She picked up the lantern and looked around the dark barn for anything they might have left. Ignoring her, he collected the blanket and slung it over his shoulder. Two could play the game of cool.

Goldie trotted back inside, shook herself and went immediately to her babies, sniffing each one to make sure no one had been fooling around while her back was turned.

After sending them an accusing look over a matted golden shoulder, she circled and settled down. "Make a place," Ann Elise said, "then we can start transporting the pups. She might not be happy about it, but she'll follow.''

Joe waited until the menagerie was installed in the back of his crew cab, then he said, ''I need to make a stop on the way. I think I might know who she belongs to.''

Sitting stiffly beside him, Ann Elise waited a full minute before answering. ''Whoever it is, doesn't deserve her. I'll take her with me.''

''To Dallas? Ten might blow your lease.''

She lifted her chin, but refused to look at him. ''Of course not. Baker's Acres is large enough.''

He happened to know that was the name she'd given her uncle's place when they'd first moved to Mission Creek from Corpus Christi. Not many acres remained, but it was still a lot bigger than a city apartment, unless it happened to open onto a park.

''Right. You're in town on a visit, staying with your sister and a bunch of other people, and you're going to present them with a flea-ridden bitch and a bunch of leaky, squealing mongrel pups. You want to stop off somewhere for some gift wrap?''

She glared at him. Less than an hour ago she had come apart in his arms, and now she was looking at him as if she'd sooner get out and walk than spend another two minutes in his company.

He shrugged. "Fine. You want 'em, you got 'em, only first I'm going to drive by Wanda's place and see if she's missing a pet."

"Fine. You do that."

He wondered fleetingly when the word "Fine" had become a swear word.

Neither of them spoke again until he reached the end of the rutted, muddy road leading to the blacktop. "Turn left," she snapped.

He turned right.

"My car's that way, remember? Or shall I get out here and walk back?"

"With or without the cargo?" He nodded to the back seat, where slurping noises indicated either bath time or suppertime.

"With," she said, and sighed. "I guess."

It was all the opening he needed. "Look, let's save the arguments until we know for sure what we're arguing about, okay? Wanda lives in a mobile home park off Wheeler Road, couple of miles from here. We'll check it out first. If Goldie's hers, that settles it."

"It doesn't settle anything. The dog's obviously been mistreated. She's got worms and fleas and ear mites—I'm pretty sure she's starting an eye infection, and she's not even wearing a collar."

"Hey, cut her some slack, will you? Wanda's

a nice woman.'' Debatable, but then, he didn't really know the divorcée who worked the day shift at Coyote Harry's and occasionally took in overnight guests of the male persuasion. He'd spent one less-than-memorable half hour in her bed a couple of years ago, and left a more than generous tip. From the rumpled bed she'd watched him leave, obviously realizing he wouldn't be back.

But she was a damn good waitress.

"I'll reserve judgment.'' Wrapping her arms around her chest, Ann Elise sat poker-faced for the rest of the drive.

"Nice sunset,'' he observed when they turned off onto Wheeler. The sun was already well below the horizon, but red and gold streaks angled up from the horizon, chasing the fast moving cloud layer that had dumped more than six inches of rain on the surrounding area over the past twenty-four hours.

A plastic bag skittered across the road and clung to a leafless bush. They passed a small bungalow with roughly a hundred separate lighted Christmas decorations in an otherwise barren front yard.

"We were supposed to finish decorating the tree after supper,'' she said quietly.

Aha. The olive branch.

"We've already done ours. Pop's a great hand at untangling all the lights, and Mom's a good director. Me, all I have to do is follow orders."

They passed a doublewide outlined completely in blue lights, with a gigantic wreath on the front door. Ann Elise sighed. She was nibbling her lower lip, and on impulse, he laid a hand on her knee. Her jeans were still slightly damp. "You cold?" he asked. "I can turn up the heat."

"No, I'm fine."

Her voice said otherwise, but he wasn't about to argue. "Hey, it's Christmas Eve," he reminded her, forcing a cheerful note to his voice. "Who'd have thought after all these years we'd be celebrating together?"

That time he got a reaction. She rolled her eyes and started to speak. Fortunately, he got a word in first. "There it is," he announced. "The one with the…overflowing garbage can," he finished lamely.

Pulling over to the side of the road, they stared at the only dark residence among a dozen or more that were lighted up and decorated with everything from a battalion of knee-high plastic elves, to candles, to rooftop sleighs and a flock of reindeer grazing on the front lawn.

From the back seat, Goldie whimpered. Without turning, Joe said, "Easy, girl, let's see what's going on before we make any hasty decisions, all right?''

It was Ann Elise who replied. ''I've already made a decision. Goldie was miles away from this place. If she was happy here she would never have left, certainly not this close to term. She'd have found a warm, dry place under the trailer, if not inside.''

Joe was squinting at his cell phone, punching in a number. ''Harry? Joe Halloran. Look, is Wanda working tonight?''

While he listened to Harry, whoever that was, Ann Elise unsnapped her seat belt and twisted around onto her knees. ''Hi, how ya doing, honey?'' she whispered. ''That's some Christmas present you've got there.'' Joe had put half the stuff into the back of the pickup, shoved everything else over to one side and folded up the seat, making a cozy nest on the blanket for the canine family.

She heard him say, ''Since week before last?''

More silence. She reached down and picked up one of the pups. Goldie licked her hand, then ignored her to nose the runt of the litter into a more favorable position. ''You're going to be one busy mama for the next few weeks,'' Ann Elise whispered just as Joe was signing off. ''From now on, you'll be eating for ten, which means we're going to have to triple your rations.''

"Well, that takes care of that," Joe said flatly. Starting up the engine, he made a U-turn and headed back out Wheeler Road. "Wanda quit work and left town over a week ago. Left owing two months rent, plus utility. Harry knew about the dog—her name's Madonna, by the way.''

"I like Goldilocks better.''

"Yeah, me, too. Anyhow, he said he drove out to see if she was sick—Wanda, that is—when she didn't show up two days in a row. Her phone had already been disconnected. He checked in with the rental office that handles the park and found out she'd split. Said he saw the dog, but couldn't catch up with her, so he called animal control. Evidently they couldn't find her, either. They never called and he never checked back.''

They drove on in silence, headed back to where she had left her car by the side of the road. The chilling thought occurred to her that it might have been stolen by now, or at least vandalized. She had insurance on the brand-new van she drove back in Dallas, but she wasn't sure it covered a situation like this.

"You know the saddest thing of all?" she murmured after a while.

"Hmm?" He slowed, cautiously easing into a

fifty-foot stretch of standing water. Conditions were improving, but they were still a long way from good.

"Well, hardly the saddest of all, but still..." She sighed. "It was the only place without a single decoration, not even a red ribbon on the mail box."

"What, you want to go back and decorate her mailbox? How about the Camden place, you want to string some lights out there, too?"

"Can't. Power's probably off."

"You got that right. Like for the past twenty years," he said, but he was grinning.

Ann Elise felt some of the awkwardness dissipate. There were still issues to be confronted between them—or not. But for right now, at least they could talk. "So what do we do with Goldie and company?"

"How about my place for now?"

"What about your family?"

"Not a problem. Pop loves animals and Mom's cat's pretty tolerant. I've got a couple of holding pens off my office, but I have a feeling they'll all end up in the house for now."

Practical or not, Ann Elise wasn't quite ready to part with her little family. Even among her animal-rescue friends, she was known as a soft touch. As in soft in the head. Taking in a rat snake with a skin condition while she'd still been trying to find a good home for the house chicken had been the last straw. The chicken had freaked and flown up onto the light fixture and the snake had crawled inside a piano she was keeping for a friend, underneath the strings, and refused to come out.

"Look, how about this," she said decisively. "I'll follow you home and we can run it by your folks. If they're willing to adopt ten strays who'll soon be eating them out of house and home, then that's fine. Otherwise, I'm taking them home with me."

"Chow's not a problem. Believe it or not, I do have a few sources."

"Ha. Hay, oats and corn?"

"Good roughage," he said, and shot her a quick grin. "What do you say we get 'em settled in at my place—then, once you're satisfied with the accommodations I can follow you home to make sure you get there all right. Maybe tomorrow you can drive out again just to see how they're doing, how's that sound?"

She didn't bother to reply, as by that time they'd reached her car. Joe pulled up behind the stranded vehicle and climbed out, coming around to open her door.

Ann Elise didn't wait, but slid down off the

high seat unassisted. She wasn't about to risk finding herself in his arms again. She had enough to deal with without another reminder.

And then she was staring at the bright red sticker someone had placed on the rear window of her aunt's middle-aged compact car. "Joe? Somebody decorated it."

Joe shook his head. "Sorry. Highway Patrol," he told her. "Shows they've been by and checked it out. If it's still here, sooner or later they'll have it towed, run the license and notify you where to find it."

"Oh." She looked so crestfallen, he almost wished he'd let her go on thinking some kind soul had decorated her car for Christmas.

"Al?" he said tentatively. She was shivering, patting her pockets, a look of sheer panic spreading over her face. "Honey, what's wrong?"

Chapter 7

"If there's a key hidden out somewhere, I can't find it," Joe said, pulling his head out from under the left front fender. He'd checked all the usual places—license plate, gas flap and all four fenders. "Catch-22. Without getting inside, I can't release the hood to check underneath."

The temperature was dropping precipitously as the last few streaks of faded lavender disappeared from the sky. Inside the pickup, Ann Elise punched in Faith's number on Joe's cell phone. Sensing her tension, Goldie whimpered.

"It's all right, girl," she said quietly. "Still busy," she called over to where he was standing,

scratching his head. "If you know of any lock-
smiths who might be willing to come out on
Christmas Eve, maybe I could call information
and get the number?"

He replaced his curled-brim black Stetson. "Or
maybe you could just come home with me and
we'll send someone out tomorrow," he countered.

"Or maybe you could just take me and my
dogs to Baker's Acres and I can get hold of a
locksmith tomorrow." The truck smelled of dog
and old leather, but at least it was warm. Joe was
outside in his shirtsleeves. Just because she'd declined the use of his coat, he stubbornly refused
to wear the thing. Chivalry gone awry.

"You're going to drag some poor guy out on
Christmas Day?"

Her shoulders drooped in discouragement. It
wasn't a lack of planning, she told herself, it really wasn't. She was an excellent planner. She
happened to have been born with an organized
mind. Virgoans were known for it.

Not that she believed in astrology, but still, being a Virgo, she'd read a few books on the subject
just to see if there could possibly be anything to
it. Members of her sun sign were also known for
their analytical qualities.

"Let me try something first," Joe said. He
sauntered across the highway, hooked a booted

foot on the running board and leaned over the tool compartment on the back of his truck.

Opening the door, she reached back inside the cab and grabbed his jacket. Virgoans were also practical. Wrapped in the oversized coat, she breathed in the scent of leather and a faint hint of something spicy while she watched him rummage around in the big aluminum compartment. Her gaze fastened on his trim backside and she wondered how long it was going to take her to get over him this time. If after fourteen years she hadn't gotten over a single kiss, she could just see herself fifty years from now, tottering around a nursing home, telling everyone she could button-hole about her brown-haired, brown-eyed lover and their one-night stand in a haystack on Christmas Eve back in the year of ought-three.

When he jumped back to the ground, she followed him to her car, where he went to work, using a flat tool that looked like a saw blade. She couldn't see what he was doing, but he was muttering curses. Okay, so she could pay for a broken window, no problem, although driving might be a tad chilly until she could arrange to have it repaired.

"Just be glad it's not one of the newer models," he said, and she nodded without the least notion of what he meant.

Then he swung open the car door and stepped away. "Your carriage awaits, m'lady."

"Oh, thank heavens," she breathed fervently, and brushed past him. Reaching inside, she snatched up her damp, rumpled raincoat, and there they were, right where she'd tossed them. Her keys, lying on top of her favorite leather purse—the one with the Betadine stains on the flap and the ragged edge where a teething pup had worked it over while its mama was being treated for a torn ear.

"I have never—*ever*—felt so stupid," she said, backing out of the car.

"No kidding. Never?"

She sent him a quelling look, then shook her head, disarmed by a smile that could melt glaciers. "All right, it was stupid, locking my keys inside. You probably won't believe me, but I have a reputation for being pretty cool in an emergency."

"Who said I didn't believe you?"

She shot him another look. "It was the double whammy," she said, checking to see that everything was still inside her purse. To think that anyone could have come by and...

"Double whammy, hmm." He leaned against the side of the car, arms crossed, one ankle hooked over the other, as if he had all the time in the world. As if it weren't practically dark, with miles to go and decisions still to be made.

She refused to rise to the bait. "The flood and Goldie," she said firmly, but she could tell by the way he cocked one eyebrow that he wasn't buying it. "Oh, let's just go if we're going." She slid in under the wheel. He knew very well what she meant. Being stopped by a flooded creek and helping to rescue a bitch in labor was enough to throw anyone off-stride, but it had been seeing him again after fourteen years that had blown every fuse in her otherwise functional brain. Not to mention what had happened in the barn. "Well? Are you going to stand there smirking all night?"

Smooth, Ann Elise. You're handling this just beautifully.

Joe had rolled down the window. Now he leaned close enough that she could feel his warm breath on her cool skin. "You know what they say." There was a distinct gleam of amusement in those clear amber eyes.

"What, trouble comes in threes?" She switched on the engine and shifted into reverse, but kept her foot on the brake. "Look, if we're going to do this thing then let's get started. I don't know about you, but I happen to have plans for the evening."

Without another word he turned and sauntered across to his pickup. She could barely see his silhouette against the darkening sky, but that didn't keep her from watching him every step of the way.

The same way she used to watch him back when she'd had to invent excuses to hang out near the field during football practice, too far away to see the sparkle in his laughing eyes, but close enough to think highly improper thoughts. She hadn't been the only girl there, either, although she'd probably been the oldest of his admirers. Cradle-robbing—that's what it was called. If he'd ever gone through an awkward adolescence, it must have been before he hit middle school. For all she knew he could have been born six foot three, with those wide shoulders, those long, lean limbs and that melt-your-heart smile.

He could've played pro football, he was that good. Instead, he'd chosen to get his DVM and come back to Mission Creek to look after his father's ranch and both his parents.

And she'd chosen to buy into an established practice, and then take it over, remaining far enough from Mission Creek so that she could see her sisters occasionally, but wouldn't have to see Joe and his perky little cheerleader every time she ventured into town.

Backing around, she waited for him to lead the
way. Had it meant anything at all to him? Those
hours together in the barn? Did it fall under the
heading of casual sex? A good time was had by
all, see you around? It definitely wasn't the sort
of thing she did on a regular basis...or ever.

Ann Elise had always prided herself on being
a pragmatist, starting soon after her parents had
been killed, when she and her sisters had had to
leave behind the only home they'd ever known
and move to a different town to live with relatives
who'd been all but strangers. She had learned to
assess a situation, set her sights on a goal and
work relentlessly toward it, never allowing opti-
mism to warp her vision.

Some might even call that pessimism, but it
was actually only realism. There were no guar-
antees in life; anyone who expected miracles deserved what they got.

"So what am I going to do about you now?"
she whispered, following the Christmas-red taillights three car lengths ahead.

They passed the turnoff that led to the Baker's
place. Joe kept on going. Ann Elise kept on following. Following the dogs, she told herself, not
Joe. Because while it might be more practical for
him to keep them for the time being, that didn't
mean she intended to relinquish control. Dogs

were her business. He dealt mostly with big farm animals. The fundamentals might be the same, but the two specialties were miles apart.

Excuses, excuses...

The Halloran place had been pointed out to her years ago. "That's where Joe Halloran lives," someone had said. A classmate. Female, and thus, as enthralled by the young athlete as she'd been.

By Mission Creek standards it wasn't a large ranch, but it was definitely bigger than Uncle Lloyd's had been, even before Aunt Beth had sold off great gobs of acreage. There was a neat sign on the gatepost announcing J. Halloran, DVM, with a rocking *H* just beneath.

At the end of a long, well-tended dirt road, the house looked as if it had started out small and been added on to over the years. The result was no particular style, but attractive and inviting, even so. There was an enormous wreath on the front door and swags of greenery laced around the porch rail. Electric candles gleamed from every window.

Joe turned into a space in front of the house and she pulled in beside him, wondering why he hadn't gone directly to the barn. He'd told her he'd set up shop in a renovated equipment shed attached to the main barn.

A small woman with a sweater thrown over her

shoulders came out onto the porch and waved. She was using a walker. Joe slid down from the truck and called out, "Hi, Mom—I brought company."

"I simply must go home," Ann Elise protested for the third time, or maybe the fourth. The dogs were bedded down for the night, not in a pen out by Joe's office, but in a mudroom just off the warm, fragrant kitchen. Joe had carried his father's rocking chair out there and Mr. Halloran was rocking, talking to Goldie and keeping watch on the pups while only a few steps away, Mrs. Halloran pressed another serving of gingerbread on Ann Elise. Homemade, not from a mix. With cranberries and a rich lemon sauce.

"Oh, I couldn't," Ann Elise protested, even as she accepted her second generous slice. As hungry as she was, she'd declined a supper invitation, but dessert was different. After all, as Mrs. Halloran—"Call me Polly"—said, it was Christmas Eve. A time for sharing.

It was even later than she'd expected when she finally got away. She'd called Faith soon after they'd arrived to tell her what had happened. Some of it, anyway. "I can't ask you to take in Goldie and her nine babies, with all you have to do," she'd said by way of explanation.

"The children would love it," Faith had protested.

"They're newborns, Faith—give them time to develop a few defenses before we let the kids at them."

"Oh. Well... I guess you'd know."

"Trust me, it's better this way." And to Polly Halloran, who was holding the coffeepot over her cup with a questioning look, she shook her head. "Look, I'll be along in about a half hour, Faith. No later, all right?"

The kitchen smelled of gingerbread and sage and coffee. Somewhere in the house, a radio was broadcasting a Christmas Eve program. She needed to be with her own family—she'd come here for just that purpose. And to say goodbye to Aunt Beth.

Yet somehow this old kitchen, a place where she'd never set foot in her life, felt more like home than any other place she could remember. The tree was a straggly cedar. It was slightly crooked, and the decorations were obviously old, more than a few of them handmade.

By a young Joe? He had an older sister who was married and living in Olean, New York, who couldn't make it home because she'd broken her ankle trying to teach her little boy to ski. Polly had insisted on showing her pictures of both her children—a tall, grinning Joe, age eleven, and a tall, grave-looking girl a couple of years older, with her father's height and her mother's pale coloring.

Reluctantly, she stood and reached for her raincoat. The day had started out chilly and damp, but not really cold. Over a sweater, the silk raincoat had been enough. Now, without asking, Joe brought her a wool-lined denim jacket that was only a dozen or so sizes too large. "It'll keep you from freezing on the way home," he said.

"My car does have a heater, you know."

"Take it," he insisted, and she did, and wrapped it around her, not so much because she couldn't bear a little cold, but because it smelled of Joe. He'd worn it. And so she would wear it, too, so she could feel close to him for just a little while longer.

He walked her out to the car and said, "I'll follow, just to be sure you don't run into any more flooded creeks."

"I don't need an escort." And when he only looked at her—that steady, level look that said so much that was open to interpretation—she grudgingly relented. "Oh, all right. But just as far as the turnoff."

He followed her all the way up the lane. In the darkness, the Baker house still looked impressive with it's light-trimmed eaves and wraparound porch, and a wealth of decorations sparkling in the clear, cold air. A moment after the headlights played over the front, the door opened, and there was Faith, with Gabriel at her shoulder.

Joe came over to the car and opened her door. "You don't have to get out," Ann Elise said, despising herself for sounding so inhospitable. As if she didn't really want him here, when she wanted him more than she had ever wanted anything in her entire life.

"Sorry. Too late. Maybe I can sneak back to the truck and get away before anyone sees me." He sounded hurt, and perhaps just a bit angry.

"Joe, I'm sorry, I didn't mean that." She caught his arm before he could walk away and held on. "Come say hello to the family. You know Faith—I think she was in one of your classes."

Faith, who had always considered herself plain, was glowing. She looked at Ann Elise, and her eyes widened. "Good Lord, what happened to you? You look like...and your sweater!"

Her sweater was drooping a couple of inches below the oversize denim coat. In Polly's warm kitchen she'd forgotten what she must look like. No wonder Joe had been staring at her all evening. "I told you, we rescued a dog in a flooded creek in the pouring rain, and then had to hole up in a barn while she delivered. The water was too high to come home right away.''

That was the short version, the only one she intended to tell. Quickly she made introductions and glanced past Gabriel to see that the tree was upright again, and complete, with angel on top. She explained to Joe, ''Jason got a little rambunctious and nearly knocked the whole thing down.'' And to Faith, ''I guess. they're both asleep by now?''

''Just barely. At least they're quiet.''

The sound of voices drifted in from the kitchen. Startled, Ann Elise whispered, ''Company? I'd better slip upstairs before anyone sees me. G'night, Joe, and thanks.''

Faith grabbed her arm. ''No you don't. Oh, Annie, guess what!''

Chapter 8

Under a spray of mistletoe hanging in the kitchen doorway, an obviously pregnant Marilou was arguing with a man who looked vaguely familiar. Hesitating only a moment, Ann Elise opened her arms and rushed forward. "Excuse the dirt, I'll clean up in a minute. Marilou? Wh-what happened?"

"You don't know?" The youngest of the Baker sisters confronted her, eyes a-gleam, cheeks flushed. She laughed, but there was a brittle edge to the sound. "Remember all those lectures you used to give me when I started my—"

"And this is Tate Carson," Faith said hur-

riedly, moving in to wave toward the man whose
face and name were familiar to anyone who followed the rodeo circuit. "He's going to be spending Christmas with us, and let me tell you, Jason
thinks Santa's already come and gone. First Gabe
and now Tate. Joe, you need to stick around and
meet my son. He's really hungry for male role
models."

Tate Carson pointed a finger at Joe. "Halloran.
Didn't you used to play for A & M? Quarterback,
right?"

Joe nodded. Faith hooked her arm through Gabriel's and beamed at the tall veterinarian. "I was
in two of your classes, Joe. I don't mind admitting
now that I used to have the biggest crush on
you."

Ann Elise stared. "You did?"

"Don't tell me you didn't," her sister teased,
brown eyes sparkling with laughter.

Ann Elise decided that whatever else he was,
Gabriel Raines was the best thing that had happened to her sister in years. There was no sign
now of either the rebellious teenager who had run
away from an overly strict uncle or the frightened
woman of a few years later who had divorced an
abusive, alcoholic husband. Since then Faith had
struggled to raise her two children alone, stub-

bornly refusing most offers of help. They'd both tried, even when Marilou had been dealing with her own problems, but Faith had been determined to make it on her own. Short on luck, but long on pride. She'd said it laughingly the last time Ann Elise had tried to give her money to pay for a new water heater.

"Look, I live here, you don't," her sister had said. "I have a great job with nice people and a lot of friends. One of those friends happens to be a plumber, so quit worrying. You worry too much—you always did."

Ann Elise hadn't even tried to refute the charge. Of course she'd always worried. As the eldest, it had always been her job to worry. She had a feeling that things were changing—that something precious was slipping away. Yet seeing her sister glowing with happiness, she couldn't help but be happy for her.

With decidedly mixed feelings Ann Elise leaned against the wall and watched the interplay between her two sisters and the men they'd brought home with them. She couldn't tell about Marilou and Tate Carson. There was definitely something there, but it felt—edgy. And Marilou was pregnant, for heaven's sake! When had that happened, and who—?

Clearly one of her sisters no longer needed her, but she wasn't at all sure about the other one. When it came to men, the Baker sisters didn't have a great track record.

"I'd better be getting back home," Joe said, and everyone chimed in to beg him to stay.

"I promised to take the folks to midnight services," he said. "Anyone want to come with me?" The invitation was general, but he was looking at Ann Elise. "How about all you folks being my guest at the Lone Star Club for Christmas dinner?"

Christmas dinner? Ann Elise couldn't think beyond the moment. "Oh, I don't know. I really need to—well, to, uh…" She gestured helplessly at her muddy jeans, her baggy sweater and her once-beautiful snakeskin boots.

"I could take you outside and hose you off," Marilou offered.

"Just point me to a bathtub and turn up that big new water heater," she said with a sigh.

In the meantime she'd figure out a way to put this thing with Joe into perspective before it took on too great a significance. Christmas dinner with both families present probably wasn't the best way. "Call me tomorrow and let me know how the babies are," she said. "If you have time."

"Babies!" Faith and Marilou chorused together.

So then they had to explain all over again about Goldie and her pups. Faith had heard part of the story over the phone, but the others were fascinated. Gabe said, "I might be able to place a few of them for you, Halloran."

Marilou said, "Oh, I want one!" Then she looked down at her expanded girth and wrinkled her nose. Tate merely looked uncomfortable.

Hmm, mused Ann Elise. Something's definitely going on here...but what?

Joe left after a murmured conversation with Gabriel, and Ann Elise made her excuses and went upstairs. She had washed up at Joe's house, but there was only so much that could be done short of a complete bath and change of clothes. Standing in the room that used to be hers, she reminded herself that tomorrow was Christmas. She was surrounded by her family—what was left of it—and that was truly wonderful. It should be enough, she told herself as she gathered up gown, robe and slippers and headed for the bathroom.

But it wasn't.

She stoppered the tub, turned on both faucets and dumped in a palmful of bath salts. Faith had Gabe now. There was definitely something between Tate and Marilou, but evidently they still had some issues to work out.

A rodeo star and a financial consultant?

Hardly a likely match.

As for Faith and her oilman, she was beginning to get the idea that Gabe Raines was more than just a bit player. She knew quality when she saw it, and those bench-made boots of his hadn't come cheap. Nor had that custom-tailored shirt.

If anyone deserved a Prince Charming, it was Faith, she told herself as she tested the temperature and stepped into the bathtub. Evidently her love of cooking had finally turned into a good thing. Somewhere in last night's conversation she'd got the impression that Gabe was going to back her in a restaurant venture. She'd been too sleepy to pay much attention.

Sliding down in the hot, sudsy water, she propped her feet against the tiled wall and closed her eyes. The house had been built long before one-piece plastic units had been invented. Parts of it still needed modernizing, but she liked it just as it was.

She tried to focus on her sisters and the children—anything to keep from thinking about Joe. But by the time she climbed out of the tub and confronted herself in the steamy mirror, she couldn't put it off any longer. It was still there, what she'd felt for him all these years. She'd managed to put it behind her, to shove it under the surface, but all it took was one look at that familiar face—that warm, quirky grin—and she'd lost it all over again. Heart, mind and any shred of sense she'd ever possessed.

Two veterinarians, for Pete's sake. They had that much in common—maybe even a few more things, but it wasn't going to work. In a few more days she'd be going back to Dallas, to her impatient clients and their trophy dogs, too many of which were overbred, undertrained and stressed to the max. In the past year alone she'd dealt with a deaf dalmation, a hydrocephalic cocker spaniel, and more than a few edgy Dobermans and mean German shepherds, all from overbreeding. At least Goldie had sense enough to dilute the gene pool.

Joe's life was here in Mission Creek with his parents and his practice and his perky little cheerleader, or whoever her successor was. Ann Elise couldn't imagine him going for long without a woman in his life. Several women, probably.

On the other hand, that might mean he hadn't

found the right one yet. "Dream on, you pathetic wimp," she whispered to the rosy image in the mirror.

Christmas Day was hectic, to say the least. The kids were hyper, but surprisingly well behaved. Magically, gifts had appeared under the tree from Santa—those were the ones with no gift wrappings. There were several fancy packages with no cards on them at all. Ann Elise knew for a fact that there had been gift cards earlier, because she'd seen them.

Over the heads of the children she caught Faith's eye and lifted a questioning brow. *What happened to the cards?*

Faith winked at her. *Who cares?*

Becky came over to where she was seated, nursing a cup of coffee. "Aunt Ann Elise, Mama said something about some puppies. Did you find some?"

"Sure did, hon." So she proceeded to tell both children all about the adventure of the previous evening, and how she and an old friend had rescued a golden retriever from a flooded creek and taken her to a deserted barn where nine puppies had been born.

Jason got in with his question first. "Can I have

one? I want a boy dog, and I can name him Fire-man.''

"Silly, you can't name a dog Fireman. I want a girl dog. I'm going to name her... What color are they, Aunt Ann Elise?''

"Why don't you call me Annalise, the way Jason does? Color? Let's see, there are two sort of grayish-brown and at least three that look like their mama. She's blond. Dr. Halloran and I called her Goldilocks.''

"Then I'm going to call my puppy Gretel,'' Becky said smugly.

Faith sat up and started to say something. Grinning, Gabe pulled her back. "As in Hansel and,'' he said softly. "Those old books of your aunt Beth's, remember? Must date back to her childhood.''

"At least,'' Faith said, and the moment passed. By the time the dogs were weaned and adoptable, Ann Elise would no longer be here. They'd have to work it out all on their own.

With Joe, she thought wistfully. In a way she wished she didn't have to go back to Dallas so soon, but of course she did. Her home was there now. Her friends, her practice—everything. She'd left Mission Creek behind when she'd gone off to college, spending most of every summer thereafter working and taking night classes.

She had deliberately scheduled around this Christmas, leaving her new assistant to handle anything that came up unexpectedly. Jen was working out even better than she'd hoped, but she was nowhere near ready to take over the practice yet.

Yet?

Where had that thought come from?

The midday Christmas meal was in ruins, the partakers sprawled around in various chairs while the children enjoyed their new gifts. Conversation was desultory. Ann Elise had insisted on cleaning up the kitchen. "Just sit down, both of you," she'd ordered when both women had started to clear the table. "Faith, you cooked the entire meal, and Marilou, you—"

"Go ahead…you were going to say—?" Her baby sister was in a better mood today. Marginally.

"I know you—you just want to nibble."

"I do not," the youngest sister protested. "There's your nibbler." Marilou pointed at Ann Elise.

"Oh, just go sit down," Ann Elise protested,

laughing. "We all know I can't cook, but at least I know how to load a dishwasher."

Faith had said, "Thank goodness we're eating out tonight." It had been Faith who had accepted Joe's invitation for all of them. "Two big meals in one day and I won't be able to get into my clothes."

The phone rang in the kitchen just as Ann Elise finished off a tiny strip of leftover turkey that was too small to have been good for anything anyway. Without thinking, she reached for the receiver while she wiped her fingers on a paper towel. "H'lo? Baker—I mean Donner residence."

"Ann Elise?"

She sank onto a stool. "Joe...Merry Christmas."

"To you, too. I was wondering—that is, it occurred to me that the kids might like to see the pups."

She laughed and hoped it sounded convincing. "They've already named two of them. Fireman and Gretel."

"I'm surprised they didn't come up with Donner and Blitzen and all the rest of the gang. So what about it?"

"You mean come there?"

"I could come get you. You all, that is. As many as want to come."

He sounded the way she felt—uncertain, but leaning toward hopefulness. "Well, sure," she said breathlessly. "I mean, you don't have to come get us. I know the way. Um...when would be a good time?"

It was decided that the children would ride with Ann Elise so that she could explain the rules concerning new puppies. Faith and Gabe would follow in his car, while Marilou took a nap and Tate watched a football game on ESPN.

The children were ecstatic. Jason took along his fire engine to show it to Joe, and Becky brought one of her new books to read on the way. "Remember, you can look, but don't touch," Ann Elise warned as they neared the turnoff. "Golden retrievers are amazingly good-natured, but new mamas are always protective. Let her smell your hand, and then—well, we'll see."

She thought of explaining how dogs could read human gestures and facial expressions almost from birth—even better than chimps could, actually, and chimpanzees were considered man's closest relative.

"We'll just play it by ear," she said, pulling up to the house.

And I'll play it by heart, she thought when Joe opened her door and handed her out. There was a moment—a single moment—when she could have stepped into his arms with no thought of tomorrow or all the yesterdays since that long-ago kiss, when he'd first imprinted himself on her heart.

"Where are they, Annalise?" Jason danced around her, his fire engine forgotten on the back seat.

"This way, son." Joe led both children, and Ann Elise brought up the rear. Joe and the children...

Down, girl!

"Mom says to tell you all when you're done admiring the pups, she has fruitcake and more gingerbread."

"I like gingerbread," piped up Jason.

"I liked it first," said Becky.

But then there were the dogs, and all that could be heard was awed whispers as both children knelt beside the ragged quilt where Goldie tended her flock.

"My mercy, already they look bigger," Ann Elise murmured to Joe.

"Just drier. Couple of real bushy ones there. Interesting gene pool. Hey, are you all right?" He looked at her with concern. "You didn't catch cold or anything, did you?"

She had a feeling he was referring more to her emotional health than her physical health, but she wasn't about to venture into that territory. "Sure, I'm fine. We didn't have a big meal, with tonight and all, but Faith's the world's best cook. I'm afraid I made a pig of myself." She pasted a smile on her face to prove she meant it. "Faith and Gabe are on their way out, too. I guess I pretty much promised the kids a pup...or two. When they're old enough. The pups, not the children."

He laughed softly and edged closer. "You'll have to be here to check them out first, see that they have all their shots."

"Heck of a house call, all the way from Dallas. You're here—you can take care of all that."

His eyes were twinkling. "Hey, show me a horse with the heaves or a cow with warble flies and I'm your guy, but canines?"

"Bull," she jeered softly.

"That's what I just said."

And he laughed, and then so did she, and taking her hand in his, he brought it up to his chest. He flattened her palm over his heart and murmured, "Feel that? That feel normal to you?"

"Only if you just climbed off a treadmill."

Slowly he shook his head. "Treadmills I can handle. Don't have time for gym work, but then, that's never been the problem."

The barn and the children seemed to fade into the distance as she read the message in his eyes. Out on the highway a car went by, windows down, radio blaring Christmas songs. Becky and Jason were arguing quietly about which pup looked like a fireman and which looked like a Gretel.

And then Faith and Gabe drove up, and introductions and holiday greetings were exchanged. Joe's dad, a tall gentleman with a crop of thick white hair and a gentle air, looked at Ann Elise and said, "And who are you, missy? You look like someone I used to know."

"I'm Ann Elise, Mr. Halloran, a friend of Joe's." *The woman you met just last night—the woman who loves your son with all her heart.*

Joe squeezed her hand and they went into the kitchen, where Polly was serving up huge slices of fruitcake and gingerbread. "This will hold you until we get to the club tonight. Here, now, don't be shy."

Gabriel, who'd claimed just the night before not to care for fruitcake, professed it the best he'd ever tasted and ate two large slices to prove it.

Polly Halloran beamed and patted Jason on the head with one knobby, arthritic hand. "Coconut, instant coffee and cocoa," she confided to Faith, who requested the recipe.

The two women launched into a conversation about cooking, and after a while Gabe took the two children back to see the pups again. Joe said to Ann Elise, "Come on, let me show you something."

He took her upstairs to his bedroom. Ann Elise half expected his mother to come hurrying after them. This struck her as one of those rare households where fifties mores still reigned.

But then he shut the door, and they might as well have been alone on the planet. "What—what did you want to show me?" she asked hesitantly, feeling wicked and wary and aroused.

He opened a desk drawer. The room was tidy, but impersonal. There was a framed photograph of his parents at an earlier age on the wall and shelves full of books, but other than that, little that even hinted at the man who slept in the bed, who stood at the window and looked down on a pasture where a few dozen purebred Angus grazed.

And then he handed her a sheaf of clippings. Puzzled, she looked at the first one. "Local woman rescues abused Labrador, owner jailed."

Another one heralded an award she'd received for single-handedly placing more homeless animals than any other rescue worker.

"Oh, for heaven's sake, this doesn't mean anything, you know that. All vets do it. Some of the best rescue workers aren't even vets, just animal lovers. I just happened to be the—"

"The woman I love," he said so quietly she almost missed it.

"And besides..." She blinked at him. "What did you say? You love me? *Me?*" Dropping the clippings in the drawer, she stared at him, afraid to believe...afraid to hope.

"Don't tell me you didn't know. You think I spent practically a month's allowance renting a tux and risked getting picked up for driving without a license just to help out a buddy who got himself into some trouble?"

She dropped down onto his bed. He came down beside her, took her hand in his and said, "Say something. For God's sake, woman, don't leave me hanging here."

"You didn't know?" she whispered. "You mean, you never even guessed—not even after yesterday?"

He looked away, and she could have sworn he was blushing. "Yeah, well...yesterday—I mean, things happen. You know, under the circumstances...''

"Not to me they don't. When I make love to a man, it's just that. Making love, not having sex. Of course I love you, you dunce! I've loved you for fourteen years—even before that!''

Closing his eyes, Joe flopped back onto the bed, his long legs dangling over the side. "I can't believe we wasted all this time.''

From downstairs, his mother called up to say that Faith and Gabe and the children were leaving. "Okay, Mom. We'll be down in a minute.''

She really needed to go back to get ready for tonight. Instead, she stretched out beside him, one arm across his waist. "Joe...it's not that simple.''

He brushed her hair back from her face. "I know. Stuff to work out, but we can handle it.''

"I've got to go back in a few days.''

"I can't leave the folks for more than a day at a time. There's a woman I can get to come help out, but...''

"I know. It's a fragile time,'' she whispered, wondering if it was any more painful to watch a loved one gradually slip away than to be faced suddenly with the fact that you'd lost both parents.

"What about...?''

She knew what he was trying to say. What about her practice, her apartment, her friends? Friends moved, and still remained friends.

As for the rest... ''For the past few months I've been toying with the idea of moving to another part of town where there aren't so many gated communities. All kinds of people have animals, but some people seem to appreciate them more.''

They were silent for a moment, and then came the sound of voices in the hall below. ''Come on, let's go say goodbye,'' Joe said. ''Just one thing, though. Could we make it soon?''

She didn't pretend not to know what he meant—or why soon was so important. ''Give me a month,'' she said. ''And I can come back home for weekends.''

''God, I love you,'' he groaned, and, wrapping her in his arms, he held her as if he would never let go.

She knew better than to kiss him. One kiss and they'd never be able to break away. ''Come on, let's hurry. I don't want your mother to worry about us and try to climb those stairs.''

Taking her hand, Joe led the way downstairs. Halfway down, he turned and said, ''Don't worry about Mom. She knew why I took you upstairs.

She's already picking out names for her grand-kids.''

Suddenly it sank in. All those sidelong glances, the teasing little smiles she'd been getting from Joe's mother. "You mean…?"

"I mean," he affirmed, and they went on downstairs, where everyone was congregated by the front door. The children had dashed back to say goodbye to Goldie and her babies, with Gabe in attendance. Polly and Faith were talking about lard versus vegetable shortening versus oil, and Mr. Halloran was rocking, gazing out the window.

"Joe Junior suits me just fine," she whispered. "To start with."

"Hey, I'm easy. Anything but Fireman and Gretel."

They both laughed, and everyone looked at them. "Well," Faith said, glancing at her watch. "We need to go home and start getting ready for tonight. I have a feeling there might be an interesting announcement made at dinner tonight."

With a look of quiet satisfaction Joe said, "I have a feeling you might be right."

* * * * *

NEW YEAR'S BABY
Kathie DeNosky

To my readers, with best wishes for a holiday season
filled with hope, happiness and love.

Chapter 1

When Marilou Baker noticed the unsavory looking character leering at her from the bank of chairs facing her in the Corpus Christi bus station, she cringed and tried her best to look disapproving and unapproachable. But that was kind of difficult to do, considering that she was almost nine months pregnant and on the verge of tears.

Sniffling, she looked around. She wasn't even supposed to be here. It was Christmas Eve day and she was supposed to be on a commuter flight winging her way home to Mission Creek to spend the holidays with her two older sisters, Ann Elise and Faith. And…to face the music.

She took a deep breath. Once she'd learned that her flight had been canceled due to bad weather, she'd been tempted to call them, make her excuses and go back to her practically empty apartment to spend the holidays alone.

Unfortunately, that wasn't an option. Not only had she missed spending Christmas with her sisters for the past three years, a special memorial service for Aunt Beth had been planned for New Year's Eve. There was no way Marilou could miss that, no matter how much she dreaded her sisters' reaction when they saw what a mess she'd made of her life. She needed to say goodbye to the woman who had raised her from the time she was six years old.

Tears welled up in her eyes at the thought of going home and Aunt Beth not being there. Even though it had almost been a year since her passing, Marilou still had a hard time accepting that her beloved aunt was really gone.

But as upsetting as it would be to attend the memorial service for a woman she'd loved like a mother, Marilou was dreading what Ann Elise and Faith would say when they saw her. They'd always been so protective of her. How would they react when she walked in just weeks away from giving birth without the prospect of a husband anywhere in sight? What would they think of her when they discovered that she'd lied to them about being engaged to Harlan Bridges?

For the past three months she'd put off thinking about how she would justify that little white lie. But time had run out. In a matter of a few hours, she was going to have to explain that she'd really believed she and Harlan would eventually marry, especially after he'd been so insistent about moving in with her. But after she'd unexpectedly gotten pregnant, he'd started pulling away—distancing himself from her emotionally, as well as physically. That's when she'd learned just how wrong her assumption had been.

Sniffling, she closed her eyes and tried not to think about what a fool she'd been. For months, she'd deluded herself into believing that Harlan would come around and see what a wonderful addition to their relationship a baby would be.

The moisture filling her eyes streamed down her cheeks and she reached for her shoulder bag to see if she could find a tissue. She'd known that Harlan tended to be a bit shallow and self-centered, but she'd honestly thought that once he got used to the idea of being a father, he'd settle down and embrace his role in their child's life.

How could she have been so blind? Had she wanted a husband and family so much that she'd overlooked the obvious?

A white handkerchief was suddenly pressed into her hands. "You look like you could use this."

Glancing up to find an extremely handsome cowboy standing in front of her, Marilou swiped at her tears with her fingertips as she shook her head. "Th-thank you, b-but I'm fine."

His deep chuckle sent a shiver up her spine and momentarily distracted her from searching for the tissue. "Darlin', if you're fine, I'd hate like hell to see you when you're not." He dropped his gym bag beside her two small suitcases, then lowered his tall frame onto the chair next to her. "Now, take this."

She stared at the handkerchief for several moments, before taking it from him to wipe the tears dripping off her chin. "Th-thank you," she said, trying her best to pull herself together. She hated crying in front of people. Her nose always turned cherry-red and her cheeks looked as if someone had slapped her.

They sat in silence for some time before he spoke again. "You know, sometimes it helps to talk about what's bothering you."

"I...don't think that would be a good idea," she said, shaking her head. "We don't know each other and you couldn't possibly be interested in my problems."

"You're right," he said, nodding. "We don't know each other. But that can be easily remedied." He extended his hand. "I'm Tate Carson and I'm headed home to the Circle C Ranch just outside of Mission Creek." He smiled. "And you couldn't be more wrong, darlin'. I am interested in hearing about what made you cry. Maybe I can help."

Tate Carson was the man being so nice to her? Marilou stared at him for several long moments. Although he'd been two years ahead of her in school, everyone attending Mission Creek High had known who Tate Carson was. He was not only the cutest, most popular boy in school, he'd also helped the school's rodeo team win the state title three years in a row. She'd heard that after he graduated, he'd gone on to become a champion bull and bronc rider on the professional rodeo circuit.

But having him witness her in a weepy moment wasn't what bothered her the most. He probably didn't even know who she was. What made her uncomfortable about the situation was that Aunt Beth had been a Wainwright, and from the day Marilou and her sisters had been taken in by her and Uncle Lloyd, they'd been told to steer clear of anyone with the last name of Carson. Marilou had never understood what the dispute had been about, but the two families had a falling out several generations back and had avoided any and all contact with each other ever since. Poor Aunt Beth would probably roll over in her grave if she knew that Marilou was even in the same building with a Carson, let alone talking to one.

Tate watched the pretty young woman study his face a moment before she slowly slipped her small, delicate hand in his. On contact, a tingling feeling streaked its way up his arm.

"I... I'm Marilou Baker and I'm on my way to Mission Creek, too," she said, her voice little more than a whisper. She quickly disengaged her hand from his, as if she'd experienced the same sensation he'd felt when their palms touched. "I'm spending Christmas and New Year's with my sisters."

"Well, Marilou Baker, it's nice to meet you." Checking his watch, he gave her what he hoped was an encouraging smile. "We've got a couple of hours before the bus leaves. What do you say we walk down to the coffee shop and grab a cup of joe?"

To his disappointment, she shook her head. "I can't drink coffee. Caffeine isn't good for the baby."

"What about some kind of juice or maybe mineral water?'' he asked, rising to his feet. ''I'm buying.''

He caught a glimpse of the sleazy-looking guy across from her. The lecherous way he looked at Marilou didn't sit well with Tate. Had the guy said or done something to frighten her? Could that be another reason she'd been crying?

The glare he turned on the derelict had the man on his feet and shuffling away in short order. Satisfied that the bum wouldn't bother her again, Tate turned his attention back to Marilou. ''Come on. It'll help get your mind off your troubles.''

''I'm fine.''

''Really?''

He didn't think she looked fine. She looked like she was at her wit's end, and he'd bet every rodeo buckle he'd ever won that within the next second or two she was going to turn on the waterworks again.

She hesitated a moment, then shook her head. ''N-no. I'm not…fine. And…I doubt…that I'll ever be.''

He watched first one tear, then another trickle down her cheek. Yep. Sure as shootin' the floodgates were about to open.

Sitting back down beside her, he pulled her into his arms. ''Aw, darlin', don't cry. It can't be that bad.''

Tate hated seeing a woman so upset, and especially one who looked like she might have her baby at any moment. He tensed. Could that be what was wrong with her? Was she in labor?

"Are you in pain?"

When she shook her head, he blew out a relieved breath and stared at the driving rain just beyond the glass doors of the bus station. He wasn't sure what the problem was, but he was mighty damned glad they wouldn't be making a mad dash for the nearest hospital in a gully washer.

While he held her, Tate ran his hand up and down her back in what he hoped was a consoling manner. Hell, what did he know about comforting a woman?

He'd been too young when his dad abandoned him and his mother to know the full extent of what she'd gone through. All he could remember for sure was that she'd looked sad and defeated when she'd explained that his father wouldn't be coming home anymore. She'd assured him that they would be fine, and they had been. But he knew it hadn't always been easy for her being a single mom with a daredevil son who took great delight in risking life and limb at everything he tried.

As he continued to hold Marilou, her heartbroken sobs made him feel sick inside. Knowing what his mom must have gone through, he had a soft spot for vulnerable women, and the one he held seemed about as defenseless as any he'd ever seen.

Stroking her silky, strawberry-blond hair, he tried to think of something encouraging to say. When nothing came to mind, Tate remained silent. There were times when it was better for a man to keep quiet and just be there for a woman. He figured this was one of those times.

"I-I'm sorry," she finally said, pulling back. "I don't know what came over me." She wiped at the wet spot on his denim jacket with his handkerchief. "I-I'm afraid I got you wet."

Tate shrugged. "It'll dry." He brushed a strand of her shoulder-length hair from her flushed cheek. "You want to tell me what the problem is? I'm a good listener and I might be able to help."

He studied her pretty green eyes. It was obvious that she was trying to decide whether to unload on him, or decline his offer and tell him to buzz off.

"Come on, Marilou," he coaxed. "You need to talk to someone about whatever this is that's got you all tore up." He purposely lowered his voice to add a gentleness that he rarely used with anyone. "Being this upset can't be good for you or your baby, darlin'."

"I suppose you're right." Her perfectly shaped lower lip trembled and he found himself wondering how it would feel beneath his.

Whoa, Carson! What the hell's wrong with you? This was definitely not the time, the place or the woman to be having thoughts like that.

"I doubt there's anything anyone can do," she said uncertainly. She looked so darned vulnerable that it was all he could do to keep from pulling her back into his arms.

"Let's go get that juice for you and a cup of coffee for me," he said. Rising from the chair, he held out his hand to help her up. "You can tell me all about it."

When she trustingly placed her soft palm on top of his calloused one, the same little charge of electric current he'd experienced when they'd shaken hands snaked up his arm and exploded somewhere in the vicinity of his solar plexus. Tate sucked in a sharp breath and did his best to ignore the sensation as he watched her awkwardly get to her feet.

"I feel like you could stamp Goodyear on my backside and replace one of the blimps with me," she said, sounding a little winded.

"You look fine to me," he said, meaning it.

Granted, Marilou was pregnant and carrying a few extra pounds, but he'd never been attracted to pencil-thin women. He was always afraid they'd snap in two if he hugged them too tight.

''How close is it to your time?'' he asked, not exactly sure what women called the end of their gestation period. He knew all about pregnant cows and mares, but women were a whole different ball game.

''I'm not due until mid-January,'' she said, smoothing the folds of her dark green dress over her rounded belly. She gave him the first genuine smile he'd seen from her since he walked through the bus station doors some thirty minutes ago. ''But I'd be more than happy if the baby came a little early.''

Tate gave her a wan smile, but remained silent as he picked up their bags. He wasn't about to tell Marilou Baker that he hoped like hell the baby held off until she was with whoever she was going to visit in Mission Creek, and he was at the Circle C spending Christmas the way he'd done every year since his mother died—watching college football on his big screen TV. Alone.

''Time to fess up, Marilou. What is it you think is so hopeless?''

Marilou eyed Tate as she took a sip of fruit

juice through her straw. Tate Carson certainly
didn't beat around the bush. But staring into this
handsome cowboy's dark brown eyes, she could
almost believe that he would be able to make
things better. Almost.

"I told a little fib."

He nodded and pushed the wide brim of his
cowboy hat up with his thumb, then leaned back
in his chair. "I think we've all done that at one
time or another." Taking a sip of his coffee, he
grinned. "But let me guess. This little white lie
came back to bite you in the butt. Am I right?"

It was her turn to nod. "I told my sisters I was
engaged to the man I was living with." She nervously fingered the straw wrapper lying on the
chipped Formica tabletop. "And I really thought
we would get married eventually."

"What happened?"

Marilou sighed. "After I unexpectedly became
pregnant, Harlan—my baby's father—started putting in a lot of extra hours at the office where he
worked." She paused. "At least, that's where he
said he was."

"He was with another woman?" Tate asked,
his voice kind. When she nodded, he asked,
"How did you find out he wasn't where he said
he was?"

"In the most humiliating way imaginable."

She glanced up to see him watching her. Her cheeks heated with embarrassment at the thought of how naive she'd been. "About three months ago, we were supposed to be on the Chanda Jordan talk show here in Corpus Christi. The segment spotlighted several couples expecting their first child."

"Isn't her show a lot like Oprah's?" he asked.

"You watch programs like that?" She found it hard to believe that a rugged, rodeo cowboy like Tate would watch a television show primarily targeted toward women and their concerns.

"Good lord, no! Those are chick shows."

Under normal circumstances, Marilou might have laughed at the horrified expression on Tate Carson's handsome face. But at the moment, she couldn't find humor in much of anything.

Shrugging one shoulder, she tore the straw paper in two. "I thought it might bring us closer together and increase his excitement about the baby. But he didn't bother to show up. I ended up being the only single mother on that stage."

Tate's large hand immediately covered hers. "I'm sorry, Marilou. That must have been awfully embarrassing for you."

"To say the least." She took a deep breath. "But the biggest humiliation came when I arrived home with a bag full of sample baby products to show him, only to discover that Harlan had moved out.''

''You mean this jerk didn't even have the balls to tell you to your face that he was leaving?'' Tate straightened in his chair. ''He's not much of a man.''

She wasn't going to argue in Harlan's favor on that count. ''He left a note on the refrigerator that he was moving in with his girlfriend, Charlene.''

''Do you still love him?'' Tate asked, gently squeezing her hand.

''No,'' she answered honestly. ''I've had a lot of time to think about it, and I'm not sure I ever really did. I told myself I loved him, but I think I was more in love with the idea of being in love. If that makes sense.'' She shook her head. ''But what really hurt was that Charlene is about as big around as a toothpick and openly brags that she'd never ruin her figure by having a baby.'' Glancing down at her rounded stomach, Marilou sighed. ''Even before I got pregnant, I was never what you'd call thin and willowy. But now—''

''You look just fine, darlin'.'' Tate snorted. ''It sounds to me like old Harlan and Charlene deserve each other.''

Marilou hadn't thought about it that way, but she had to agree. ''I think you're probably right.

It would be a toss-up as to which one of them is more shallow.''

"So if you're okay with him being out of the picture, it's facing your sisters that's upsetting you?" he asked, sounding genuinely interested.

She nodded and once again felt the heavy weight of guilt press against her chest. "I'm the youngest and...I feel like I've let them down. They've always been so protective of me, I'm afraid they'll be terribly disappointed over the mess I've made of my life.''

"They expect you to come home with a fiancé, don't they?" he asked, looking thoughtful.

"Yes." She took a deep breath, in order to tell him the rest of it. "And then there's the little matter of them not even knowing that I'm pregnant.''

He whistled low as he gazed at her over the top of his coffee cup. "That's going to be kind of hard to hide.''

"Thank you for telling me," she said, dryly. "I hadn't thought of that.''

They sat in silence for several minutes before he slowly set his coffee cup on the table. "The way I see it, you have two choices," he said calmly. "You can go home and face your sisters alone, or you can go home on the arm of a fiancé.''

"Yeah, sure. Like fiancés grow on trees." She shook her head. "I told you it was hopeless."

"Hey, I know I'm no prize, but—"

"You mean..." She had to stop to clear her suddenly dry throat. "...you're offering to pose as my fiancé?"

He grinned. "Unless, you have some other guy in mind."

Marilou's heart skipped a beat. Tate Carson was one of the best-looking men she'd ever seen, and as it turned out, one of the nicest. But they'd barely met. How could they convince Ann Elise and Faith that they were in love, engaged and expecting a child together? And what would they say when they found out he was a Carson?

"We don't know each other well enough," Marilou said, slowly. "What if they asked me things about you that I can't answer? Things like how you take your morning coffee, and what your favorite food is."

He grinned. "That's easy, darlin'. I'm a Texan, born and bred. I like my coffee black, and my steak burnt. As for the rest, we've got..." He checked his watch. "...an hour before the bus leaves, then another couple of hours' ride to get to Mission Creek. I figure I can fill you in on the basics." His grin widened. "You can wing the rest."

"This is insane," she said, rubbing her suddenly throbbing temples with her fingertips. "It has disaster written all over it, and I would just be supporting one lie with another."

He sat forward and took both of her suddenly cold hands in his. "I've already called my ranch foreman and told him to leave my truck at the bus station so I'll have a way to get home. All I'll have to do is take you by your sister's place, make an appearance as your intended, then come up with an excuse about needing to check on things at my ranch and leave."

"It sounds pretty simple," she said slowly. She wondered if she might be losing her mind, but she was actually considering his offer. "But won't they wonder why we aren't spending Christmas Day together?"

"I can call tomorrow morning and tell you that I have a cold or something and that I don't want to expose you to it because of the baby."

He made it all sound so logical, as if it was the perfect solution to her problem. "You really think we can pull this off?"

"Trust me," he said, grinning. "It'll work like a charm."

Chapter 2

"This is never going to work," Marilou said as she and Tate hurried through the pouring rain from his truck to the big wraparound porch at the front of the Baker ranch house.

"Yes, it will," he said, sounding so darned confident she felt like screaming. He helped her up the steps. "What's my favorite color?"

"Blue?"

He shook his head. "Red."

"What do I do for a living?" she asked.

"You're a banker?"

"No, I'm a CPA," she said, feeling more apprehensive by the second. "Do you see what I'm talking about? We can't even remember the easy things about each other.''

''We'll do fine.'' At the sound of someone in the house approaching the front door, he put his arm around her shoulders. ''Just act like you couldn't be happier, and the rest will take care of itself.''

''That's what you think,'' she muttered. ''You don't know my sisters. This is going to be like a CIA interrogation.''

When the door opened and she caught a glimpse of her sister, Faith, for the first time in three years, Marilou forgot all about their deception and reached out to hug her.

''Marilou, you look absolutely radiant...'' Faith's voice trailed off when the baby inside of Marilou's swollen stomach chose that moment to kick. Stepping back, Faith's eyes grew round as she stared at where Marilou's waist used to be. ''...and pregnant.''

Before Marilou could say a word, Faith eyed her, then glanced at Tate. ''Is this Harlan?'' She'd no sooner gotten the words out than she turned pale and gasped. ''Good heavens, you're Tate Carson!''

''Yes, ma'am.'' Tate removed his arm from around Marilou's shoulders to extend his hand to Faith. ''And you must be...''

Faith shook his hand. "I'm Faith Donner."

Marilou could see the shock and confusion in her sister's eyes. She was going to want answers, and as soon as possible.

"Would you mind if we take this reunion inside?" Tate asked. "I'd like to get Marilou out of this damp air. We don't want her catching a cold this close to having the baby."

"Oh, of course," Faith said, ushering them into the foyer. They all stood staring at each other for what seemed like an eternity before Faith finally cleared her throat. "While I make hot cocoa, why don't you two slip off your coats and make yourselves at home?"

"That's not necessary," Marilou said as Tate helped her take off her all-weather coat, then removed his denim jacket and cowboy hat.

"Yes, it is," Faith said firmly. "You need to warm up and a steaming cup of cocoa should do the trick."

When her sister was out of earshot, Marilou sighed heavily. She knew exactly what was running through Faith's mind. She was going to review what Marilou had told her about her fiancé, then decide on the best way to find out what was going on without being overly obvious.

"That went pretty well," Tate said, sounding

quite pleased as he hung their coats on a row of wooden pegs beside the door.

"It's not over yet." She stared down the hall toward the kitchen. "Right now Faith is trying to decide on the best way to discover what's going on without coming right out and asking."

"Is that so?" He ran a hand through his thick, dark brown hair as if pondering the information, then smiling, placed his hand to the small of her back to urge her forward. "We'll just have to see what we can do about that."

Marilou stopped short. "What do you have in mind?"

His smile caused her heart to skip several beats. "Sometimes, the best defense is a good offense, darlin'." Taking her hand in his, he started down the hall. "We're going to answer her questions before she has a chance to ask them."

"This is never going to work."

"Sure it will," he whispered close to her ear. "You just have to think positive, darlin'."

A shiver streaked up her spine and she wasn't sure if it was caused by Tate's warm breath on her sensitive skin, or the trepidation she felt about telling her sister another falsehood.

As Faith took mugs down from the cupboard, Tate placed his hand on her rounded stomach about the same time the baby kicked.

Marilou nodded. "I'm nervous, but otherwise—"

"I mean physically," he said, looking concerned. "That kick was pretty damned hard. Did it hurt?"

His obvious concern was touching, but standing in her sister's kitchen talking to Tate Carson about how it felt to have her baby move inside of her was more than a little disconcerting. "I'm fine. Really."

When Faith turned to face them, Tate cleared his throat and stepped behind her. Reaching around, he clasped his hands over her swollen stomach. "Marilou and I know you're pretty shocked about all this. But we weren't exactly sure how to tell you about the baby, or about our being together."

Marilou almost jumped out of her own skin at the feel of his large hands resting just below her breasts. He was taking this loving couple thing a little further than she'd anticipated.

But she didn't have time to dwell on it when Faith turned her *I want straight answers, and I want them now* look on both of them. "The last I heard, Marilou was engaged to some man named Harlan Bridges."

Thinking fast, Marilou nodded. "I made up that name because I wasn't sure how you'd feel about

Tate. You know Aunt Beth always warned us never to trust a Carson. I was afraid you'd be upset when you found out.''

"You know, that's something I've never understood," Faith said, placing a dollop of marshmallow cream on top of the steaming mugs of hot cocoa. "The disagreement between the Wainwrights and Carsons happened almost a hundred years ago. Does anyone even remember what it was about?''

Marilou shook her head. "I don't think I ever heard Aunt Beth say." She turned to Tate. "Do you know what the dispute was over?''

"Nope." He nuzzled her hair with his lean cheek, sending a wave of goose bumps shimmering over her skin. "And as far as we're concerned, it has nothing to do with us. Right, darlin'?''

"R-r-right," Marilou stammered. Tate really seemed to be getting into the role of loving fiancé, and it was making her a nervous wreck.

Smiling warmly, Faith handed a mug to Marilou. "I think he's right. We're not Wainwrights by blood, and I don't think we should be expected to carry on something that should have been forgotten a long time ago. As long as you're both happy, and committed to each other and the baby, that's all that matters.''

"We are," Marilou said, breathing a bit easier when Tate released her to take the mug Faith handed him.

"I can't stand to be away from Marilou for more than a day or two," he said, nodding.

"How do you manage when there's a rodeo you need to compete in?" Faith asked, blowing on her cocoa to cool it.

"I fly in just before the event starts, then take the first flight back home as soon as it's over," he said, giving Marilou a look that curled her toes inside her sensible black flats.

"That's so romantic," Faith said, sighing.

Marilou stared at her sister. She'd been so nervous about facing the music, and the questions she would be asked, that she hadn't noticed her sister's contented expression. But Faith looked happier and more carefree than Marilou had seen her since she married that snake of an ex-husband, Earl Donner, ten years ago.

Before Marilou could comment on her sister's obvious happiness, a tall, broad-shouldered man walked right in through the back door and over to where Faith stood. Shaking hands with Tate, he introduced himself. "I'm Gabriel Raines. And you must be Harlan Bridges."

"That's my alias," Tate said, grinning. "My real name is Tate Carson."

As he shook Marilou's hand, Gabriel looked confused. "But I thought Faith said your name was—"

"I'll explain later," Faith said, kissing the man's cheek. Turning back to Marilou and Tate, she smiled. "Gabriel and I are engaged to be married in February."

Marilou experienced a momentary stab of envy. Why couldn't she find the same kind of happiness? Was she destined to go through life searching for, but never meeting her Mr. Right?

As if sensing her emotions, Tate put his arm around her shoulders. "Congratulations to both of you."

Her uncharacteristic feelings quickly passing, Marilou smiled as she rubbed her aching lower back. "I think it's wonderful that you've found happiness together."

Faith put her cup of cocoa on the well-worn counter. "We have a week to play catch-up. Right now, we need to get you settled in your room and off your feet." She reached out to touch Marilou's shoulder. "You look like you're ready to drop, sweetie."

Tate checked his watch. "I think I should probably be going. It'll take me a good forty-five minutes to get on the other side of Mission Creek and out to the Circle C."

Marilou caught the look that passed between Faith and Gabriel, and she had a good idea of what was running through their minds. But before she had a chance to divert their train of thought, Faith stepped forward and hugged first Marilou, then Tate.

"I know your mother passed away several years ago," Faith said, her voice filled with compassion. "Do you have any plans for the holidays, Tate?"

He shook his head. "Nothing besides driving over here to see Marilou."

"Well, you do now." Faith grinned. "It's Christmas Eve and there's no reason for you to have to commute back and forth between here and your ranch in this nasty weather."

Marilou swallowed hard and tried to salvage the situation. "There aren't any extra rooms."

"You can both stay in Marilou's old bedroom." Faith smiled. "There's a double bed, and after all, you are engaged and expecting a baby together. It's not like the two of you just met."

"Tate?" Marilou hoped he was as quick with an excuse why he couldn't stay as he'd been with his fabrication of why they'd kept her pregnancy a secret.

"I don't want to impose," he said, shaking his head. "I'll just—"

"Nonsense." Faith looped one arm with Marilou's and the other with Tate's. "You said you couldn't stand to be away from Marilou, and with her so close to having the baby you need to be with her." Starting down the hall, she added, "Besides, you're practically family now. You belong here with us for the holidays, Tate."

Marilou looked helplessly over the top of her sister's head at Tate. But all he did was give her a sheepish grin.

And just that quick, she knew that short of giving away their deception, she had no other choice but to spend the night in the same bed with Tate Carson.

When the bedroom door closed and he heard Faith start back downstairs, Tate turned his attention on Marilou. She looked fit to be tied as she rubbed the small of her back and slowly lowered herself to the side of the bed.

"Now what are we going to do?" she asked, looking at him expectantly.

He ran a hand around the back of his neck and tried to think of something to say that wouldn't make the situation worse. When nothing came to mind, he shrugged. "It looks like we're going to have to play this out, or else come clean about the whole thing."

"If you hadn't laid it on so thick about hating to be away from me, we might not be in this predicament right now," she said, shaking her head. "What on earth got into you down there in the kitchen?"

Walking over to the padded window seat, he sat down and propped his forearms on his knees. What *had* gotten into him? How could he explain something he didn't understand himself? Hell, he was still trying to come to grips with how good she'd felt in his arms, and how easy it had been to say what he had about not wanting to be away from her.

"We're supposed to be in love," he finally answered. "If I hadn't acted like I cared for you it would have raised a red flag the size of Rhode Island with your sister."

"I suppose you're right." She tried to hide a huge yawn behind her delicate little hand. "Otherwise, she'd have seen right through our story."

Noticing the shadows under her eyes, a protective feeling swept over him. He'd bet she hadn't slept worth a damn last night from dreading the showdown with her sisters today.

"We'll just take this one day at a time and deal with whatever happens, darlin'."

She frowned. "What bothers me the most about all this is that the lie just keeps growing."

He rose from the window seat and walked over to kneel down in front of her. Taking her cold hands in his, he tried to reassure her. "If it's any consolation, I think it's about as big as it's going to get."

"Let's hope," she said tiredly.

When she yawned again, he smiled. "You've had a pretty tough day, Marilou. Why don't you take a nap and forget about everything for a while?"

"But—"

"No 'buts' about it," he said firmly. "You need to rest."

"I am pretty tired," she finally admitted.

Brushing a strand of hair from her cheek, Tate smiled. "Just stretch out and relax. As long as we keep playing the happy couple, there shouldn't be any more questions."

"When do you plan on getting married?" Faith asked, handing Marilou a bowl of mashed potatoes to be carried to the table.

Marilou was relieved that her sister had already turned back to the counter to pick up a platter of fried chicken and hadn't seen her reaction. She'd almost dropped the bowl of potatoes, and she was sure there wasn't a bit of color left in her cheeks.

So much for Tate's theory that there shouldn't be any more questions.

"We thought we'd wait until spring," she answered, quickly. She tried not to think of how much bigger her little white lie had become in the past few hours, or that her sisters would never forgive her if they discovered the deception.

Faith looked uncertain. "I don't mean to pry, but why are you waiting?"

Fortunately, Marilou had an easy and truthful answer to that question. "I've always wanted to have an outdoor spring wedding in the Mission Creek Inn's gazebo."

Her sister grinned. "The one in the garden behind the inn?"

Marilou nodded. "From the time I was a little girl, I've dreamed of being married there."

"It is beautiful," Faith said wistfully as they carried the rest of the food to the table. "Especially when the bougainvillea are in bloom."

Relieved that her sister had accepted her explanation, Marilou put the bowl she held on Aunt Beth's sideboard and went in search of Tate. She had to tell him about the excuse she'd given for their not getting married right away, just in case someone mentioned it during dinner.

She found him watching television with Faith's children, Becky and Jason. When she and Tate arrived, they'd been in the attic playroom that Uncle Lloyd had built for Marilou and her sisters after they came to live with him and Aunt Beth.

"Oh my goodness, look how much you've grown," Marilou said, completely forgetting the reason she'd walked into the living room. She hadn't seen her niece and nephew in three years—not since Becky was six and Jason was three. "I can't believe how much you've changed."

"Aunt Marilou!" Becky cried, jumping up from where she'd been sitting on the sofa. Rushing over to her, Becky took Marilou's hands in hers, then stood back and surveyed her aunt's rounded belly. "Are you planning on having the doctor induce your labor?"

Marilou's jaw dropped. "Becky, how on earth do you know what being induced is?"

Behind the wire-rimmed frames of her glasses, an intellect far beyond her nine years sparkled in the little girl's brown eyes. "I read all about it in *Cosmo.* Some career women arrange the birth of their babies so that it fits into their schedules."

"Your mother lets you read magazines like that?" Marilou asked, astounded. "Isn't that a bit advanced for you?"

"Yes, it's much too advanced for her," Faith said, walking up to stand next to them. "Becky got hold of one at the library a few weeks back

and that's all she talks about lately." She reached
out to lovingly stroke her daughter's long, curly
brown hair. "But we talked about it and agreed
that she won't be reading any more women's
magazines until she's older. Right, sweetie?"

Nodding, Becky shrugged. "I'll wait until I
meet a major hunk and need advice on relation-
ships before I read it again."

"I think she's twenty-something disguised in a
child's body," Marilou said, laughing.

Faith groaned. "I have a feeling I'm going to
have white hair before I turn thirty."

When Jason got up from where he'd been sitting on the carpet in front of the television to walk
over to his mother, Faith put her arm around him.
"Do you remember Aunt Marilou, Jason?"

The little boy nodded shyly. "She's the lady in
the picture with me and Becky when we were
little."

Marilou smiled at her nephew. "You've grown
a lot since that photo was taken. I wouldn't have
recognized you, Jason."

"I know who he is," Jason said, giving her an
angelic smile and pointing toward the armchair
Tate was sitting in. "He's Tate Carson. I watch
him ride bulls and horses on TV."

Not wanting to intrude, Tate had silently
watched the exchange between Marilou and her

family. But when Jason mentioned his name, Tate stood up to join them. "Do you like to watch rodeo, Jason?"

Jason nodded so vigorously his curly blond hair bounced on his forehead. "My new daddy says he'll take me to a rodeo sometime. He's gonna take me fishin' down at the creek, too."

Tate knelt down to bring himself to eye level with the little boy. "How about I get tickets for your whole family and take you behind the chutes before the rodeo starts?"

"Wow! That would be cool," Jason said, his big brown eyes lighting up with excitement. "I can't wait to tell my daddy."

"Where is Gabriel?" Marilou asked. "Isn't he joining us for dinner?"

"Gabe will be here as soon as he can," Faith said, her eyes brightening at the mention of her fiancé. "He's having some problems with a leaky roof on the building he's renovating for his new restaurant in Mission Creek and doing some last minute Christmas shopping."

"Dinner's getting cold," Becky reminded.

Observing the two sisters side-by-side, Tate had to admit they were both very pretty. But there was a softness about Marilou that seemed to set her apart—something that appealed to him in a way that he couldn't quite explain. Come to think of it, he was probably better off not knowing.

"I'm starved and something sure smells good," he said, in an effort to get his mind off of his pretend fiancée.

As they crossed the foyer to the dining room, Becky stopped. "Aunt Marilou, you walked right under the mistletoe." The little girl giggled and pointed toward the ceiling. "You know what that means."

"Becky's right," Faith said, nodding. "You have to kiss. Centuries ago, a lot of European countries recognized it as a promise to marry."

"Th-that's just folklore," Marilou sputtered, her cheeks turning the prettiest shade of pink Tate had ever seen.

"It's tradition," Faith added, her smile wide.

He wished he could take a picture of Marilou at that very moment. Her green eyes were about as wide as a pair of half dollars and her perfectly shaped mouth opened and closed like she wasn't quite sure what to say. Damned if she wasn't about the cutest thing he'd ever seen.

Grinning, he wrapped his arms around her and pulled her as close as her swollen belly would allow. "Faith's right. It is tradition. And you know me, darlin'. I'm a real traditional kind of guy."

Chapter 3

Marilou couldn't believe that Tate was actually going to give into her family's chiding. After all, they were little more than strangers and only playing the part of a happy couple. But as his arms tightened around her and his firm, warm lips touched hers, she stopped thinking about the fact that they barely knew each other and brought her hands up to rest on his wide shoulders.

At first soft and tender, he nibbled and teased, then gradually increased the pressure, demanding that she respond. Without thinking, she parted her lips and as he slipped his tongue inside to taste and explore her sensitive inner recesses, Marilou could have sworn she felt the earth move and fireworks ignite within her soul.

Until that moment, she'd been so concerned with the front they presented, she hadn't had time to think about how sexy Tate Carson was, or that his touch made her tingle from head to toe. But as he kissed her like she'd never been kissed before, it all came rushing forward like an ocean wave crashing onto a rocky shore.

As his tongue stroked hers, her knees began to wobble and she had to clench the fabric of his chambray shirt to keep from melting into a puddle at his big-booted feet. His hands splayed across her back, warmed her through her brushed cotton jumper and had her wondering what it would feel like to have his calloused palms caressing her bare skin.

Lost in the warmth of his kiss and the sensual feel of being held in his strong arms, Marilou forgot all about their audience, or that the show she and Tate were putting on was for their benefit. But as the sound of her family's applause penetrated her addled brain, Marilou's cheeks heated and she quickly pulled back.

Glancing up at Tate, she found that he looked as startled as she felt. It was little consolation, all things considered. Even though it was obvious he was experiencing the same physical reaction to her that she was having for him, this just wasn't a good time in her life to be tingling over anyone.

"I think...that fulfilled...the traditional kiss under the mistletoe," she finally said, cringing at the breathless sound of her own voice.

"I'd say that more than met the requirement," Faith said dryly. "I was beginning to wonder if I shouldn't ask Becky and Jason to leave the room."

"I'm hungry," Jason complained. "Can we eat now? Or are we gonna have to watch more mushy stuff?"

"No, honey, you don't have to watch any more 'mushy stuff,'" Faith said, laughing. "We're going to sit down at the table right now."

When Marilou started to follow the others into the dining room, Tate took hold of her arm to hold her back. "Marilou, I—"

Shaking her head, she lightly touched her index finger to his mouth in order to stop him. "We'll talk later."

She'd never felt anything as powerful as Tate's kiss, and that's what confused her. In all of the time she and Harlan had been together, she hadn't felt anything even remotely close to what she had when Tate's lips touched hers. And at the moment, she wasn't prepared to discuss what she didn't understand.

* * *

His stomach full of the best-tasting food he'd had since his mother passed away almost ten years ago, Tate helped the Baker sisters clear the table, then wandered back into the living room to watch the evening news. But as the meteorologist predicted a break in the weather and a clearing trend for the weekend, Tate tuned out the drone of the man's nasal twang and allowed himself to think about the kiss he'd shared with Marilou under the mistletoe.

What would he have said to her if she hadn't shut him up?

He stared blindly at the Christmas tree in the corner, the striking contrast between the dark green of the Douglas fir and the twinkling colored lights lost on him. Thinking back on it, he'd come close to telling her that in all of his twenty-eight years he'd never experienced anything like the kiss they'd shared. All that would have accomplished was to convince her that she'd brought some kind of nutcase home to play the part of her intended.

He grunted. She'd probably have pitched his sorry butt out in the rain faster than that big brindle bull had thrown him during the fourth round at the National Finals.

Come to think of it though, maybe he did have

one or two screws loose. He had suffered a few concussions during his thirteen years of rodeoing. It was the only thing he could think of that would explain his uncharacteristic reaction to Marilou, and why he'd volunteered to act as her fiancé.

Hell, from the moment he'd laid eyes on her in the Corpus Christi bus station, all he'd wanted to do was take her into his arms. But what he was feeling went beyond wanting to hold and kiss her. For some reason, he felt a deep need to take care of her and to make sure that nothing made her cry ever again.

That's what had him questioning his sanity more than anything else. How could he be this attracted to a woman he'd just met? A woman who was about to give birth to another man's baby?

He shook his head. It just didn't make sense.

Lost in the analyzation of his probable insanity, it took a moment for Tate to realize that someone was calling his name. Rising from the chair, he went into the hall to find Marilou standing by the kitchen doorway.

"What's up, darlin'? Are you feeling okay?"

"I'm fine," Marilou said, nodding. But before she could ask if he'd thought of an excuse why he couldn't stay, the front door opened and they turned to see what the commotion was about.

To Marilou's shock, her always impeccably dressed, never-a-hair-out-of-place older sister, Ann Elise, stood there looking for all the world like a very muddy, soaked-to-the-bone mess. The tall, good-looking man standing beside her looked little better. But as she continued to watch her sister, Marilou noticed that Ann Elise's smile was brighter and there was a definite sparkle in her blue eyes. Marilou didn't think she'd ever seen her oldest sister look happier.

"Excuse the dirt, I'll clean up in a minute," she said, rushing forward to wrap her arms around Marilou. "What happened to you?"

"You don't know?" Marilou asked, laughing nervously as she hugged her sister back. "Remember all those lectures you used to give me when I started my—"

Tate suddenly put his arm around her shoulders and rested his other hand on her rounded stomach. "What Marilou is trying to tell you is that we have a little cowboy or cowgirl on the way."

Marilou felt her cheeks turn beet-red, and she prayed for the floor to open up and swallow her. Unfortunately, it didn't happen. No telling what she would have said if Tate hadn't stopped her.

"This is Tate Carson," Faith said, hurrying down the hall from the kitchen about the same time Gabriel walked through the open doorway.

"He's going to be spending Christmas with us, and let me tell you, Jason thinks Santa's already come and gone. First Gabe and now Tate. Joe, you need to stick around and meet my son. He's really hungry for male role models."

"Halloran," Tate said, pointing his finger at Joe. "Didn't you used to play for A & M? Quarterback, right?"

Joe nodded. "And didn't you win your third bull-riding championship at the National Finals just a few days ago?"

Marilou listened as everyone caught up on who went to school together and about both of her sisters having a crush on Joe when they were in high school. And the more she heard, the more nervous she became. There was no way she and Tate would be able to carry off the ruse he'd proposed.

Her nerves ready to snap, Marilou gasped when the baby cut loose with a mighty kick right under Tate's hand.

His arm tightened around her as he stared down at her, his eyes filled with awe. "Are you okay, darlin'?"

Bless her heart, Faith chose that moment to step forward and take charge. "Why don't we go into the kitchen and I'll get everyone a cup of cocoa?"

Joe cleared his throat. "I guess I'd better be

going. I promised to take the folks to midnight services. Anyone want to come with me?''

Ann Elise gestured at her disheveled appearance. ''I need to—well, to, uh...''

Thankful everyone's attention was on her older sister and not her and Tate, Marilou offered, ''I could take you outside and hose you off.''

Ann Elise laughed. ''Just point me to a bathtub and turn up that big new water heater.'' As Joe turned toward the door, she added. ''Call me tomorrow and let me know how the babies are. That is, if you have the time.''

''Babies!'' Marilou and Faith said at the same time.

After Ann Elise and Joe explained about the dog and her litter of puppies, Marilou watched her sister follow Joe to the door. She, Tate, Faith and Gabriel discreetly moved into the kitchen.

''Unless I miss my guess, I think we'll be getting a new brother-in-law in the not too distant future,'' Faith said, grinning.

Relieved that the focus of attention was off her and Tate, Marilou smiled. ''I think you might be right.''

''I have your dinner in the oven to keep it warm,'' Faith said, taking Gabriel by the arm.

''She's the best cook in the county.'' Gabriel

sounded proud as any man could be. "Maybe the whole damned state."

Grinning, Tate nodded. "Almost as good as Marilou."

Faith looked at him like he'd sprouted another head. "Marilou? Cook? She can barely boil water without scorching it."

"Oh, I do a little better in the kitchen than I used to," Marilou said slowly.

Thankful that she'd covered his blunder, Tate put his arm around her and gazed into her emerald eyes. Her expression clearly told him that she wanted him to shut up and not waste time doing it.

"Her specialty is Tex-Mex," he said, without a second thought.

Her not so subtle elbow to his ribs warned him that he was venturing into a dangerous area. But what the hell? Riding wild horses and rank bulls made him something of an adrenalin junkie, and he thrived on walking that fine line between safe and hazardous.

Smiling, he couldn't resist adding, "Marilou's changed a lot since she met me."

"You mean besides the obvious?" Gabriel asked, grinning and pointing to Marilou's stomach.

Tate couldn't resist pushing his luck. "Here

lately things have been changing from one minute to the next.''

"One of the biggest changes being how early I get sleepy," Marilou said, yawning. She gave him a meaningful look. "Why don't you help me upstairs to our room, Tate?"

Unless he missed his guess, when they got to the bedroom she was going to let him know, in no uncertain terms, just how much she appreciated his sense of humor. Damned if he'd had this much fun in a month of Sundays.

"Yeah, that would probably be best," he said, placing his hand at the small of her back to guide her toward the stairs. For some reason that he couldn't explain, and probably wouldn't want to analyze too closely, he liked touching her. "We'll see you all in the morning."

Marilou was ready to explode by the time she reached her room—their room. If she hadn't thought to fake that yawn and ask him to help her up the stairs, no telling what kind of trouble Tate would have gotten them into.

As soon as he closed the door, she turned on him. "What were you thinking?" Shaking her head, she held up her hand. "Don't answer that. There couldn't possibly have been anything running through your mind."

"Not true, darlin'." His charming grin caused her heart to skip a beat, and she had no doubt he'd used that expression many times before to extricate himself from trouble. "I was just having a little fun. And it made us appear to know more about each other in the process."

She stopped pacing and closed her eyes as she tried for patience. Counting to ten, she finally felt in control enough to speak in a normal tone. "You don't understand, Tate. My sister deemed me a hopeless case in the kitchen years ago. Faith has been trying to teach me to cook for as long as I can remember and I failed miserably every time."

He frowned. "Surely you can't be that bad at it."

"Wanna bet?" Marilou walked over to lower her bulk onto the window seat. Rubbing her throbbing temples, she shook her head. "I still can't make anything more complicated than canned soup. And most of the time I manage to scorch that."

"You're kidding, right?"

"No, I'm not. Give me columns of numbers and I can crunch them with the best. Put me in a kitchen and you're asking for the fire department to show up."

Walking over, he sat down beside her. "It's not

a big deal, Marilou. Unless your sister asks you to cook something, she'll never know the difference.'' He took her hand in his, and at the touch of his skin against hers, a shiver coursed through her. ''You've got to lighten up, darlin'. Otherwise, they're going to figure out that we aren't what we're supposed to be.''

Overwhelmingly exhausted from the emotional roller coaster she'd been riding all day, she yawned for real this time. ''I guess you're right.''

''Why don't you stop worrying so much and get ready to go to bed?'' The gentleness in his voice warmed her all the way to her soul.

But as she thought about changing into her gown and snuggling under the patchwork quilt Aunt Beth had given her on her tenth birthday, a sudden tension gripped her. She'd used the excuse that she was tired to get Tate away from Faith and Gabriel. But she really hadn't thought about what would happen once they got to her room and faced having to sleep in the same bed.

Tate apparently picked up on her apprehension. ''Don't worry, darlin'. I don't bite.'' He gave her a grin that caused her heart to skip several beats. ''Much.''

The visual that ran through her mind from that one little word sent a jolt of electric impulses to places that had no business tingling. Unable to think of a thing to say, she nodded, then rising to her feet as gracefully as her protruding stomach would allow, she poked around in the dresser drawer where she'd put her things earlier. Gathering what she needed, she waddled into the adjoining bathroom as quickly, and with as much dignity as she could muster.

After a quick shower, she pulled on her long, flannel granny gown and stuffed her arms into her purple chenille robe. Glancing at herself in the mirror, she nodded her approval at the image staring back at her. She knew it was utterly ridiculous to think that any man could be attracted to her in her current condition, but there was nothing wrong with a little insurance. If her advanced pregnancy wasn't enough to keep Tate Carson on his side of the bed, her choice of nightclothes certainly would.

Taking a deep breath, she opened the door. "Your turn. I put a—"

She'd started to tell him that she put out a fresh towel for him, but the sight of Tate standing in her bedroom in nothing but low slung jeans, rendered her speechless.

"Think you'll be warm enough there, Marilou?" he asked, his grin teasing as he strolled past her on his way to take a shower.

She glanced down at her long robe and gown. "I...uh, yes."

Once the door closed behind him, she sank down on the side of the bed and barely resisted the urge to fan herself. Good Lord, the man had a gorgeous body. His muscular shoulders were impossibly wide, his pectoral muscles thick and his flat stomach sported enough ridges to make a bodybuilder proud.

When she'd lived with Harlan, he'd made a habit of lounging around the apartment without his shirt. She'd always suspected that he was trying to impress her with his physique. But never in Harlan's wildest dreams had he ever looked as good as Tate.

Removing her robe, she pulled the quilt and top sheet back, then got into bed. Her granny gown might keep Tate on his side, but what was going to keep her on her side?

The baby gave a mighty kick as if to remind her. "Okay, okay," she said, rubbing her taut belly. "It was just a thought."

"Did you say something?" Tate asked, opening the bathroom door.

Marilou's mouth went completely dry and she did her best to keep from staring as he walked into the room in a pair of boxer-briefs. He didn't look the least bit self-conscious. What he looked was fantastic.

"Is that what you're wearing to bed?" she asked, when she finally found her voice.

She watched him glance down at the navy blue cotton hugging him like a second skin. "Yeah, I figured…" His voice trailed off as an amused expression replaced his frown. "I could wear what I usually sleep in."

The mischievous light in his chocolate-brown eyes should have warned her, but before she could stop herself, she asked, "And that would be?"

"Skin and a big old smile."

If she'd gotten a visual before when he said he didn't bite much, it couldn't compare to the image dancing through her mind now. She swallowed hard and shook her head. "Those are good."

"Are you sure?" He hooked his thumbs in the waistband. "I don't want you to be unhappy with what I sleep in, darlin'."

"No. Please. What you're wearing is fine," she said hurriedly, lying back against the pillow. She pulled the quilt up to her chin and forced herself to keep her eyes on the ceiling.

If someone had told her this morning that she would be sharing the same bed with Tate Carson that very night, she'd have told them to seek help. Now, she was the one wondering if she might not

need a little psychiatric help in order to make it
through the night and still maintain a scrap of her
sanity.

The bedside lamp was switched off and she felt
the opposite side of the mattress dip as Tate sat
down on the side, then stretched out beside her.
Her whole body tensed and she scrunched her
eyes shut. Why hadn't she ever noticed before
how crowded a double bed was with two people
in it? With Tate's wide shoulders, and her pregnant bulk, there was no more than an inch or two
between them.

"This was your bed when you grew up here?"
he asked, sounding far more relaxed than she was.

"Y-yes." She slowly opened her eyes, thankful
that the room was dark and he couldn't see the
heat she was sure colored her cheeks.

"It's pretty comfortable."

"I always thought…oooh."

She'd started to agree, but the sudden tightness
in her calf had her moaning in pain. Apparently
she'd been so tense it had caused a muscle spasm.

"What's wrong, Marilou?" He immediately
switched on the lamp. "Is it the baby?"

"L-leg…c-cramp," she moaned.

"Which one?"

"L-left…oow."

Before she knew what was happening, he threw

the covers back, jerked her long gown up above her knees and reached for her left leg. If she'd been able to do anything besides moan, she might have told him not to touch her. But his strong fingers felt like magic as he worked the tightness from the convulsing muscle, and as the pain eased, she found she didn't want him to stop.

"Is that better?"

She nodded. "Y-yes, thank you."

"What caused your calf to cramp?" he asked, the concern in his voice evident as he pulled her gown back down and the quilt up over them.

Staring up at him, she decided there was no way she'd tell him that it was his body a scant two inches from hers that caused her to tense.

"In the past few months I've had to start sleeping on my side with a pillow behind me and another one in front for support," she answered, settling on a half truth.

She did have to sleep with the pillows in order to keep her lower back from bothering her while she slept, so she hadn't lied. It just wasn't the reason for the muscle spasm. And as humiliating as it was to admit that her stomach was so big she needed something to help prop it up, it was far less embarrassing than telling him that being in the same bed with him made her a nervous wreck.

"There's only two pillows here," he said, frowning. "Are there more in the closet?"

"I looked earlier, but there weren't any," she said shaking her head.

She watched him look around the room, then smile as he got out of bed and crossed the room to the quilt stand in the corner. Once he'd removed the colorful coverlet, he got back in bed.

"Turn on your side facing away from me."

"What are you going to do?"

He smiled. "Just do it, okay?"

Marilou wasn't sure what he had in mind, but when she did as he instructed, Tate handed her the quilt. "It's not as soft as a pillow, but it should help support the baby."

Touched by his thoughtfulness, she positioned the cover. "It does feel better. Thank you."

He switched off the lamp, then she felt the mattress move as he got comfortable. Sighing contentedly, she closed her eyes and started to relax.

But a split second later, her eyelids flew wide open and her startled squeak echoed through the dark room at the feel of his body aligning with hers. "Wh-what—"

"Shh, darlin'." Putting his arm over her belly, he snuggled against her. "I'm going to support your back."

Chapter 4

When Tate positioned himself behind Marilou, he hadn't thought much beyond helping her sleep comfortably. But the feel of her soft feminine backside pressed against him from shoulders to knees, quickly had him thinking of other things they could be doing in bed and none of them involved sleep.

His mouth went as dry as a desert in a yearlong drought and he had to take several deep breaths to calm himself. He couldn't believe his thoughts were straying in *that* direction. Marilou was expecting a baby for God's sake. Since when did he find himself attracted to pregnant women?

But regardless of how insane the idea was, he found that it was all too true. He did find Marilou irresistible. He also knew her pregnancy didn't have a thing to do with it. He would have been drawn to her no matter what.

"I don't think this is a good idea, Tate," she said, sounding breathless.

Unable to resist, he pressed a kiss to the top of her head. "Hush, darlin'. I'm just trying to help you get comfortable."

He gave himself a mental pat on the back for sounding practical and unaffected. Unfortunately, his lower body stirring against hers made a complete liar out of him. Her sharp intake of breath let him know she felt it, too.

Before she could pitch a full-fledged hissy fit, and bring everyone in the house running to see what was going on, he whispered close to her ear, "Just relax, Marilou. I can't hide the fact that I'm attracted to you, but that doesn't mean I'm going to act on it."

"You're attracted to me?" She sounded like she didn't believe him.

"You bet." He pressed his rapidly changing body closer to hers. "I wouldn't be this hard if I wasn't. Now, go to sleep, darlin'."

"Tate?" The sound of her soft voice saying his name sent a surge of longing straight to the part of him that he was trying desperately to bring under control.

Closing his eyes, he barely managed to keep from groaning as he willed himself to calm down. "What, Marilou?"

"Thank you…" She yawned. "…for giving up your holidays to help me."

Tate swallowed hard. He couldn't tell her that he'd jumped at the chance to take on the role of her fiancé, or that he'd only put up a token protest when her sister insisted that he stay, rather than spend another Christmas alone in his big empty ranch house. Fortunately, he was spared having to say anything. Marilou had fallen asleep.

The baby beneath his palm moved, and Tate couldn't help but wonder what it would be like if he really was the father of her child. His heart stalled. What was wrong with him?

He'd never given a thought to how he'd feel about a woman being pregnant with his baby. But he sure as hell was thinking about it now. And the idea of Marilou being the mother of his child caused a longing to invade his soul that robbed him of breath.

Forcing himself to think of something—anything—else, he focused on how well he'd ridden at the National Finals and how he'd invest the money he won. He already had a sizeable nest egg socked away, but with the money he'd won in the past two weeks, and the investments he'd made in oil futures, he'd officially topped the two million mark. Now he could seriously think about retiring from rodeo competition by the time he turned thirty, and carry out his plans for fixing up and enlarging the small ranch he'd inherited from his mother.

Yawning, he relaxed and felt the peaceful oblivion of sleep begin to overtake him. But as he drifted off, his last thoughts were of what it would be like to have Marilou and the baby helping him turn the Circle C Ranch into a home where they would celebrate many holidays to come.

The next morning, Marilou smiled and snuggled against the warm male body at her back. It was nice to be held by a man while she slept, even if it was just in a dream.

But when the strong arm thrown possessively over her enlarged stomach drew her closer and her fantasy man kissed the sensitive hollow behind her ear, reality flooded her mind and her eyes popped wide open. Good Lord, what had she been doing? How could she have forgotten that the man pressed to her back, the one who at that very moment nuzzled her neck, sending shivers coursing up and down her spine, was Tate Carson?

"Morning," he said, his warm breath causing a wave of goose bumps to skip across her skin. She felt his lower body stir against hers. "Did you sleep well, darlin'?"

"I…um, yes."

"I did, too." He rubbed his hand over her taut belly. "But I'm not so sure about the baby." His firm male lips tenderly moved over the sensitive skin along the side of her neck. "Sometime during the night, it felt like he was trying to do the Texas Two-Step in there."

"I guess I was so tired, I slept right through it," she said, wondering if that breathless female voice was really hers. Was it normal for a woman in the final stages of pregnancy to feel the degree of desire that she had thrumming through her veins?

She was saved from any further speculation when someone started pounding on the bedroom door.

"Aunt Marilou? Uncle Tate?" Jason shouted from the other side. "Get up and come downstairs. Santa Claus came and it's time to open presents and my mom says we can't start without you."

"How did he manage to get all that out without

taking a breath?'' Tate asked, laughing. He kissed
her shoulder, then rolled away from her. ''We'll
be down in a couple of minutes, little buddy.''

''Hurry!'' Jason's voice faded as he ran toward
the stairs.

Deciding it would be best to ignore the fact that
she had been snuggling against him, or that he'd
been responding in a very masculine way, Marilou hauled herself up to sit on the side of the bed.
''Uncle Tate? Where did that come from?''

''Yesterday evening before supper, he and
Becky asked me if I was going to be their uncle.''
He rose from the bed, crossed the room and
started digging around in his gym bag. Pulling out
a fresh pair of jeans and shirt, he shrugged. ''I
told them yes, that if you and I got married, I
would be their uncle.''

A pang of longing shot through Marilou that
she didn't understand. Why did the fact that they
were just putting on an act, and wouldn't actually
be getting married, make her want to cry?

''Hormones,'' she muttered as she reached for
her robe and shoved her arms into the sleeves.

''What was that, darlin'?''

Her cheeks heated and she avoided looking at
Tate as she grabbed a dark red maternity dress
from the closet and waddled toward the bathroom
to change. ''Nothing. Just talking to myself.''

* * *

"Jason, this is from Aunt Marilou and Tate," Gabriel announced, handing a brightly wrapped package to the boy.

Surprised, Tate looked at Marilou. "You put my name on the gifts you're giving to everyone?" he asked, quietly.

"It would have seemed odd if I hadn't," she whispered back.

Watching Gabriel pick up another package, a warm feeling filled his chest, and Tate reached over to take her delicate hand in his. "Thanks, darlin'."

"Tate, this is from me, Faith and the kids," Gabriel said, passing the present across the coffee table where Tate sat with Marilou on the couch.

Shocked, Tate accepted the package. "I—" He had to swallow around the sudden tightening in his throat. Not since his mother's passing almost ten years ago had anyone cared if he had something to unwrap on Christmas morning. "Thanks," he finally managed.

"I hope it's the right size and color," Faith said, hopefully. "When I called Gabe yesterday afternoon to have him pick it up, I guessed at the size." She smiled at her husband-to-be. "He picked out the color."

Tate's hands shook slightly as he tore the wrapping from the box and lifted the lid. Nestled inside was a warm-looking dark brown sweater. "The color's great," he said, meaning it. He checked the tag, then grinned at Faith. "And the size is perfect."

As everyone continued to open gifts, Tate enjoyed the warmth and closeness of the Baker sisters' family Christmas. It was an experience he knew he would never forget, nor did he ever want to.

Glancing over at Marilou as she opened a present from Ann Elise, a longing stronger than any he'd ever felt filled his chest. Her delightful laughter, the sweetness of her smile sent his blood pressure soaring and had him wishing he could celebrate every Christmas with her.

Tate continued to watch Marilou, and couldn't help but wonder how a nice woman like her could get mixed up with a sleazy jerk like her ex-boyfriend, Bridges. The man didn't have any idea how truly special she was, or what he was missing. But Tate knew.

He put his arm around her shoulders and hugged her. "Thank you, darlin'."

"For what?" she asked, treating him to a smile that caused his temperature to rise.

He leaned close. "For sharing your family with

me. This is the best Christmas I've had in a long time.''

''Really?''

''Really,'' he said, smiling.

She kissed his cheek. ''I'm glad.''

As he gazed into her emerald eyes, his heart slammed against his ribs and he felt like he just might be drowning. Could he be falling for Marilou? Was it possible for something like that to happen this fast?

''I have a treat for everyone,'' Ann Elise said, drawing everyone's attention.

''Did you bring the puppies?'' Jason asked, his face lighting up at the thought.

''No, sweetie,'' Ann Elise said gently. ''They won't be ready to leave their mother for a couple of months. But if it's all right with your mommy and daddy, you can have one as soon as they're weaned.''

Jason immediately turned his attention to his mother and Gabriel. ''Can I have one? Please? I'll take good care of it. I promise.''

Tate watched Faith and Gabriel exchange glances before Gabriel grinned. ''I think we can handle having a puppy.''

''Yippee!'' Jason shouted, jumping to his feet to hug the man who would soon be his father.

''What were you about to say, Ann Elise?''

Faith asked as she accepted a huge hug from her son.

"Every year the Lone Star Country Club has a special dinner party for its members and their guests." She grinned at Jason. "Santa will be there for the kids and they'll have dancing for the adults. Joe has invited us all to go as his guests. We might even make it a new family tradition."

When everyone agreed they'd like that, a deep sense of loneliness swept over Tate. He wouldn't be taking part in the celebration next year, nor would he be part of any other family gatherings. His being with them at Christmas was a one-time shot.

"Tate, are you all right?" Marilou asked quietly.

Gazing down at her, his stomach twisted into a knot at the thought of never spending another Christmas with her. But she wouldn't want to hear that. Not now anyway. Maybe not ever.

He clenched his teeth against the emptiness clawing at his gut, then forced a smile as he took her hand in his. "I couldn't be better, darlin'."

Seated at the long table the Lone Star Country Club's staff had set up for her family when they first arrived, Marilou watched Jason and several other excited children as they waited for Santa

Claus to make his appearance. Many of the adults were already dancing to the country-western band that had set up right after dinner had been cleared away.

Glancing at her niece seated quietly beside her, Marilou asked, ''Aren't you going to join the other children, Becky?''

''I'm too old for Santa Claus, Aunt Marilou,'' the little girl answered, shaking her head. ''He's sooo five minutes ago.''

''How old did you say you are?'' Marilou asked, laughing.

''She's nine, but she's making me feel like I'm ninety,'' Faith said, leaning over to straighten her daughter's unruly brown curls. Pointing to a couple of girls at the edge of the group of children, she asked, ''Aren't they your friends from school, Becky?''

Glancing in the direction her mother indicated, Becky nodded. ''That's Molly and Jennifer.'' She stood up, and Marilou could tell Becky was trying to maintain a dignified air, despite the excitement of seeing her friends. ''Maybe this soirée has some hope after all,'' she said before hurrying over to the two girls.

Marilou laughed as she watched her niece cross the room. ''Soirée? Where does she come up with this stuff?''

Faith rolled her eyes. "I don't know, but it's making me old way before my time."

"I hope you're not feeling too old to dance," Gabriel said, walking over to join them. He held out his hand to Faith. "Let's take a trip around the dance floor and see if I can still do a decent Dallas Shuffle."

"I hate to leave Marilou here by herself," Faith said reluctantly. "Where's Tate?"

Gabriel pointed to the group of children by the huge Christmas tree. "Jason is showing off Tate to all of his friends."

Faith frowned. "I'm not sure I like—"

"A lot of exciting things have happened to him in the past couple of weeks and he deserves to enjoy it," Gabriel said gently, pulling Faith to her feet. "Let him have his bragging rights tonight. He's a good kid. He'll get his priorities straight once he comes back down to earth."

"Now I know why I'm going to marry you," Faith said, smiling.

"And why's that?" he asked.

"You're so wise," Faith answered softly.

"Not really. Contrary to popular belief, I wasn't born in my mid-thirties."

"You weren't?" Faith asked, winking at Marilou.

Gabriel laughed. "Believe it or not, I was a little boy once, too."

Faith kissed him, then turned to Marilou. "Will you be all right by yourself?"

"Of course," Marilou said, forcing a smile and hoping they couldn't detect the sadness that had overtaken her.

Watching her sister and Gabriel join the other dancers doing the Dallas Shuffle, Marilou bit back a sob. Faith had Gabriel. Ann Elise had Joe. She didn't have anyone.

The baby kicked her as if to tell her to stop feeling sorry for herself.

Rubbing at the little knee or elbow raising a bump on her stomach, she wished that she had someone she could rely on to help her through the tough times she knew were coming. She'd tried to share her fears about childbirth and the apprehension every mother has about their baby being healthy with Harlan. But her concerns had fallen on deaf ears. The man simply hadn't cared anything about her or the baby, and couldn't be bothered with lending emotional support when she needed it most.

What would happen once the baby was born? Could she handle being a single parent? Faith had done a wonderful job with Jason and Becky, but now that Gabriel was going to be helping her,

Marilou knew everything would be much easier
for her sister.

Her gaze strayed over to Tate. He was surrounded by a half dozen of Jason's friends and
seemed to be having the time of his life interact-
ing with the little boys. From his actions, she
could tell he was instructing them on how to ride
a bucking horse or a bull.

Somehow she knew that Tate would never be
like Harlan. Tate would be right beside the mother
of his child, lending his support and doing everything he could to make it easier for her. And unlike Harlan, Tate would be there for his child, too.

"He's going to be a wonderful father some
day," she whispered to herself. The sudden realization that the woman in Tate's future wouldn't
be her made Marilou feel empty inside.

Shaking her head to dislodge the thought, she
wondered what had gotten into her. It was true
that she was more than a little attracted to Tate,
and he'd told her that he was attracted to her. But
that's as far as anything would ever go with them.
She barely knew him and, although he was a wonderful man, her judgment had proven more than
a little faulty where men were concerned.

"Are you all right, darlin'?"

Marilou jumped at the sound of Tate's voice.
She'd been so preoccupied with thoughts of the

baby and her miserable track record with men, she hadn't noticed his approach.

"I'm fine," she lied, smiling up at him.

"Good." He reached down and tugged her up into his arms. "Let's go show the good people of Mission Creek how to Waltz Across Texas."

Marilou laughed, enjoying the feel of Tate's arms around her once again. "You've got to be joking. It would look like you were dancing with a hot air balloon."

His easy grin faded. "Marilou, I don't know why you're so worried about your weight. You're pregnant. You're supposed to be bigger than normal. But even if you weren't ready to have a baby, it wouldn't make a damned bit of difference how big you are. You can't change the fact that you're a beautiful, sexy woman."

Staring up at him, Marilou could almost believe he meant every word he said. "Th-thank you."

"There's no need to thank me for telling the truth, darlin'." He walked her out onto the dance floor, then took her into his arms. "Just let me know if you get tired or your back starts to bother you."

As the band played "All I Want For Christmas Is You," Tate moved her around the floor with expert care. She loved to dance, but it had been ages since she'd had the opportunity. "You're a very good dancer."

"So are you," he said, pressing a kiss to her temple.

Suddenly aware that they were no longer playing a role, Marilou stared up at him. "Tate, what are we doing?"

The possessive look in his chocolate-brown eyes stole her breath. "I'm not real sure, darlin'. But I can tell you this much, I think we started something under the mistletoe last night. And I'd like to see where it goes."

Chapter 5

When the band suddenly stopped playing the slow country song they'd been dancing to and started playing "Here Comes Santa Claus," Tate led Marilou off the dance floor. But when they reached the table with the rest of the family, they discovered that someone had taken one of the chairs and there weren't enough seats for everyone.

"We'll have to find another chair," Joe said, standing up to offer his chair to Marilou while he looked around for one that wasn't occupied.

"Don't worry about it. Marilou can sit on my lap," Tate said, seizing the opportunity to continue holding her.

"Tate—"

Before she could protest, he sat down in the only empty chair at the table, then pulled her onto his lap. "Are you comfortable?"

She put her arm around his shoulders to steady herself. "Yes, but I'm too heavy."

He wrapped one arm around her back to hold her in place, took her free hand in his and shook his head. "No, you're not. You're just right." Kissing her cheek, he smiled and rested their linked hands on her swollen stomach. "Besides, I like holding you and the baby."

Faith and Ann Elise both gave him an approving smile, but said nothing as everyone turned their attention to Santa Claus "ho-ho-hoing" his way across the room to the group of excited children gathered around the Christmas tree. As Tate watched Santa hand Jason a bag filled with candy, he felt Marilou relax against him.

"Next year, your baby will be over there with the other kids," he whispered, wishing he could be here to see it.

He felt a tremor pass through her as she nodded, and knew he was having the same effect on her that she was having on him. Considering her advanced state of pregnancy, it was completely insane, but Tate wanted her like he'd never wanted any other woman. In fact, if he was honest with himself, he'd wanted her from the minute he saw her in the Corpus Christi bus station. And unless he was way off base—and he was damned near positive he wasn't—she wanted him, too.

When every child in the big ballroom had their treat from Santa, the band once again began to play Christmas songs with a country-western flare.

"Would you like to dance again, darlin'?"

She nodded. "Yes, I'd like that very much."

Helping her to her feet, he took her small hand in his and led her out onto the dance floor. "If you get tired, let me know."

Her smile sent heat streaking through his veins as she brought her arms up to circle his shoulders. "I will."

Tate pulled her as close as her stomach would allow. She felt good in his arms, and he found himself wondering what it would be like to hold her after she had the baby, to feel her breasts pressed to his chest. His groin tightened and he found himself having to concentrate on the dance steps that were normally second nature to him.

When the baby kicked him several times just above the belt buckle, he laughed, relieving some of his building tension. "It looks like someone else wants to dance."

Her cheeks colored a pretty pink. "I've decided

the baby is going to be a ballet dancer or a foot-ball player, depending on whether it's a girl or a boy.''

"One of the guys on the circuit and his wife found out way before she had the baby that they were having a boy. I think he called it a sono-something or other." He frowned. "Hasn't your doctor done one of those yet?"

"They're called sonograms. And yes, I've had several," she said, laughing. "But I told the doc-tor that I didn't want to know the sex of my baby. Call me old-fashioned, but I like the idea of wait-ing to find out when the baby is born."

He tightened his arms around her and kissed the tip of her cute little nose. "I like old-fashioned."

As the band started another song, he noticed her rubbing the lower part of her back. "You're getting tired, aren't you?"

"A little." She smiled. "Tiring easily is one of the hazards of an advanced pregnancy."

He was glad that each couple had driven sep-arately and they wouldn't have to inconvenience anyone by asking them for a ride home. "Let's go."

"Where?" she asked, clearly confused. "Back to the table?"

"Nope. Home."

"But—"

"No buts about it, darlin'." He led her over to where her sisters and future brothers-in-law were seated, watching Jason and Becky play with their friends. "We're going to head back to the house. Marilou's tired and I don't want her overdoing things." Turning to Joe, Tate reached out and shook the man's hand. "Thanks for inviting us. We really enjoyed the party."

"We'll do it again next year," Joe said, grinning.

Tate knew better. But forcing a smile, he nodded. "We'll look forward to it."

Faith stood up to hug Marilou. "Going home is probably a good idea. You've had a busy day and I'm sure you're ready to drop in your tracks." Turning to hug him, Faith smiled. "Thank you for taking such good care of our little sister, Tate."

Gazing down at the woman by his side, he smiled. "You don't have to thank me. Taking care of Marilou is my pleasure."

Thoroughly perplexed, Marilou lowered herself to the side of the bed and kicked off her slippers. How could she be pregnant and still feel such an intense level of desire? Were her hormones that out of sync?

But as Tate emerged from the bathroom, she knew there was a very simple explanation for the overwhelming tension flowing through her veins, and he was standing right in front of her wearing a pair of black boxer-briefs. She also realized that she'd feel this way even if she wasn't pregnant.

She'd spent hours being held by the sexiest man she'd ever met, and if that wasn't enough to send her libido into orbit, nothing would. Good heavens, any woman with a pulse would have been reduced to warm pudding after an evening of that.

"This is insane," she muttered, lying back against the pillow. Hadn't her ill-fated relationship with Harlan taught her anything?

She closed her eyes and tried to remind herself that she couldn't trust her judgment where men were concerned. But something deep inside told her that Tate was different.

"Did you say something?" he asked as he slipped into bed.

"No. You must have imagined it," she lied.

When he turned onto his side, she opened her eyes to find that he had propped himself up on one elbow and was staring down at her. "Marilou, there's something I've been meaning to do all evening."

The heat she saw in the depths of his dark brown eyes took her breath. "Wh-what?"

"I've been meaning to tell you how pretty you are." Her heart skipped a beat as he tenderly touched her cheek with his index finger. "I was the envy of every unattached man in Mission Creek tonight."

She laughed nervously. "Oh, I can't believe that. I'm as big as a beached wha—"

Placing his finger to her lips, he nodded. "It's the truth, darlin'. I caught several guys checking you out while we were dancing." He brushed his lips across her forehead. "And don't talk like that about yourself. Like I've told you before, you're a beautiful, sexy woman, who just happens to be pregnant."

Unable to find her voice, all Marilou could do was gaze up at him. He certainly knew what to say to make a woman feel better about herself.

"There's something else I've been meaning to do all evening, too, darlin'," he said, treating her to a smile that caused her to tingle in some of the most interesting places.

"What would that be?" she whispered.

"Kiss you," he said, lowering his head.

At the first touch of his mouth to hers, Marilou's eyes drifted shut and she wrapped her arms around his neck. As much she'd tried to deny it, she wanted to feel Tate's lips on hers again, wanted to experience the heady rush of sensations she'd felt when he kissed her under the mistletoe.

Tate coaxed her to open for him, and when she did, he slipped his tongue between her parted lips to reacquaint himself with her. Marilou's heart skipped several beats and her temperature soared as he teased her with strokes that imitated a more intimate union.

Shivers of delight slid up her spine when he rained tiny kisses from her chin, down the column of her throat to her collarbone. But when he cupped her breast in his large hand, she opened her eyes to find him staring down at her.

"Do you like that, Marilou?"

"Yes," she whispered. How long had it been since she'd felt a man's touch? Harlan had pulled away from her physically, as well as emotionally long before he ever packed up and moved out of her apartment.

"Do you want me to stop?" Tate asked.

"No." Heaven help her, but that was the last thing she wanted.

His mouth returned to hers and as he kissed her with a passion that stole her breath, he unbuttoned the top of her flannel gown to slip his hand inside. The combination of his tongue mating with hers and the touch of his calloused palm covering her bare breast sent warm ribbons of desire from her head all the way to her toes.

Breaking the kiss, he gave her an encouraging smile as he removed his hand from her nightgown to lift the tail of the garment. "Raise your hips, darlin'."

"Tate, I'm afraid my figure isn't very inspiring right now."

He smiled as he lowered the covers, then slowly raised her gown over her rounded belly. Instead of the look of disgust she'd seen on Harlan's face when he'd noticed that her pregnancy was starting to show, Tate had a look of awe in his eyes.

"You're gorgeous," he said, leaning down to press a kiss to her taut skin. The baby chose that moment to move, and smiling, Tate rested his cheek against the spot. "Don't get all excited, little one. It's just me. You know, the guy you kicked all evening while he danced with your mom."

Tears flooded Marilou's eyes as she listened to the tenderness in his voice. "You're a remarkable man, Tate Carson."

Shaking his head, he moved back up beside her to take her in his arms. "Not me. You." He gave her a kiss that sent a wave of longing straight through her, then nibbling his way to her ear, he whispered, "Now, turn over on your side and face me. The weight of your womb can restrict circulation if you stay on your back too long."

Distracted by his insight about the last trimester of a pregnancy, Marilou did as he directed. "How did you know about that?"

"While you were taking a nap yesterday afternoon, Faith asked if I'd had a chance to read anything on pregnancy and birth." He shrugged. "When I told her that I hadn't had time, she gave me a couple of books she had read when she was pregnant with Becky and Jason. She even marked the pages she thought would be the most informative."

Marilou felt heat color her cheeks. Leave it to her thoughtful sister to lend a helping hand. "I'm sorry you were put in that situation. All things considered, that must have been extremely embarrassing for you."

"To tell the truth, what she told me, and the few pages I read before you woke up, were pretty amazing." Tate tenderly ran his hand over her bare stomach. "It left me with a deeper appreciation of what you've gone through the past nine months."

The feel of his warm palm on her taut skin and the sincerity she detected in his softly spoken words caused her heart to skip a beat and made her insides feel as if they'd turned to melted butter. As unlikely as it seemed, she believed that Tate meant every word he said. And equally incredible was the feeling that she wished he was the father of her baby.

Before she could fully comprehend what that might mean, Tate's mouth captured hers in a kiss that seared her all the way to her soul. As he teased her with his tongue, he slowly moved his hand down the stretched skin of her abdomen, sending tiny currents of need skipping along every nerve in her body. When his hand dipped inside the waistband of her panties to gently caress her, Marilou gasped at the exquisite sensations radiating from his tender touch.

"Easy, darlin'. Does that feel good?"

She nodded, and if she could have found her voice, she would have told him that she wanted to touch him, too. But incapable of forming a single word, she simply placed her hands on his chest and did a little exploring of her own.

Tracing the thick pads of his perfect pectoral muscles, she circled each flat nipple with her fingertips, then leaned down to kiss each in turn. She smiled when a shudder ran through his big body and a groan rumbled up from deep in his chest.

"I'll give you all night to stop that," he said, sounding out of breath.

Smiling, she trailed her index finger down the shallow indention dividing his abdomen and the ridges of muscle covering his trim stomach. He was in excellent physical condition and she loved the way his warm masculine skin felt beneath her palms.

"Damn, darlin', I think you're going to kill me." His hands still caressed her, but he'd scrunched his eyes shut.

"Do you want me to stop?"

Tate's eyes flew open. "Hell, no! If you do, I'm pretty sure I'll die right here on the spot."

The smoldering heat in Marilou's emerald gaze held him captive as she ran the tip of her talented little finger around the rim of his navel, then along the fine line of dark brown hair that led to the waistband of his underwear. The room suddenly felt a good ten degrees warmer than it had only moments before. But when she lightly traced the front seam of his briefs down to the opening, his pulse took off at a gallop and sweat popped out on his forehead and upper lip. He was harder than he'd ever been, and if she kept this up, he was pretty sure he'd be reduced to a cinder in nothing flat.

"Tate?"

"Wh-what…darlin'?" All of a sudden his vocal cords didn't want to work.

"Would you mind taking these off?" she asked softly.

His heart slammed against his ribs like an out of control jackhammer. "I don't want you to feel pressured. I'll just go jump in a cold shower—"

She lightly brushed his mouth with hers, effectively stopping anything else he'd been about to say. "I want to."

Tate stared at her a moment, searching to make sure he hadn't misunderstood. But the look on her face convinced him that he hadn't, and he quickly got out of bed, removed his underwear, then retrieved a small packet from one of his jeans pockets.

Rolling the condom into place, he got back into bed and gathered Marilou into his arms. He smiled at her confused expression. "It will make things a little easier…afterward."

He watched understanding dawn in her expressive green eyes as he lowered his mouth to hers. Kissing her with every emotion he had filling his soul, but wasn't quite ready to name, Tate let her know how much the moment meant to him.

As he explored the sweet taste of her, she slid her hands down his chest to his flanks, then beyond. At the first touch of her soft hands on his heated flesh, he felt as if his head just might come right off his shoulders. Breaking the kiss, he struggled to draw air into his starved lungs and fought to maintain what little restraint he had left. He knew beyond a shadow of doubt that in all of his twenty-eight years, he'd never been this turned on before.

Positive that he couldn't take much more, Tate caught her hands in his and brought them up to his mouth to kiss each one of her fingertips. "We're going to have to slow down just a little, or I'm going to finish the race before the starting gun goes off."

"I like the way you feel, cowboy." Her sexy little grin didn't help his control one damned bit.

He closed his eyes and counted to ten, then twenty. When he finally felt a small amount of his sanity had returned, he remembered something from one of the books.

"Has your pregnancy been normal?"

She slowly nodded. "The doctor said I'm as healthy as a horse. Why?"

Relieved to hear that she'd had an easy time carrying the baby, Tate slowly slid his hand down her hip to the top of her thigh. "I know that making love the conventional way is out of the question because it might be uncomfortable for you." He let his hand stray to the apex of her thighs. "But the book mentioned there are other ways of being intimate that are perfectly safe for you and the baby.''

She didn't say a word, but her slight nod and the sweet smile curving her sensuous lips as her hands found him was all the answer he needed. Groaning, Tate took her into his arms to kiss her, showing her how much her trust meant to him, letting her taste the need that she'd created within him.

Fighting to maintain the slender hold he had on his control, Tate slowly slid his hand between them, then touched her as she touched him. The tension inside his body increased with each movement of her small hands, and Tate was determined to give her the same pleasure that she gave to him.

As he parted her to find the tiny nub of her desire, Marilou sighed. But when he gently began to stroke her, a soft moan of pleasure escaped her lips and she shivered against him.

Heat and light danced behind Tate's closed eyes, and he struggled to prolong the feelings building within him, even as he raced to end them. Only when he felt Marilou tremble and whisper his name as she crested the wave of pleasure did he surrender his control and give into his shuddering climax.

Holding her close as they both drifted back to reality, Tate knew beyond a shadow of doubt that he'd never felt closer to a woman than he did to Marilou at that very moment. And from the trusting way she'd let him caress her body, he was certain she felt the same way about him.

Chapter 6

Marilou dabbed at her eyes with a linen hand-kerchief and leaned against Tate as they walked toward the door of the chapel at the Mission Creek Cemetery. The New Year's Eve afternoon memorial service had celebrated her aunt's life with fond memories shared by family and close friends. But it had been the special message her aunt had written just before her death that left everyone in tears. Aunt Beth had wished Marilou and her sisters a life filled with health, happiness and a love as pure and strong as the love she'd shared with their Uncle Lloyd.

"I always knew Aunt Beth cared for Uncle

Lloyd, but I never realized how deeply,'' Faith said when Marilou and Tate joined her, Gabriel, Ann Elise and Joe on the chapel steps.

''Uncle Lloyd was so authoritative, I used to think they were mismatched,'' Ann Elise said, shaking her head. ''But the more I think about it—''

''They…complemented each other,'' Marilou said, her voice breaking. Tate's arm tightened around her shoulders, and when she glanced up, the understanding in his dark brown gaze touched her in ways she'd never imagined.

''We'll be back in a few minutes,'' he said, pressing a kiss to the top of her head. ''There's something we need to get from the back of my truck.''

As her sisters continued to talk about their memories of the aunt and uncle who had taken them in after their parents' deaths, Marilou watched Tate and the other two men walk toward the parking area.

With broad shoulders, narrow hips and wide-brimmed Resistols pulled down tight against the chilly winter wind, it was easy to see that all three men were true Texans. But there seemed to be something about Tate that set him apart from Joe and Gabriel—something that made him special. At least to her.

She bit her lower lip. How was she ever going to survive without him in her life?

Over the course of the past week, they'd shared childhood memories, future plans and become closer than she'd ever imagined. Tate had even driven her to his ranch on the other side of Mission Creek to show her the home he'd grown up in, and where he intended to raise his own family one day. He'd told her of his plans for the Circle C and asked her opinion on several ideas he had for remodeling the interior of the house. And each night as he held her in his arms, making her feel more cherished than she'd ever felt before, she found herself wishing more and more that she would be the woman sharing it all with him.

Rubbing at the strained muscles in her lower back, she sighed heavily. In reality, she knew that a relationship with Tate was never meant to be. But that still didn't keep her from wishing that things could be different.

"Where did Becky and Jason go?" Ann Elise asked, interrupting Marilou's wistful thoughts.

"They left with Sue Ellen Monroe," Faith answered. "They're attending a New Year's sleepover that her children, Tiffany and Brock are having."

When Faith stopped to give her an odd look, Marilou frowned. "What?"

"How long has your back been bothering you?"

Marilou laughed. "Eight and a half months. But who's counting?"

"It won't be much longer, sweetie," Faith said sympathetically.

Ann Elise suddenly pointed past Marilou's shoulder. "I love that man."

When she turned around, Marilou watched Joe and Gabriel walking toward them, carrying a large wreath on some sort of easel-like stand. Tate walked beside them, holding a smaller arrangement of flowers.

"Tate suggested that we get flowers for you girls to put on your aunt's grave," Joe said as they stopped in front of the women.

"We agreed it was a good idea, so we all chipped in on it," Gabriel added, nodding.

"That was so thoughtful of you," Marilou said softly when Tate stopped beside her. She touched the arrangement he held. "Is that for your mother's grave?"

"I know it's windy and pretty cold, but I thought we could walk over to that side of the cemetery after we take care of placing the wreath in front of your aunt's new headstone." He paused as he took her hand in his. "That is, if you feel like it."

She kissed his lean cheek. "Yes, I'd like to visit your mother's grave with you."

Ten minutes later, after they'd helped the other two couples place the wreath on Elizabeth Baker's grave and bid them goodbye, Tate put his arm around Marilou's shoulders and they slowly walked over to the far end of the Mission Creek Cemetery. Dropping to one knee, Tate brushed a collection of dead leaves from the edge of a small marker and replaced them with the silk roses he'd purchased earlier in the day.

He wished his mother could have met the woman standing beside him. Maria Carson would have loved Marilou almost as much as...

Whoa, cowboy! Swallowing hard, he shook his head in an effort to clear it. He'd come damned close to thinking in terms of the "L" word.

But as he straightened and met Marilou's steady emerald gaze, his chest tightened and it felt as if someone had delivered a sucker punch to his gut. If he hadn't done it already, it wouldn't take much to fall in love with her.

They'd spent the past week talking, laughing and growing closer than he'd ever been with any woman. They'd told each other stories about their childhood, talked about their likes and dislikes, and shared their dreams for the future. And each night as he held her in his arms the intimacy between them had grown. But did he love her?

Hell, how would he know? He didn't have anything to compare it to. He'd never been in love before.

"Your mother was very young when she passed away," Marilou said softly. She glanced down at the tombstone. "She was only thirty-nine. What happened?"

Distracted from his disturbing introspection, Tate nodded. "She was in a ranching accident." He took a deep breath against the tightness suddenly filling his chest. "After my dad left us high and dry, Mom and I ran the ranch. Then after I graduated, I took off on the rodeo circuit to earn money to keep us going. One weekend, while I was gone to a rodeo in Waco, she tried to pull a stump out of the ground with a tractor. It...turned over on her."

"Oh, how terrible," Marilou said, placing her soft hand on his arm. "I'm so sorry, Tate."

With a lump the size of his fist clogging his throat, he simply nodded and pulled her into his arms. They stood for several minutes just holding each other before he felt her shiver against him.

"You're cold," he said, rubbing his hands up and down her back. Stepping back, he pulled her open coat as close together as her stomach would allow. "Let's go back to Faith's and see if we can get her to make some of her world class cocoa to warm you up."

"That does sound nice," Marilou said, smiling up at him.

He watched her rub the lower part of her back. "Another backache?"

She shook her head. "Actually, I think it's the same one."

He put his arm around her, kissed the top of her head and steered her toward his truck. "I'll give you a back rub when we go to bed tonight, darlin'."

"Mmm. A cup of Faith's cocoa *and* a back rub." She laughed. "Aren't you afraid you're going to spoil me?"

"Nope. You deserve to be pampered." He stopped to give her a kiss that left them both gasping for breath. "And I'm finding that I enjoy being the one who does the pampering."

Even though the nagging ache in her back seemed to be getting worse, Marilou enjoyed spending New Year's Eve with her family. After one of Faith's scrumptious dinners, they'd divided up into teams and played a heated game of Monopoly. She and Tate had won, with Faith and Gabriel coming in a close second. Ann Elise and

Joe had been too busy discussing plans for their new animal clinic to really get into playing.

"Have you and Tate given any thought to living at the Circle C after the baby is born, Marilou?" Gabriel asked as they all gathered in the living room. He switched on the television to await the New Year's broadcast from Times Square in New York City. "I could use a good CPA for my new restaurant."

"We'll be needing an accountant for our expanded practices, too," Ann Elise added, looking hopeful.

Marilou wasn't sure what to say. Nothing would please her more than living close to her sisters. But if she moved back to Mission Creek, everything would get extremely complicated.

She could cover her and Tate not being together by telling everyone that things just didn't work out between them. But how would she explain his not helping her raise her baby without making him look like a complete jerk?

"With Tate being away nearly every weekend for a rodeo, we would be close enough to help with the baby," Faith said, seating herself on the arm of Gabriel's chair.

"I'm not sure—"

Marilou stopped to glance at Tate sitting next to her on the couch, silently begging for another one of his quick, and completely reasonable, explanations. But he remained silent, as if he, too, was interested in her answer.

Hoping to end any further discussion of the matter, she shook her head. "We…um, really haven't had a chance to make any definite plans."

"Marilou and I are still looking at our options," Tate said, reaching out to take her hand in his.

His hand gave hers a gentle squeeze and his reassuring smile warming her all the way to her toes, had her wishing that what he said was true—that they really would be planning a future together. She wasn't sure how or when, but sometime over the past week, she'd let down her guard and fallen head over heels for Tate Carson.

Time seemed to stand still at the unsettling realization, and needing a moment to collect herself, Marilou struggled to get off the couch. "One thing about being pregnant, you get to visit a lot of bathrooms," she said, hoping the excuse would cover her sudden need to be alone.

Tate was immediately on his feet to help her up. "Are you feeling all right?"

"I'm fine. I just—" She stopped suddenly as a warm, wet sensation began to spread down her legs.

"What's wrong, darlin'?" Tate asked, looking alarmed.

Glancing down at the front of her maternity slacks, Marilou's cheeks heated with embarrassment and she forgot all about the need to have a moment alone. "I think...my water just broke."

After her announcement there was a momentary pause, then everyone jumped to their feet and started talking at once.

"Oh, God," Tate groaned.

"Are you in pain?" Ann Elise asked.

"No," Tate answered, looking pale.

Ann Elise shook her head. "Not you, silly. I'm talking to Marilou."

"My back hurts." Marilou tried to remember what the doctor had told her about back labor. "But it does seem to have started coming and going."

Faith nodded knowingly. "I had a feeling this afternoon at the memorial service that you were having more than just a normal backache."

"Carson, it looks like you're going to start the New Year off as a brand-new daddy," Joe said, grinning.

Gabriel slapped Tate on the shoulder. "Hang in there, kid. You'll do just fine."

"Who had the first?" Faith asked.

Gabriel gave Marilou a sheepish grin. "I did."

"You were all betting on when I'd have the baby?" she asked incredulously.

"Hey, why didn't someone let me in on it?" Tate asked, his complexion returning to its normal shade.

"You want to be in on the next pool?" Joe asked.

Tate nodded. "Sure. What are we betting on this time?"

"The hour Marilou has the baby," Ann Elise answered. "I'm saying it will be sometime between eight and nine tomorrow morning."

"How did I get to be blessed with such a sensitive family?" Marilou asked dryly.

Her comment froze everyone to the spot, and as she looked from her sisters to her brothers-in-law-to-be, to Tate, she couldn't help but laugh. They all looked like naughty children caught with their hands in the cookie jar.

"Oh, what the heck." She groaned as the ache in her back intensified. "Count me…in. I'll take the hour…between four and five…in the morning."

Chapter 7

On the drive from the Baker place to the Mission Creek hospital, Marilou asked Tate to stay with her through the birth of her baby, and he'd told her that nothing would keep him from being there for her every step of the way. But when they arrived at the hospital, he felt like a fish out of water.

As soon as they finished filling out the paperwork, a nurse, who's name tag identified her as Christina Brooks, appeared with a wheelchair, helped Marilou into it, then started down a long corridor with her. Tate was left standing in the reception area holding a small overnight case, wondering what he was supposed to do next. He wasn't sure if he should follow them, or drop the little suitcase right there in the middle of the floor and run like hell in the opposite direction.

"Come on, Dad," Nurse Brooks said, looking over her shoulder at him. "You've got a job to do, too."

It took a moment for Tate to realize she was talking to him. *He* had a job to do? What was the woman talking about? And where the hell was the exit anyway?

But when he spotted the sign above a door on the other side of the lobby—the arrow looking for all the world like an open invitation to freedom— Tate turned and followed Marilou and the nurse. The thought of what his "job" might entail scared him more than the biggest, meanest, pissed-off bull he'd ever had the misfortune to ride in the past thirteen years on the rodeo circuit. But Marilou needed him and he wasn't about to let her down. He'd do whatever it took to make this as easy for her as possible.

"Tate, we'll be in the waiting room," someone called from behind him.

When he looked over his shoulder, he found Faith, Gabriel, Ann Elise and Joe walking toward him.

"The women decided they'd rather wait here at the hospital than at home," Joe said, grinning.

As soon as the group reached him, Faith placed her hand on his arm. "I don't want to frighten you, but things might get a little intense during Marilou's labor." Her sympathetic expression made the hair on the back of his neck stand straight up and a knot to form in the pit of his stomach. "Feeling helpless is normal for a father, and you may find that you'll need to take a few minutes break from time to time. Let me know if you do and I'll go in to coach her through the contractions, while you collect yourself and catch your breath."

"Thanks, Faith. I'll remember that," Tate said, meaning it. He didn't like having to admit it, even to himself, but he just might have to take her up on her offer. Watching Marilou in pain was going to be the hardest thing he'd ever had to do.

"Whenever possible, come out and give us periodic updates on how everything is progressing," Ann Elise added.

"Will do."

Before he could change his mind and go running for the exit like a coyote with a tail-end full of buckshot, Tate turned toward the double doors that Marilou and Nurse Brooks had disappeared through only moments before. Checking in at the nurse's station in the obstetrics unit, he impatiently checked his watch as another nurse, whom he was sure had done time as an army drill sergeant at some point in her life, gave him strict orders about the do's and don'ts of the birthing room. He was supposed to be there for support and encouragement. He wasn't, under any circumstances, supposed to get in the way.

After what seemed like an eternity, the woman abruptly stopped the lecture and pointed toward a door a little farther down the hall. "Ms. Baker is in room 224 if you'd like to go in now."

Without hesitation, Tate strode purposefully into the room where Nurse Brooks had already helped Marilou change and was in the process of helping her get into bed. Setting the overnight case on the nightstand, he smiled and took hold of Marilou's hand. "You still doing okay?"

"I think so," she said, looking a little nervous.

"You're right on time, Dad," the young nurse said cheerfully.

Every time the woman called him "Dad," a warm feeling filled Tate's chest and sent a longing through him that defied logic.

"I'm just getting ready to hook up the fetal monitor, then I'll do a quick ultrasound to make sure everything is going well.'' The nurse pulled the sheet down below Marilou's rounded belly, then pushed the flimsy hospital gown up to just below her breasts.

''Is this normal procedure?'' Marilou asked, looking concerned. ''The nurse/midwife conducting the childbirth classes I attended said that an ultrasound was usually only done during labor if the doctor suspects there's a problem.''

''It's probably just hospital policy, darlin',''' Tate said, hoping that was the case. He watched in total fascination as Nurse Brooks squeezed a big gob of clear gel onto Marilou's stomach, then placed something that looked like a microphone right in the middle of it and started smearing it around.

''Since the obstetrician who'll be delivering your baby is different from the one you've been seeing throughout your pregnancy, he's going to want an idea of what's going on in there,'' the nurse explained. She smiled and pointed to a screen resembling a small television set. ''See, there's your baby.''

Tate frowned as he tried to concentrate on what the nurse might be seeing that he wasn't. All he could decipher on the small screen was a bunch of twitching gray areas that didn't even come close to resembling a baby.

"I'll be back in just a moment," the woman said, her easy expression fading.

"What's wrong?" The fear in Marilou's eyes just about tore Tate apart.

"Is there a problem?" he asked. The knot in his gut felt as if it grew to the size of a basketball when Nurse Brooks hurried from the room without answering.

Turning his attention to Marilou, Tate brushed a tear from her pale cheek. "Did your doctor indicate there might be a problem before?"

"No." Her voice was little more than a whisper and he could tell she was close to losing it.

"Then it's probably nothing," he said gently, hoping that was the case. "Maybe there's something wrong with the machine."

Marilou's grip suddenly tightened on his hand as she closed her eyes and started taking deep breaths. He could tell from the sweat beading her forehead and the deep rose coloring her cheeks that the pains were getting a lot stronger. Just knowing she was hurting caused him to feel ill.

As the contraction passed and she opened her eyes, a tall man Tate judged to be somewhere in his mid- to late-thirties walked into the room holding a metal chart. The stethoscope draped around his neck and the blue scrub suit indicated that he was probably the obstetrician.

"I'm Doctor Martinelli and I'll be delivering your baby," he said, walking straight to the monitor on the other side of the bed. "How are you doing, Marilou?"

"Please tell me if there's something wrong with my baby," she pleaded.

The tremor in her voice and the fear in her eyes broke Tate's heart. If someone didn't tell them something, and damned quick, he was going to invite the good doctor out into the hall for a private consultation. By the time Tate got finished with him, the man would be damned glad to answer their questions.

"Let's take a look and see what we've got here," the doctor said as he picked up the microphonelike instrument and started smearing it around in the clear gel on Marilou's belly. The grim set of his mouth didn't reassure Tate one damned bit. "It appears the fetus is breech."

Marilou groaned and Tate wasn't sure whether it was from the doctor's news or from the current contraction.

"What does that mean in terms of problems for

Marilou and the baby?'' Tate demanded, feeling sick inside.

Martinelli met Tate's gaze head on. ''It might mean that we'll have to perform a C-section. But since it looks like it's a face presentation, and the baby is still up high and to the right of the cervix, there's a good possibility we'll be able to get it into the proper position for Marilou to deliver naturally.''

''What does that entail?'' Tate didn't like the idea of her being put through any more pain than necessary. If they were taking a poll, he'd vote for the quickest, least uncomfortable procedure possible.

''I'll have a resident use an ultrasound to monitor our progress while I try to get the baby turned the right way,'' Martinelli answered, reaching for a box of latex gloves. ''It's all done externally and shouldn't cause Marilou an extreme amount of discomfort.''

''Not another one,'' Marilou said, groaning. Her hand tightened around Tate's as another wave of pain swept over her, and he wasn't sure he wouldn't need a couple of finger splints before this ordeal was over with.

''Let's see how far along you are,'' Martinelli said, pulling on the glove.

When the man lifted the bottom of the sheet to examine Marilou, Tate wasn't sure whether to turn his head, or step out into the hall. In the end, he focused his attention on stroking her strawberry-blond hair and murmuring words that he hoped were encouraging. He could tell the examination was uncomfortable for her and he wanted to do whatever he could to lend her his strength and support.

The doctor's sudden epithet sent a chill slithering up Tate's spine. "You're dilated to eight centimeters and we'll have to work fast if we're going to get the baby turned," Martinelli said, lowering the sheet. He stripped the glove off and started for the door. "I'll get one of the residents and be right back."

As the doctor walked from the room, Tate blew out the breath he hadn't been aware of holding. He wasn't quite sure what to do next. In light of the problem facing her, Marilou might want one of her sisters by her side.

"Would you rather have Faith or Ann Elise in here with you, darlin'?"

"No. I want you with me." She bit her lower lip a moment before she whispered, "Please don't leave, Tate. I need you."

Gazing down at her, he saw a mixture of pain

and fear clouding her pretty emerald eyes, but he also saw the trust that he'd walk through hell before he betrayed. "I love you, darlin'. There's nowhere else I'd rather be than right here with you."

A tear trickled down her cheek as she reached up to touch his jaw with trembling fingers. "I love you, too, Tate Carson."

Emotion filled his chest and he leaned down to kiss her with every ounce of feeling he possessed. When he raised his head, he smiled. "We're going to get through this just fine. I promise."

"I need…to push," Marilou panted.

Tate watched the doctor stare at the ultrasound monitor as he mashed on the side of her belly. "Not yet," Martinelli said, his gaze glued to the fuzzy-looking picture on the screen. "We're almost there, but I need you to hold off just a little longer, sweetheart."

She groaned. "I…can't. I have…to push."

Tate had never felt more helpless in his entire life than he did at that very moment. The contractions were coming faster, lasting longer and at times seemed to overlap. He'd gladly take her place if it meant that she'd finally get some relief. But since that was impossible, he intended to make sure she did everything the doctor and nurses had told them would make this whole ordeal easier for her.

"Come on, Marilou," Tate said, cupping her face with a shaky hand. He turned her head until their gazes met. Her eyes were clouded with pain and he had to swallow hard to get the words past the lump clogging his throat. "You can do this. Just look at me and concentrate on how much I love you."

He wasn't sure if he was doing the right thing, but after a second or two her eyes focused on his and she began blowing quick, sharp breaths through her mouth. "That's it, darlin'. You're doing great."

What seemed like an eternity later, but couldn't have been more than a couple of minutes, the doctor stopped pushing against Marilou's stomach to stare at the monitor. Grinning, he gave them the thumb's-up sign. "The baby is in position and we're good to go. You can start pushing now, Marilou."

Tate felt relieved and scared to death all at the same time. They'd passed one hurdle, but they still had to make it through the delivery.

But Marilou didn't give him a chance to dwell on his conflicting emotions. Without waiting for any further instructions from the doctor, she scrunched her eyes shut, grabbed her knees and started pushing with all her might.

When she lay back against the pillow to catch her breath, Tate kissed her forehead. "What can I do to help you through this, darlin'?"

"Support my shoulders…with the next… contraction," she said, panting from the exertion.

"You got it," he said, determined not to let her down.

"Here comes another one," she said, her voice strained.

Taking hold of her shoulders, Tate helped her lean forward as she redoubled her efforts with the next round of pushing. He couldn't blame her for wanting to get to the end of the ordeal as soon as possible. With the doctor shoving around on her stomach between every contraction, she'd been through hell.

Tate was so busy helping Marilou that he failed to notice the flurry of activity going on around them. But when he glanced up, he noticed that several things had changed. Carts had been wheeled into the room with a variety of sterile instruments neatly laid out on top, the bottom part of the bed had been removed, and some kind of poles with strange looking troughs had been attached to each side of the bed frame.

Then everything seemed to go into fast forward. The sheet covering Marilou was shoved aside, Doctor Martinelli took his position to deliver the baby, and the nurses took over coaching Marilou. Tate had no idea why one of the women insisted that he put on a pair of latex gloves, then move to the end of the bed with the doctor, but remembering the lecture from the crusty old nurse, he did as he was told.

"I need for you to give me a big push, Marilou," Martinelli said.

Standing beside the doctor, Tate was struck absolutely speechless as he watched the top of the baby's head appear, then slowly emerge from Marilou's body. He'd never experienced anything as terrifying or as amazing as watching her give birth.

"Step a little closer, Dad," Martinelli instructed. "Now put your hands down here to help catch your baby."

As if moving through a dream, Tate followed the doctor's orders, and within a matter of seconds, the baby slid out into his waiting hands. Time stood still as he gazed down at the squirming infant, but when she opened her eyes to look up at him, he instantly fell in love with the baby girl everyone thought he'd fathered.

"Is my baby all right?" Marilou asked, her voice sounding surprisingly strong for all she'd been through.

Glancing up, Tate's vision blurred as he smiled at the woman he loved. "She's fine, darlin'."

Marilou looked stunned. "I have a little girl?"

He nodded. "You sure do. And she's just as beautiful and perfect as her mother."

"She's absolutely gorgeous, Marilou," Ann Elise said, leaning over the hospital bassinet to touch her new niece's baby soft cheek. "I think she's going to look like Tate when she gets older."

Marilou glanced over at Tate sitting across the room with Joe and Gabriel. When their eyes met, his smile caused her heart to skip a beat. She'd fallen hopelessly in love with him, but could he really love her?

He'd been the first to confess his feelings, but that had happened during a very stressful moment in her labor. Did he mean it? Or had it been something said due to the emotional intensity of the situation?

"Have you two picked out a name for her?" Faith asked, bringing Marilou back to the present.

"Not yet," Tate answered, his gaze never waivering from Marilou's. "That's something we have to talk about this afternoon." He winked, warming her all the way to her soul. "Among other things."

"I don't know about everyone else, but I intend to spend this afternoon taking a nap," Gabriel said, yawning. "I'm getting too old for these all-night New Year's parties."

"They are kind of rough," Joe admitted, grinning.

"Not nearly as rough as the New Year's party Marilou and Tate attended," Faith said sympathetically. Leaning over, she hugged Marilou. "We're going to leave now. You and Tate need some time alone with your new angel."

When Faith stepped back from the side of the bed, Ann Elise took her place. Giving Marilou a hug and a light kiss on the cheek, she smiled. "Get some rest, sweetie."

The men stood up to shake Tate's hand.

"In a few years, you're going to have a line of boys a mile long, just waiting for a smile from that little girl," Gabriel laughed.

"Congratulations, Carson." Joe smiled at Ann

Elise. "One of these days, we'll be adding to the family."

Marilou and Faith both spoke at once. "Ann Elise, are you—"

Their sister shook her head. "Not yet. But Joe and I have talked about getting pregnant right after we get the new practice opened."

Grinning, Gabriel cleared his throat. "Faith and I have been talking about that possibility, too."

Her smile radiant, Faith walked straight into her husband-to-be's waiting arms. "We're going to start trying as soon as we get married."

"Who's going to keep track of the bet this time?" Marilou asked, grinning. "I'll say Faith's pregnant by Easter."

Joe laughed and pulled an ink pen and paper from his coat pocket. "As the winner of the last pool, I'll keep track of this one."

By the time everyone selected the months they thought Faith and Gabriel's baby would be conceived, congratulated Tate and Marilou on the birth, and left for home, the baby woke up to nurse.

Marilou watched Tate gently pick up her daughter, then walk over to sit down on the side of the bed, facing her. When he handed the baby to her, his expression took her breath.

"Thank you, Marilou."

"For what?"

"Everything." He reached out to cup her cheek with his large palm. "This has been the best Christmas and New Year that I've ever had."

The love she saw shining in his dark brown eyes made her heart skip a beat. "I feel the same way, Tate."

As if he'd read her earlier thoughts, he smiled. "I meant what I said when you were in labor, darlin'. I love you more than life itself."

Her chest filled with emotion. "I love you, too. So very much."

He looked down at the baby in her arms. "And I love her." Touching the infant's soft cheek with his finger, he glanced back up at Marilou. "It was one of the proudest moments in my life when Ann Elise said she thought the baby looked like me." His expression turned serious. "Does Bridges have dark hair?"

Marilou couldn't help it. She laughed as she remembered how sensitive Harlan had been about his hair, or more accurately, the lack of it. "What little hair Harlan has left is pale blond."

Tate grinned. "So she really does look like she has my hair?"

"Yes."

He held her gaze for several long seconds, then cleared his throat. "Marilou, what do you think about making all this real?"

Afraid to hope, Marilou wanted to make sure she understood. "You mean—"

"Everything," he said before she could ask. "The engagement, my being the baby's daddy—I want it all, darlin'."

Moisture blurred her vision as she nodded. "I want that, too."

A wide grin spread across his handsome face. "Marilou Baker, will you marry me and let me be this little girl's daddy for real?"

"Oh, yes," Marilou said through her tears.

Tate's arms were immediately around her and the baby. "Darlin', you've just made me the happiest man in the whole damned state of Texas."

The baby chose that moment to protest the delay in getting her next meal.

When he released them, Tate smiled. "*Our* daughter is going to work herself up into a real hissy fit if you don't feed her."

His referring to the baby as *their* daughter made Marilou's heart soar. Happier than she'd ever imagined, she arranged her gown and lifted the baby to her breast.

Tate moved to sit beside and slightly behind

Marilou, then wrapping his arms around her and the baby, he pulled them back against his wide chest. "I want to hold both of you for the rest of my life," he whispered close to her ear.

With Tate holding her and the baby, they spent most of New Year's afternoon deciding what to name their daughter, when they were going to get married, and where they were going to live.

"I'll call the Mission Creek Inn tomorrow and see if we can reserve the garden for the first Saturday afternoon in May," Tate said.

Marilou's breath caught. "How did you know I've always dreamed of getting married there?"

He smiled. "I overheard you telling your sister."

"I love you, Tate Carson. You're the most thoughtful man I've ever met."

"I just want to give you your dreams, darlin'." He tightened his arms around her and the baby. "Are you sure you want to live on the Circle C? It's a lot different than living in Corpus Christi."

Marilou didn't have to think twice. "Corpus Christi is my past. My future is here with you and the baby."

"I'm glad," he said, kissing the side of her head. "While I was out yesterday morning to get the flowers for your aunt and my mom's graves,

I stopped by and arranged for a contractor to start work next week on all the remodeling ideas you had for the ranch house.''

''You did?'' She glanced over her shoulder at him.

''Yep.'' He grinned. ''By the time you're on your feet, the work crew will have everything ripped out and they'll be ready for you to pick out what you want.''

Before she could tell him she didn't care what the house had in it as long as they were together, there was a soft knock on the door.

''How is Mission Creek's newest resident and her parents?'' a well-dressed woman of about fifty asked, entering the room.

''Couldn't be better,'' Tate answered cheerfully.

''Wonderful,'' the woman said, smiling. ''I'm Laura Kingston. I work in the records office here at the hospital and I need some information for your daughter's birth certificate.''

''What do you need?'' Tate asked.

Ms. Kingston smiled. ''Have you decided on a name for your daughter?''

''Her name is Maria Elizabeth,'' Marilou said, smiling down at the baby in her arms. Their choice of what to name the little girl had been easy. She and Tate had decided on Maria for his mother and Elizabeth after Aunt Beth.

"I also need your names," Ms. Kingston said.

"My name is Marilou Baker, and the baby's father's name is—"

"Tate Carson," he said, sounding as proud as any first-time father possibly could.

Marilou turned her head to kiss his lean cheek. "I love you, Tate Carson."

"And I love you, darlin'," he said, his slow smile promising a lifetime of undying devotion.

Happier than she'd been in her entire life, Marilou held their daughter close, and snuggled into the arms of the man she loved with all of her heart and soul. She had everything she'd ever dreamed of, and all because she'd decided to come home for the holidays.

*   *   *   *   *

USA TODAY bestselling author

LINDSAY McKENNA

From the master of romantic adventure come two of the Morgan's Mercenaries stories that started it all!

Legendary commander Morgan Trayhern and his family are in danger, and only his team of fearless men and women can save them.

MORGAN'S LEGACY

Coming to stores in February 2004.

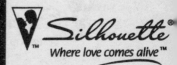

Where love comes alive™

**The Wolfe twins' stories—
together in one fantastic volume!**

USA TODAY bestselling author

JOAN HOHL

Double WOLFE

The emotional story of Matilda Wolfe plus an original short
story about Matilda's twin sister, Lisa. The twins have
followed different paths...but each leads to true love!

Look for DOUBLE WOLFE in January 2004.

"A compelling storyteller who weaves her tales
with verve, passion and style."
—*New York Times* bestselling author Nora Roberts

Where love comes alive™